Murder on the Hour

ALSO BY ELIZABETH J. DUNCAN

Murder on the Hour

A PENNY BRANNIGAN MYSTERY

Elizabeth J. Duncan

Minotaur Books

A Thomas Dunne Book

New York

A THOMAS DUNNE BOOK FOR MINOTAUR BOOKS.
An imprint of St. Martin's Publishing Group.

MURDER ON THE HOUR. Copyright © 2016 by Elizabeth J. Duncan.
All rights reserved. Printed in the United States of America. For information, address St. Martin's Press, 175 Fifth Avenue, New York, N.Y. 10010.

www.thomasdunnebooks.com
www.minotaurbooks.com

Library of Congress Cataloging-in-Publication Data

Names: Duncan, Elizabeth J., author.
Title: Murder on the hour : a Penny Brannigan mystery / Elizabeth J. Duncan.
Description: First edition. | New York : Minotaur Books, 2016. | Series:
   A Penny Brannigan mystery ; 7 | "A Thomas Dunne book."
Identifiers: LCCN 2015045812| ISBN 9781250074232 (hardcover) |
   ISBN 9781466885844 (e-book)
Subjects: LCSH: Brannigan, Penny (Fictitious character)—Fiction. | Women
   private investigators—Fiction. | City and town life—Wales—Fiction. |
   Murder—Investigation—Fiction. | Heirlooms—Fiction. | BISAC: FICTION /
   Mystery & Detective / Women Sleuths. | GSAFD: Mystery fiction.
Classification: LCC PR9199.4.D863 M87 2016 | DDC 813/.6—dc23
LC record available at http://lccn.loc.gov/2015045812

Our books may be purchased in bulk for promotional, educational, or business use. Please contact your local bookseller or the Macmillan Corporate and Premium Sales Department at 1-800-221-7945, extension 5442, or by e-mail at MacmillanSpecialMarkets@macmillan.com.

First Edition: April 2016

10 9 8 7 6 5 4 3 2 1

For Eirlys Owen

Acknowledgements

Many people contributed to the publication of this book, and I am grateful to all of them.

In Wales, thank you to Eirlys Owen for her plotting suggestions and encouragement given generously over tea and cake, to Daniel Casey of Snowdonia Antiques for sharing his expertise on longcase clocks and secret hiding places, and to Sylvia and Peter Jones for so many wonderful days out, including the excursion to the stunningly beautiful Ynys Llanddwyn where the last scene of the book is set. I thank them, too, for the time they spent proofreading this work. They caught many errors and suggested dozens of improvements.

In New York, thank you to the St. Martin's Press editorial team of Anne Brewer and Jennifer Letwack for shepherding this work through the publishing process and to my agent, Dominick Abel, for his insight and wisdom.

And while I do strive for accuracy, any errors are mine.

On the home front, love to Riley and Lucas who so kindly share Bentley, Charlotte, and York.

Murder on the Hour

One

"What's everyone looking at?" asked Evelyn Lloyd as she and her friend Florence Semble picked their way across the cobblestones of the Llanelen town square. They joined the small crowd gathered in front of the newsagent's and as a blonde woman in a bright green spring cloth coat backed away, Mrs. Lloyd was able to get close enough to read the poster in the window.

"Oh, my word," she said, turning to Florence. "*Antiques Cymru* is coming to town. It says they'll be doing appraisals and filming the television show right here in Llanelen! Saturday, May ninth. It's to be held up at Ty Brith Hall. How exciting! Now, let me think. There must be something of value in all those old things Arthur's auntie left us." She touched Florence lightly on the arm. "Her set of best china! That's got to be worth a bob or two! Twelve of everything, including what she called fruit nappies. Fruit nappies! Nowadays, nobody would call those little bowls nappies, that's for sure. And who'd have twelve people for dinner these days? Or in her day, for that matter. I doubt she even knew twelve people, and she's the one who owned the china."

"Well, it's not until May, so you've got a couple of months to think about it," Florence replied. "We'll have a good poke round the attic and you might find something better between now and then that would be worth bringing in for an evaluation." She reached into her handbag for a pen and the little notebook in which she kept a running to-do list. "Put *Antiques Cymru* in diary and order tickets," she scribbled.

A smaller, regional version of a national television program, *Antiques Cymru* travelled exclusively throughout Wales, filming in towns and villages where local experts evaluated fine art, stamps, coins, books, jewellery, textiles, ceramics, collections of memorabilia, and amusing oddments, decorative or useful, that defied any category.

The two women continued on their way and had almost reached the Llanelen Spa when Penny Brannigan, one of its co-owners, approached them from the other direction.

"Oh, Penny," said Mrs. Lloyd, with just the slightest hint of annoying smugness. "You'll never guess. *Antiques Cymru* is coming to town. Florence and I are heading home this very minute to see what we can dig out that might be of value. You see those people turn up with what they thought was an old bit of tat and it turns out to be worth a fortune. Maybe that'll be me!"

"Maybe it will," agreed Penny. "So the signs are up, then. Good."

"Yes, we saw the sign in the newsagent's window just now,"

said Mrs. Lloyd, her eyebrows arching in puzzlement. "Wait a minute. How did you know about the signs?"

"Because I asked for them to be put there," replied Penny. "Emyr asked me if I'd help out with the event, and I said I would. Someone gave him the wrong information in a telephone message and at first we thought it was the big national antiques program, but it's *Antiques Cymru,* with its focus on local items of interest."

"Well, you might have told me," grumbled Mrs. Lloyd. "I shouldn't have to find out about an important event like this from a sign in a shop window when the organizer is known to me personally."

"Sorry, Mrs. Lloyd. I'm not really the organizer, though. The television production company takes care of everything. It's their show." She exchanged a quick smile with Florence and prepared to move on. "Well, mustn't keep you." She held up a brown envelope. "My turn to do the bank run."

A few minutes later she pushed open the door of the bank and joined the short queue. The man just ahead of her had turned around when the door opened and raised a hand at Penny in a small, friendly gesture. He was Haydn Williams, a hill farmer, known throughout the area for his prize-winning sheep and beautiful singing voice. In his mid-forties, he was tall, with refined features that included friendly eyes that gave him a quiet, sensitive look. He lived alone just outside town, on a narrow country road, in the same grey stone farmhouse with a grey slate roof where his parents, grandparents, great-grandparents, and several generations before that had raised their families and tended countless flocks of prize-winning sheep.

"Good to see you, Penny. How are you? Recovered from the St. David's Day concert?"

"Just about, thanks, Haydn. What's new with you?"

"Oh, not much. It's always busy on the farm this time of year, with lambing season approaching. You should come up and see them this year. You could bring your sketchbook."

"I'd love to! If there's anything cuter than a lamb, I don't know what that is. Oh, and by the way, *Antiques Cymru* is coming to town in May. I'm helping out with the event and I especially wanted you to know about it as you've got so many wonderful traditional Welsh pieces up at the farm. Please consider having one or two of them evaluated. The organizers are hoping to see some lovely furniture and I know you've got some."

"I guess all that lot would be considered antiques now. I never take any notice of them. It's just the furniture I grew up with. The Welsh dresser's been in the kitchen longer than even my grandfather could remember."

As she handed him a flyer promoting the show, the door opened and the woman in the bright green coat who had been looking at the sign in the newsagent's window a few minutes earlier entered. Penny and Haydn smiled a greeting at her, and then resumed their conversation as the woman took her place in the queue behind Penny.

"Now Haydn, if you've got a large piece of furniture you'd like appraised, such as that Welsh dresser, you contact the show ahead of time and they'll inspect the piece at your home. Then, if they want it on the show, they'll make arrangements to transport it safely up to the Hall."

Haydn's eyes flickered past Penny and appraised the woman in the green coat and then returned to meet Penny's amused gaze.

"That sounds good," he said as the woman in the green

coat leaned slightly around Penny and pointed at the flyer in Haydn's hand.

"I've just seen the poster in the newsagent's window," said Catrin Bellis. "I'm sure everybody's wondering what unknown treasure they've got hidden away in their attic just waiting to be discovered."

At that moment the customer being served wrapped up his business and with a nod to both women and one last appreciative glance at Catrin, Haydn stepped up to the wicket. Penny and Catrin shuffled forward.

Catrin Bellis was about the same age as Haydn. Her platinum blonde hair was styled in a pixie cut and she wore soft makeup, expertly applied, that gave her a healthy, natural look. She smiled at Penny, revealing a row of even, white teeth. Penny's eyes moved down to look at her hands, but they were covered in black leather gloves. Something of a late bloomer, Catrin had only recently started coming to the Llanelen Spa. Until a few months ago, her hair had been a mousy brown of uneven length flecked with grey, her eyebrows unshaped, and her hands and fingernails rough and uncared for. And following her makeover at the hands of the Llanelen Spa's experts in hair and skin care, came the welcome and novel discovery that men found her attractive. Even Haydn Williams, whom she'd known all her life and who hadn't paid the slightest bit of attention to her since they were children, was starting to sit up and take notice. And she liked the way that made her feel.

"We're hoping for a good turn out to the Antiques event," Penny said. "Do you think there's something in your home you could bring along to show the appraisers?"

"Oh, I'm sure there is," replied Catrin. "And I don't think you need to worry about people turning up. This will be one of the biggest events in Llanelen in a very long time. Possibly bigger even than the last visit by the Prince of Wales, and that's saying something. Everyone in town has probably heard about the show by now. You know what this place is like."

Two

This place is Llanelen, located on the picturesque River Conwy in North Wales. Penny had arrived in the pretty market town about twenty-five years ago as a young Canadian fine arts graduate, fallen in love with the area, and stayed on as the days turned into months, and then into years. About eighteen months ago, she and her friend and business partner, Victoria Hopkirk, had renovated a dilapidated stone building with what estate agents like to call "splendid views" across the river to the ancient hills that cradle the town and reopened it as the Llanelen Spa. The cool, stylish Spa had quickly become a destination for local women as a restful place for pampering, taking care of body and soul, and for Evelyn Lloyd, the town's former postmistress, it was the perfect place to keep up with local news, or, if you prefer, to pick up and spread local gossip.

Mrs. Lloyd settled herself in the client's chair and lowered her fingers into the soaking water as the first step in her bi-weekly manicure. She used to come every week, but lately, as part of her belt-tightening efforts, had decided once every two weeks was enough.

"I saw Catrin Bellis in front of the newsagent's looking at the *Antiques Cymru* poster," Mrs. Lloyd remarked. "I've no doubt she'll have a few bits and pieces in that house of hers she could bring. Her parents didn't have a lot of money, but her mother did have good taste and looked after her things."

Penny nodded as she picked up Mrs. Lloyd's hand and began shaping her fingernails. "I'm sure there are many households in this area with valuables that people don't know they have. From what I've seen, people around here tend to live in the family home for generations and hang on to their ancestors' property."

"True," said Mrs. Lloyd, "but I think you'll find that's changing. Many young people nowadays don't want all that heavy furniture, sets of dishes, large paintings, longcase clocks, and what have you. The children grow up, move away, and they live in small flats in cities . . . there just isn't room for all those old-fashioned things. And I'm sure most of the stuff in the charity shops comes from the grandmother's house. She dies and the family has no room for all her stuff. Have you ever noticed how much royal memorabilia there is in the charity shops? Coronation mugs, jubilee biscuit tins, royal wedding this and that. All that's got to be from house clearings after a grandparent died. Young people don't collect that stuff."

She leaned forward to see what Penny was doing.

"All rather sad when you think about it, really," she said, settling back in her chair. "Still, I'll definitely be at the Antiques show. I haven't decided yet what I'm going to bring. I was thinking about Arthur's aunt's Carlton Ware dinner service but Florence said there might be something else and she'd have a good look round."

"I wonder if Florence will bring anything," Penny said.

"Florence?" Mrs. Lloyd scoffed. "What on earth could she possibly have that would be of value?"

"Well, that's the beauty of it," said Penny. "You never know."

"That's right," agreed Mrs. Lloyd in a friendly fashion, "you don't. Well, getting back to Catrin Bellis, I don't think I've ever seen such a transformation in a woman. She used to be so, well, what we used to call plain, and now, she's all glammed up. Even had her teeth done, I believe. Who has white, even teeth like that around here? No one. And the men are really starting to take notice. And when I say 'men,' that includes men who should know better."

Penny raised an eyebrow and Mrs. Lloyd mouthed, "Married."

"Or so I've heard," Mrs. Lloyd went on, "and I saw her myself walking down the street with a," she lowered her voice again, "married man."

"Oh, but that doesn't mean anything," said Penny. "You know how easy it is to bump into someone you know, you realize you're going in the same direction, so you walk off together."

"Well, that's true," acknowledged Mrs. Lloyd, "but there's walking down the street together and then there's 'walking down the street together' if you see what I mean."

"No," said Penny, trying not to laugh. "I don't see what you mean. Unless you mean there's walking down the street together at seven in the morning, which some might well find suspicious, and then there's just your regular walking down the street together at any old time of day."

"That's exactly what I mean!" said Mrs. Lloyd. "Well, sort of, I guess."

"Anyway, I saw Catrin in the bank this morning," said Penny. "She puts the rest of us to shame, really. Wears makeup when she's just out and about on errands." A light smile crossed her face. "Even just walking down the street. Most of us consider ourselves dolled up if we bother to put on lipstick."

"I can remember the old days when women would wear a dress and put on a hat just to go shopping," said Mrs. Lloyd. "Gloves, too, for heaven's sake. Mind you, that's going back a good few years. More than I care to remember, actually. I guess going into town was more special back then."

Penny smiled and reached for the bottle of nail varnish Mrs. Lloyd had chosen.

"Got everything? Gathered up all your bits and pieces? Want to put your coat on before we do this?"

Mrs. Lloyd slid her arms through the sleeves of her spring coat and sat down again.

"I don't think Catrin had much of a life while her parents were alive," she continued. "So maybe that's what's brought all this on. Very religious, they were, and so strict with her. Much too strict. You've got to let young people have fun. She was never allowed to go to the dances or young people's outings when she was a teenager, and not allowed to train for anything so she could get a decent job. Such a shame. If only those kinds of controlling parents knew how their children would go wild at the first opportunity. And who can blame them? The girls often end up in the family way and the boys in trouble with the law."

She peered at the polish Penny was applying. "Yes, that's a nice colour. Has a lovely touch of spring in it."

"I heard somewhere that Catrin looked after her parents for years," Penny said.

"That's right," said Mrs. Lloyd. "They kept her at home and she never had much of a life, really. They were well into their forties when she was born and they died quite close to each other. She hasn't been on her own that long and in some ways, she's like a much younger girl living on her own for the first time. Enjoying her freedom and turning into the woman she wants to be, not what her parents thought she should be."

"She's quite girly," said Penny. "Likes pretty things and loves coming here for hair and nails." She laughed. "Our kind of girl, really."

"I think at one time Haydn Williams's parents had hopes the two might get together," said Mrs. Lloyd, "but her parents seem to have quashed any chance of that happening."

"Well," said Penny, "if the way he looked at her in the bank today is anything to go by, they might still get together. He seemed rather interested in her."

"Oh, that'll be the new hair," said Mrs. Lloyd. "Men can be so shallow that way, I find."

Penny laughed. "She's lost a fair bit of weight, too," said Penny. "All in all, I think she's doing a great job of making the best of herself. I might take a page out of her book and lose a few pounds myself."

Three

Catrin Bellis entered the dark, outdated kitchen, dropped her small bag of shopping on the green linoleum floor, and filled the kettle. While the water heated she put away the groceries and a few minutes later walked into the sitting room with a cup of tea on a small tray. While her parents were alive the tea would have been accompanied by a couple of biscuits or a home-baked scone or tea cake but now that she was free to do as she pleased, biscuits were not allowed in the house. Neither was meat. Her father had been a butcher and how she hated the sight and smell of meat. The very idea of the traditional roast beef Sunday lunch her mother served after chapel, with the roast potatoes and sprouts, followed by a stodgy pudding, made her nauseous. Now, she might have an occasional fillet of grilled salmon with some green beans and new potatoes, but for the most part her diet was vegetarian.

She'd been nervous in the supermarket this morning when she inserted her bank card into the little machine to pay for her groceries. How embarrassing it would be to have it declined in full view of the people behind her in the queue and the teenage cashier. But she'd been careful what she'd put in her shopping basket, keeping a running total as she went and her transaction had gone through. Going forward, though, she'd have to be much more careful with her money.

She thought, not for the first time, that perhaps she should sell the house. She'd probably get a good price for it, and she could use that money to buy a small flat. Even though the house wasn't large, she could easily get by in a smaller space. She didn't need two bedrooms, for a start.

And maybe she should even consider leaving the town and relocating to a larger place where there'd be more opportunities. But opportunities for what? She had no training to do anything. What kind of job could she hope to get? Here, in Llanelen, at least she knew a few people. There, in a larger town, she'd know no one. And property prices were rising, so it might be best to hang on to the house for the time being. Perhaps she could take in a lodger, a single woman perhaps. She could rent out her parents' old bedroom. She'd barely set foot in it since her mother died.

She wished her father had been open about the family finances but he didn't think women needed to know about that sort of thing, or much of anything at all, for that matter. Her mother was just as much in the dark as she was when her father had died. Neither woman knew where the banking papers were kept, or his will, or any of the important papers. Eventually Catrin had found a metal box with what looked like important papers in it, so she took them to the bank and had a friendly chat with the new manager who pored over the papers. While she sat anxiously in the hard wooden visitor's chair, listening to his wheezy breathing, he studied the documents, turning them face down on his desk with stubby fingers as he finished with each one. Finally, he refolded the last piece of paper and placed them all back in the metal box. He clasped his hands together, placed his arms on his desk up to his elbows, and leaned forward.

Her father had left everything to her mother, the banker informed her, but eventually all assets would come to her, and when her mother died unexpectedly just a few months after her father, they did. She had no delusions that her mother had died of a broken heart, like the couples you read about in the papers when one partner couldn't live without the other. Her mother had just seemed unsure how to be in the world without her father telling her what to do and how to do it every five minutes. In Catrin's opinion, her mother just gave up.

After her father had sold the butcher shop, he invested the proceeds in safe financial instruments that weren't due to mature for another three years. They were earning about as much interest as could be expected, the banker told her, but if she cashed them in now, there would be heavy penalties.

She wished she had someone besides a bank manager she scarcely knew to advise her, someone with her best interests at heart, someone who cared only for her well being and happiness. There had been someone, once, but her father had made sure that came to nothing. A lad had walked home with her after school, but instead of inviting him in for a cup of tea and a bun as other mothers would have done, her mother had closed the door sending the boy away and Catrin to her room. You know what your father's like, she'd said, and we must obey his

15

wishes. Of course the lad had taken no more notice of her. There'd been another boy a year or two later but her parents had not permitted them to walk out together and he eventually married Tegwen, a schoolmate of hers, who was still her closest friend. He and Tegwen were now the parents of two teenage daughters and he was active in the local Rotary and served on the town council. She'd thought of him over the years and wondered why her parents had been so determined to stand in the way of her happiness. She envied Tegwen her happy family life. How different her life would be now if she had a home of her own, a nice little place in the country maybe, filled with the love of a decent man and their children.

She sighed and taking her tea with her, went upstairs. The wooden stairs creaked beneath her feet. At the landing, instead of turning left into her little room with its sloping ceiling, she turned right and pressed down on the latch that opened the door to her parents' slightly larger bedroom.

The curtains were kept drawn, so she pulled them apart, letting in a weak stream of afternoon sunlight that cast a slanted shaft of light across the bed and onto the floor. The air felt stale and close; it was obvious that the room was unoccupied. The furniture was solid and heavy, with two oak chests of drawers, part of a set, against one wall. The taller one with five drawers had belonged to her father. On top of the shorter one, which had belonged to her mother, sat two framed photos and a silver-backed hairbrush. She picked up a photo and tilted it toward the window. Her mother, her hair upswept in a beehive hairdo and wearing a sleeveless summer dress, gazed lovingly at the little girl in her arms. Catrin's eyes filled with tears as she set the faded colour photo back on the chest of drawers and picked up the hairbrush.

Her mother had never asked for much, but had always longed for a dressing table with three mirrors, lots of drawers, and a matching stool that tucked away when not in use, but her stern father had refused to have such an item of furniture in the house, saying it catered to a woman's vanity and would set a bad example for Catrin.

Hairbrush in hand, Catrin sat on the edge of the bed. The worn mattress on its ancient, metal bedsprings sagged beneath her weight. They should have been replaced years ago, and if she did get in a lodger, she'd have to find the money for a new set of box springs with a decent mattress. She looked down and ran her fingers lightly over the handmade quilt that had covered her parents' double bed for as long as she could remember. When she was very small and home from school sick, her mother had wrapped her in the quilt and kept her downstairs on the sofa where she could keep an eye on her as she went about her tasks. But she'd made sure Catrin was back upstairs in her bed by the time her father came home and the quilt returned to its place on their bed.

The pattern was a simple geometric design of turquoise triangles on a white background. Catrin had never really thought about it before, but now she considered it rather modern in its choice of colour and its clean, uncluttered design.

She was sure her mother must have told her who had sewn it, but she couldn't remember—either her grandmother or great-grandmother. Probably her great-grandmother as a young girl, as the initials JB in a circle had been carefully embroidered on the bottom layer. Her great-grandmother's maiden name was Jane Bellis, so it was likely her. That's the trouble with family history, Catrin was starting to realize. When your parents are telling you about your grandparents

17

and great-grandparents you don't care. And then, when you're older and you do care, your parents are no longer alive to answer questions or recount family history.

She stood up and opened the wardrobe door. It was past time—she should have got rid of this lot months ago. She pulled out her father's Sunday best suit and his white shirts and laid them on the bed. She'd bundle them up in the morning for the charity shop, although they were so worn and outdated she doubted anyone would want them. Her mother's skirts and dresses would be a little more difficult to part with, but they had to go, too. She'd bring in some bags tomorrow and get that done. There was no point in holding on to these garments and the memories they held any longer.

The last thing she saw before she closed the door was her father's suit on the bed. She shifted it onto the room's only chair and then surveyed the quilt as an idea began to nibble at the edges of her mind.

But for now, she'd better hurry if she was to catch the 2:10 bus as her friend Tegwen didn't like to be kept waiting. It was all very well for her; her husband had bought her that little car to run about in. But if Catrin was just a minute or two late, Tegwen would punish her for about half an hour with cool indifference. Then she'd warm up and the two would be best friends again, just like they'd been in their school days, laughing and chatting about everything in general and nothing in particular.

Four

I'm not late, am I?" said Catrin anxiously, sliding into the seat opposite Tegwen. "I know how you hate to be kept waiting." With the exception of an elderly couple seated at the window, the two women had the café to themselves, as the lunchtime rush was over and the after-school crowd had yet to arrive.

"No, you're all right," Tegwen replied, "I got here early." About the same age as Catrin, Tegwen wore her dark, shoulder-length hair styled in loose curls that framed a round, open face. "What are you having?"

"Just a coffee for me."

"Oh, but they have St. Clement's cake today and I wanted a slice. You'd better have one to keep me company."

"Not for me, thanks," said Catrin. "I've been reading how harmful sugar is and I really am trying to cut back."

"Well, that's not very friendly," pouted Tegwen. "How can I have a slice of cake if you don't? I'll look a right pig."

Catrin shrugged. "I doubt anyone will notice," she said, glancing at the elderly couple who sat wrapped in the silence of decades as they gazed out the window. And then, as Tegwen's nose wrinkled in disapproval, Catrin heard herself blurting out, "Well, maybe we could share one, then."

Tegwen brightened at the suggestion. "Yes, of course we can." She handed Catrin a ten-pound note. "Here, you go over to the counter and get me a latte and piece of cake out of that." Catrin took the money and returned a few minutes later with two coffees and a white plate with a piece of cake on a brown serving tray.

Catrin smiled at her companion as she set the latte and the slice of cake in front of her. Tegwen did not return the smile, but frowned as a look of something Catrin couldn't make out flashed across her grey eyes. Catrin placed the change from the ten-pound note in front of Tegwen as she sat down.

"You're so lucky you don't have a family to worry about, Catrin," Tegwen sighed, ignoring the change and picking up the fork. She sliced the pale orange icing off the cake to save for last. "It's just one thing after another."

"Is there a problem with the girls?" Catrin asked, wrapping her hands around the less expensive plain coffee she'd bought for herself. It would have been a nice gesture, she thought, if Tegwen had told her to pay for her coffee out of the ten-pound note.

"No, not the girls, no," said Tegwen, tucking into the cake, all thoughts of sharing apparently forgotten. "Well, just the usual. You have no idea how difficult teenage girls are these days." Actually, Catrin had a fair idea what was involved, having listened to Tegwen often enough going on about her two daughters and their insatiable demands for new clothes, makeup, and top ups for their phones. And how the girls were never off those phones, never lifted a finger to help out around the house, or showed the slightest bit of gratitude for all the things their parents gave them. And who raised them to be that way, Catrin was tempted to ask.

"Of course, you never got married," Tegwen continued, gesturing slightly with the fork held in fingers that bordered on chubby. "Lucky you just got yourself to worry about." She took a sip of her latte and then licked a bit of foam off her top lip and shot Catrin a sly, measured look.

"Anyway, it isn't the girls I want to talk about today. It's Brad."

"Oh, yes." Catrin didn't want the conversation to go in this direction. There was something so unpleasantly intimate about listening to the details of someone else's marriage. Tegwen sometimes recounted squabbles or disagreements she had with her husband, usually to do with his working long hours at his insurance business or having to spend his evenings visiting clients in their homes. What did Tegwen expect? She didn't work outside the home and apparently someone had to pay for the expensive items on the girls' ever growing list of wants.

Tegwen cleared her throat and ran a hand under her chin. "This is a bit difficult, so I guess the best thing is for me to be direct. Apparently, there are rumours. A good friend of mine told me that Brad's been seen with a woman, and well, I wondered if it was you."

"Me?" Catrin's eyebrows shot up.

"Well, yes, you. Apparently the woman has short blonde hair and wears a green coat. You always liked him and now that you're, well, coming out of your shell, shall we say, men are starting to notice you. And you don't have much experience of them, so you might easily be . . ."

"If that's what you think, Tegwen, then obviously you don't think much of me." Catrin stood up. "Or your husband, either, for that matter."

"No, wait, Catrin, I didn't mean it like that. Please sit down," said Tegwen, reaching out to her. The elderly couple turned their heads toward them and Tegwen lowered her voice. "I'm sorry, that came out all wrong. I'm very worried, that's all. I've heard things, and I don't know what to do. I thought I'd ask you if you knew anything."

"You weren't asking me," said Catrin, as she sank reluctantly back into her seat. "You were practically accusing me of having an affair with your husband."

"There's just no one else I could think of that fit the description," said Tegwen, with a forced, shallow laugh.

"Have you spoken to Brad? He's the one you should be talking to, not me. But since you have asked me, then no, I haven't heard anything."

"It's just that you spend time at the Spa, and I thought you might have picked up something there. The place is filled with women, and they, well, they do talk."

Catrin shook her head.

"No, I haven't heard anything. But I think you should talk to Brad and hear what he has to say." A gloomy silence settled over them and in its awkwardness they finished up their coffees and gathered up their things, just as the café began to fill up with the after-school crowd.

"I'd offer you a lift home," Tegwen began, "but I have to pick the girls up from school."

"Of course you do," said Catrin stiffly. "No worries. I'm fine on the bus."

Normally, there would have been a quick hug and an exchange of "see you soon," but Catrin plunged out through the café door and did not look back.

As she waited for the bus, words from the conversation tumbled round in her mind like clothes in a dryer. She'd been feeling uncomfortable with Tegwen for some time. They just didn't seem to connect the way they used to. Catrin was tired of listening to the endless complaints about the daughters and husband. And to her, of all people! Didn't Tegwen realize how much she longed for a family of her own? And although she'd never said anything, Catrin sensed that Tegwen disapproved of the improvements she was making to her physical appearance and the way she was taking better care of herself—especially the weight loss. She was always going on about how hard it was for her to lose weight, and her complexion was looking very dull and the skin on her neck was starting to sag and Catrin had to reassure her that she looked as good as, if not better, than other women her age.

When is it time to end a friendship, she wondered. When the things you don't like about someone begin to overwhelm the good things? And then the answer came to her. When it just isn't fun anymore.

Five

Two weeks before *Antiques Cymru* was scheduled to visit the town, Haydn Williams received a telephone call. The advance team was going to be in the area and was interested in the item of furniture he had described in his submission to them. Could he make it available for a pre-show inspection? Certainly he'd replied.

"Come in. Never mind the shoes," Haydn said. "Come in, do." The evaluator from the television program entered his warm kitchen with its flagstone floor. A black and white Border collie, asleep in his basket beside the Aga, roused himself and stood up to greet the visitor.

"That's our Kip," said Haydn. "Don't mind him. He's very friendly, aren't you boy?" Kip wagged his feathery tail and the stranger gave him a friendly pat.

"I've just made a pot of tea, if you'd like some," Haydn said.

"Indeed I would. That would be most welcome. Thank you." He held out his hand. "Daniel Casey." Haydn handed him a mug of tea and then gestured to a door on the far side of the kitchen. "Just through here," he said. "There's a little ante-room."

Daniel Casey stood for a few moments, examining the well-proportioned, finely crafted piece of furniture with his eyes. It stood just a little over three feet tall, with a graceful silhouette that included an angled top.

After taking several digital photographs from all angles he turned to Haydn. "It's a lovely English fall-front walnut bureau. I'll have a better idea how old it is in a minute or two, after I've had a closer look, but it could be Queen Anne period. Have you emptied it?"

As he'd been asked to do, Haydn had removed all its contents so every inch of the bureau would be easily accessible for the evaluation.

"Well, let's see what we have here then, shall we?" said Casey. He waved a hand in front of the bureau. "It has a configuration of two drawers over two, with one long thin drawer for paperwork." The two bottom drawers were each the width of the bureau; above them were two drawers, each half the width.

Casey pulled out one of these drawers and turned it slightly so Haydn had a clear view of it.

"The dovetails run all the way down to the front of the drawer's facing, so that shows it's an early piece," he said, pointing to them. "Plus, the sides and bottom are made of oak and if you look at the grain on the bottom, you can see that it runs front to back. On the later pieces, it ran side to side. So this is an early piece. I'd place it about 1730, or possibly even ten years earlier."

"That old?" said Haydn. "I never would have thought."

"Now, then," said Casey, "let's see what secrets this bureau holds."

He tugged on two small brass knobs just above the drawers, and two pieces of wood slid out. He then lifted the cover of the desk toward himself and rested it gently on the pulls. With the desk open, he proceeded to examine the interior.

He pushed back a wooden bar on top of the work surface, revealing a space below the main body of the desk. "This is called the well," he told Haydn. "And again, you can see that the grain runs front to back, so that's good. This was the place to keep deeds or other documents you'd want close to hand."

"And a good way to keep down the clutter," Haydn said. "Just chuck all the bits and pieces in there, close the lid, and the desk top is nice and tidy."

The upright part of the bureau featured three pigeonholes on each side of a small locked door with two columns separating the pigeonholes from the door. A little gold key was in the lock. He turned the lock and peered inside. Empty.

Below the pigeonholes was a small drawer. He ran his hands along the top of the pigeonholes, feeling his way behind a bit of decorative woodwork.

"These are called canopies," he said, referring to the delicate work that framed the top of the pigeonholes. "There's nothing behind there, so that tells me we have to look elsewhere for the hidden compartments."

He took out each drawer and finding no place to set them, handed them to Haydn. He reached his hand in the spaces where the drawers had been and flicked a little tab. This freed the box with the lock in it and he gently pulled it out. It resembled a small wooden safe.

"And now," said Casey, "we come to the real secret compartment. The box has a false back." He turned it around so Haydn could watch as he slowly raised the back of the box, revealing a hidden compartment.

"Oh, wow!" said Haydn as Daniel removed a wooden box from the back and then slid a little latch to open it. "I never knew that was there. Is there anything in it?"

"No," said Daniel. "I'm sure it's been used for storage at some point, but nothing here now."

"What sort of things would have been kept there?" Haydn asked.

"Well, a few centuries ago, people didn't have nearly as much stuff as we do now. But the gentleman who owned this bureau might have kept his property deeds or family wills—that sort of thing. And sometimes these compartments come with little locks, so he could have kept things he didn't want his missus to know about—letters from the mistress, maybe."

He pulled out two more drawers, set them on the floor and then peered into the innermost depths of the bureau.

"What's the most interesting thing you've ever found squirreled away in one of these things?" asked Haydn.

"I guess the neatest thing I ever found was a pearl-handled opera glass. That tells you something about the status of the person who once owned it, doesn't it?"

He bent over and picked up a drawer. "Well, that's it for the bureau," he said as he slid the drawer back into place and reached for the other one. "All secrets revealed. What can you tell me about this bureau? How did you come to have it?"

"It's always been there," Haydn replied. "I've lived in this house all my life and it was there when I was growing up. My father told me it was there when he was a lad, so it was here in my grandparents' time and probably long before that."

Daniel Casey took a sip of tea and ran an affectionate, knowledgeable hand along the top of the desk. "I'm always happy to see one of these lovely pieces of furniture," he said, "and the longer they've been in the same family, the better."

As he finished speaking, from another room came the mellow tones of a clock chiming five times. Casey checked his watch. It was exactly 5 P.M.

"You've got a clock?"

"Oh, yes. Longcase."

"I wouldn't mind a look at it, since I'm here. Would that be all right with you?"

"Of course. Just through here." Haydn opened a door off the anteroom and led the way into a small sitting room. Daniel Casey stepped back fifty years into a parlour that Haydn's mother and grandmother would have used only on the most special occasions—after a funeral, perhaps, or when the vicar came to call. A fine layer of dust covered the furniture and the room had the musty smell of a room rarely used. An upright piano with brass candle holders attached to its upper front board stood in one corner. A faded burgundy sofa with crocheted antimacassars along the back was positioned against the far wall, resting on an almost threadbare carpet. In the opposite corner to the piano stood a longcase clock.

Casey approached it and once again took several photographs. He stood back and with his arms folded, took in the clock from top to bottom. Haydn remained silent. Finally, Casey spoke.

"And how long has this been in your family?"

"Well, that one I do know a little more about. According to my father, it's been in the family since it was made."

Casey nodded and a slight smile twitched at the corner of his lips. "Do you know how long ago that was?"

"Sometime in the 1800s?"

"Go back another hundred years. It was made about 1760 or perhaps a few years later by John Owen himself, one of the most famous clockmakers in all of Wales. This clock is a stunning example of his work. The beautiful brass dial engraved with sunflowers is exquisite." Casey grinned. "That's what I love about this job. You just never know when you get up in the morning what the day will bring."

He pulled a small notebook out of his pocket and wrote a few lines.

"Wonderful that it's been in your family that long. And it's still keeping perfect time. These clocks are sensitive—they have to be level and they like a nice moderate temperature, so obviously it's very happy where it is and it's been well cared for." He ran his hands down the side of the clock. "The cabinetry is perfect. No swelling or buckling."

"It's oak, I believe," said Haydn. "The cabinet was made from oak trees that grew in this area, my father told me. My mate told me after I wrote in to your program about the desk that I should have mentioned the clock as it was apparently made locally and the program likes to feature local artifacts."

Casey raised his arms and gently lifted the hood off the clock, exposing the time-keeping mechanism behind the dial.

"What are you doing?" asked Haydn.

"Checking to make sure that the mechanism and the cabinet are of the same period and were made to go together.

Sometimes you see the wrong mechanism in the wrong cabinet, but that's not the case here. This clock is everything it should be. And then some."

He slid the hood back into place and then, with his arms straight in front of him, ran his hands down the sides of the clock with his fingers curled around the back of it until he had almost reached the base. When his hands were about a foot from the floor he stopped, leaned to the left side of the clock, and turned it gently, exposing part of the clock's back and with two fingers, extracted a piece of rolled paper.

"This was hidden in the hollow of the decorative moulding," he said handing it to Haydn who unrolled it, examined it for a moment, and then held it out to Casey.

"A rough map of some kind," Casey suggested. "Well, half a map. You can see where it's been torn in half. Drawn by a child, perhaps? That's the sort of thing kids do, isn't it?"

"I've no idea what this is or how it got there," said Haydn. "I've never seen it before. But my mother was a meticulous housekeeper and I'm surprised she never found it."

Casey returned the clock to its original position flush against the wall, stepped back, and offered his hand to Haydn. "Well, that's all for today," he said. "It's been a pleasure meeting you and thank you for showing me your beautiful pieces. I'll have a little chat with the team and we'll be in touch to let you know what happens next."

"Can you tell me a little about the pieces?" Haydn said. "What did you think of the bureau?"

"Very nice." He smiled. "I can't say too much yet, but you'll get our professional opinion soon. You'll just have to be patient."

"I guess I will. Well, if that's everything, I'll show you out," said Haydn.

When Casey had left, Haydn poured himself a large whisky and sat at the kitchen table staring at the map.

It was crudely hand drawn in pencil on a piece of lined paper. The person who had made the map had indicated a couple of buildings with square boxes, wavy lines indicating what Haydn guessed was meant to be a river, and odd circles on sticks that he took to be trees. Oval shapes on four sticks he thought might be sheep and the lines surrounding them could be stone walls. There were two initials in the lower left corner: WW. He thought it likely that the W stood for Williams, his surname, and if so, the map must have been made by someone in his family. He returned to the little-used parlour and from a small table in the corner picked up a large black book he rarely touched: the family Bible. In the back, carefully entered by various maternal ancestors, were the names of his parents, grandparents, great-grandparents, and so on, going back to the early 1800s. The entries contained the dates of their births, christenings, marriages, and deaths, all written in an old-fashioned script. The ink had faded but the names were still legible. The last entry was the date of his own christening, August 30, 1970, written in his mother's hand. If and when he married, his bride would enter the date of their marriage and then, in the years that followed, the particulars of their children, if any, although he had to admit that was looking increasingly unlikely. His thoughts turned to Catrin Bellis. How pretty she'd become lately. He wondered if maybe he should ask her out. Where would he ask her to go? He knew very little about her—what she liked or didn't like. The pictures were always a safe bet as long as it was something appropriate and not too violent or with what they called sexually explicit content. And then something nice to eat afterward so they could talk and get to know each other a little better. Or maybe if she liked flowers and walking, they could spend an afternoon at Bodnant Garden and then have tea. That sounded like a nice idea. Now all he had to do was find the courage to ask her.

He took another sip of whisky and turned his attention back to the piece of paper on the table. Something puzzled him. That Daniel Casey appraiser fellow had given the bureau a thorough going over, showing him all those little hidey holes where someone could easily have hidden the map. So the question was: why would someone who wanted to hide something as simple as a piece of paper choose the clock when he might have used all those secret compartments? Surely the bureau would have been a much more logical place. He gave his head a little shake and drained the last of the whisky.

"Come on, Kip," he said to the Border collie who'd been watching him from his cozy basket. "Time for the pub." Kip sat up eagerly, gave a few hearty thumps of his tail, and a few minutes later the two set off on their daily walk down the narrow lane that led to town.

Six

*H*aydn! Kip! Good to see you, boyo! We got yours in."
One of the ruddy-faced men seated around an oak table
in the main room of the Leek and Lily pointed at the full glass
awaiting Haydn. He returned his friends' greetings while he
hung up his coat and let Kip off his lead. The dog immediately
made for the fireplace and lay down in front of the open fire, his
paws stretched out toward it.

"Cheers," said Haydn, raising his glass to his friends and then
taking a long, welcome sip. He set his glass down and took a
slow look around the room. "Not too many in tonight," he remarked.

The Leek and Lily, with its uneven floorboards, whitewashed
walls hung with horse brasses and sporting prints, exuded a
sense of awareness of its timeless place in local history. No

modern flat screen televisions or noisy, flashing gambling machines disturbed the pub's warm, relaxed atmosphere, establishing it as a place to gather for a cozy chat or a spirited discussion, to drink good ale and eat hearty, traditional food like bangers and mash, and steak and kidney pie.

The low-beamed ceiling ensured a jolly noise level at the bar, and local men had been polishing the chairs and tables with their bottoms and elbows for over a century. Although women were welcome here, most of its customers tended to be men.

Like Haydn, the men who greeted him were hill farmers, men whose families had raised sheep for generations on the rugged slopes that kept watch over the town. Life was robust and challenging for these farmers in their flat cloth caps, chunky sweaters, baggy trousers, and Wellington boots. Their workdays started early and usually ended late, moving forward in endless, timeless rhythm with the changing seasons. Lambing was well underway for this year and for the past two or three weeks the farmers had barely had time to draw breath. But now, in the time before they have to mark and vaccinate the sheep, they could relax a little, and once again enjoy an evening down the pub with friends as a small reward for all the hard work of the previous weeks.

The men discussed the news of the day for a few minutes, and then Evan Hughes, seated on Haydn's left, turned to him and asked, "How did you get on with that *Antiques Cymru* fellow? It was today he was coming to check out the bureau, wasn't it?"

"Aye," said Haydn. "He checked it over, all right, and even showed me secret compartments I didn't know were there. But then he asked to see the clock and, to be honest, I think he was more interested in it than the bureau. You were right; I should have told him about the clock since it's a local piece and the bureau is English."

"Is it a Watkin Owen?" asked the man directly across from Haydn.

"No," said Haydn. "It's an authentic John Owen and it's been in my family since Adam were a lad. Lived all its life right here in Llanelen, it has."

"What did he tell you about it?" Evan Hughes asked.

"Not that much, really," said Haydn reaching into his pocket. "But when he pulled it out a bit from the wall and reached round the back, he found this." He held up the piece of paper. "Rolled up, it was, and stuffed into the moulding that goes round the base of the clock."

"What is it?" asked one of the men. "It doesn't look like a banknote from where I'm sitting!" The others laughed and Haydn shook his head.

"No, it isn't. It looks like one half of a map." He passed it to the man on his right who glanced at it, then passed it on. It circulated around the table until it came to Evan Hughes.

"What do you think this is meant to be?" he asked, tilting the paper to catch the light while he peered at it, and then turning it over so he could see if anything was written on the back.

"I have no idea what it is or where it came from," replied Haydn. "He found it just before he left, the fellow did. I haven't a clue what it means or how long it was hidden in that clock. But a long time would be my guess."

They marveled at the map for a few minutes and then the conversation moved on to the most important element in a farmer's life: the weather. The long-range forecast predicted a hot, dry summer, which boded well for their hay making. Too much rain before the mown hay can dry properly and it becomes a rotten, inedible, wasted mess, leaving the farmer with nothing to feed his ewes over the winter. Evan Hughes drained the last of the beer in his glass and set it on the table.

"It's your turn to get the round in, Haydn," one of the farmers said to him.

"Same again all round, is it?" Haydn asked. A chorus of agreement answered his question, although most said they'd just have half a pint this time as they were driving and you couldn't get away with driving home from the pub with some drink in you like you could in the old days. Kip raised his head as Haydn walked past him on his way to the bar, then lowered it as soon as he realized it wasn't time yet to go home.

Haydn paid for the drinks for everyone at his table and returned to his place. "She's bringing them over," he said. Seeing the empty seat beside him, he turned to the man on his right.

"Evan hasn't gone home, has he? I did hear that his wife was a bit poorly. She wasn't in church on Sunday and it's not like her to miss a service."

"No, no," the man reassured him. "Just gone to the gents. He'll be back." The barmaid arrived at their table balancing a tray laden with glasses. She set down five beer mats and placed a glass on top of each one, picking up their empty glasses as she worked her way around the table. She then wiped up the wet rings that had formed on the table where glasses had been set directly on it.

"Coming back, is he?" she said when she reached Evan Hughes's place. Just as she finished her question the man himself appeared and picked a glass off her tray.

"Thanks, love," he said as he sat down.

She moved on to the last man and then paused and looked down. After serving him, she bent over and picked a piece of paper off the floor. "This belong to any of you?" she asked, holding it up.

"Oh, aye, that's Haydn's map," said one. She handed it to Haydn and he set it on the table.

"I wouldn't put it there if I were you," said Evan Hughes. "The table's damp from the glasses and if there's a spill your map's had it."

"Good point," said Haydn. "I haven't had a chance to really study it, yet." He folded it in half and put it back in his pocket.

Evan Hughes was the first to leave. "The missus wants me home early tonight to put together some new shelving for her flower arranging room. Have you seen how complicated the instructions are for something like that?" He shook his head. "Well, good night, lads. See you soon." The men said good night and he opened the door and was gone. As he left, two newcomers entered the pub.

Haydn waved at Penny Brannigan, who was accompanied by Emyr Gruffydd, the local landowner who was well known to everyone in the pub. They all called out greetings to him as he and Penny made their way to a quiet table in the corner.

"What are you having, Penny?" he asked.

"Oh, a glass of white would be perfect, thanks."

He rejoined her at the table a few minutes later with a glass of wine in each hand. He set hers down in front of her, and then sat down.

"Right," he said, "as he raised his glass to her. "How are things going for *Antiques Cymru*? No problems, I hope."

"Everything's going very well," she replied. "The show obviously has a lot of experience with this sort of thing and is

39

very clear about what they need from us. Which isn't much. They're providing everything and doing everything, so all I need do is be there early in the morning just to make sure the production team has everything it needs."

"Good. I knew when I asked you to take this on that I could count on you."

"The logistics are fine," said Penny. "It's the weather I'm worried about."

"I expect they've dealt with a bit of rain before," said Emyr. "But let's hope for a sunny day."

Seven

*C*atrin had been pleasantly surprised to discover that letting go of a long friendship was easier than she'd thought it would be. When she hadn't heard from Tegwen for over a month, she picked up the phone several times to call her, then each time set the phone down again, the call unmade. Calling Tegwen wasn't something she wanted to do; it felt like a duty or obligation. And the longer she put off doing it, the less she wanted to do it.

Her life had moved on in another important way, too, and one that she couldn't have imagined just a few weeks earlier. She couldn't believe her luck when the local chemist offered her a part-time job behind the makeup counter.

"My wife suggested we offer you the job," the chemist said when he hired her. "She thought that since you spend so much time in front of our makeup counter, you'd do very well behind it. She wants to spend more time at home, so we'll see how things work out. If you get on well, this could become full time."

Catrin always arrived a few minutes early for work, eager to slip on her crisp, white smock. The anticipation and excitement of cutting open the small brown boxes and pulling out a dozen lipsticks or packets of eye shadow in the newest shades felt better than Christmas. She enjoyed arranging the products on the shelves in appealing, artistic displays. But most of all, she loved helping customers find the product that was perfect for their colouring, lifestyle, and budget. It wasn't long until women began heading straight to the makeup counter for a consultation before dropping off their prescription.

Within a couple of weeks the chemist had told Catrin sales were up considerably and he was very pleased with her work.

"Keep that up Catrin," he'd said, "and my wife will find herself out of a job."

"Can't come soon enough," laughed his wife with a warm smile at her protégée. Catrin blushed and went back to her task of preparing their order of summer products.

"Coral will be the next big lipstick colour," she said to the chemist's wife. "Should I order in an extra half dozen?"

"Good idea. I'm sure you'll be able to sell them. And when you've finished that, you can go for lunch," she said. A few minutes later Catrin hung up her smock on the little hook behind the dispensary door, smoothed the flirty skirt of her red and white polka dot dress, and left the shop.

With her newfound extra income she could have bought her lunch, but preferred to bring her own and, if the weather was fine, eat it picnic style sitting on a bench in the churchyard overlooking the river watching the swans drift lazily with the current. She enjoyed a cup of freshly brewed coffee with her lunch, and stopped into the little café on the town square.

"Hello, Catrin," said a male voice behind her just as she was about to place her order. "You're looking very summery today."

She turned and smiled. "Oh, hello, Brad." She turned to the barista and asked for an Americano. "Make it two," said Brad to the woman at the counter, holding out a five-pound note, "and take them both out of that."

"It's very kind of you, but I'd really rather pay for my own," protested Catrin.

"It's just a cup of coffee, Catrin," he said. "No big deal."

The woman handed them their coffees and a few moments later they stood on the cobblestones of the town square.

"Well, thank you for this," Catrin said, raising her cup slightly. "I don't have long for lunch, so I'd best get on."

"Going back to the shop, are you?" asked Brad. "I'll walk back with you."

"Actually, I was going to . . ." She caught a glimpse out of the corner of her eye of a woman with grey hair leaving the post office. Mrs. Lloyd's head turned toward them and she walked briskly in their direction. "Yes," Catrin said, "I'm just going back to work." She tipped her head in Mrs. Lloyd's direction. "I don't know what people have been saying, but I don't want to give anyone reason to talk, and I don't want anyone getting the wrong end of the stick. It's probably best if we aren't seen together."

Before Brad could reply, Mrs. Lloyd was upon them. She smiled at each one in turn, said hello, and then continued on her way to the Llanelen Spa.

Her appetite gone, Catrin set off at a fast pace to the shop. She replaced her lunch in the little fridge and tipped the untouched coffee down the sink. Honestly, what was the world coming to when you can't even stop to say hello to a man in the street without rumours starting up that there's something going on between you. She didn't even fancy Brad. She'd been that surprised when Tegwen had asked if they'd been seeing each other. She hadn't known how to tell her, in a tactful way, that she wouldn't fancy Brad if he was the last man on earth. So full of himself. He reminded her of her father, in the worst possible ways. And Mrs. Lloyd coming along just when she did was really bad luck. Catrin shuddered.

It wasn't until she had slipped on her smock that she felt calmer and back in control. As she approached the makeup counter, the chemist's wife threw her a grateful look.

"Oh, look," she said. "Here's Catrin back early from lunch. Catrin, this lady would like to know how to create a smoky eye, whatever that is. Can you help her?"

Catrin put on her best professional smile. "Of course." She made a mental note to suggest to the chemist that a proper makeup chair and large mirror would pay for themselves in no time.

Mrs. Lloyd pushed open the door to the Llanelen Spa. Tegwen Driscoll stood at the reception desk, tucking her credit card in her purse. A mischievous smile played at the corners of Mrs. Lloyd's lips.

"Hello, Tegwen. Just saw your husband getting a coffee in the square."

"Oh, yes. He likes to get out of the office for a few minutes every now and then. Stretch his legs."

Mrs. Lloyd laughed. "Oh, is that what you call it, now. Well, it certainly seemed to be doing him good. He looked very happy."

Tegwen gave her a puzzled look. "Your hair looks very nice," Mrs. Lloyd said as Tegwen brushed past her on the way out.

Mrs. Lloyd walked down the hall to the manicure room. Penny gave her a welcoming smile as she entered and waited for her to settle herself in the client's chair.

Since Penny had been so dismissive of her suggestion a few weeks ago that Catrin had an admirer, who just happened to be married, Mrs. Lloyd decided not to mention what she'd just seen in the town square. And more importantly, what she'd just heard.

Eight

The day of the *Antiques Cymru* show dawned cloudy but with a forecast of bright sunshine and unseasonable warmth.

Twenty-four hours earlier, as lorries filled with recording equipment, cables, and sets had rumbled through the town's narrow streets, townsfolk turned over their attics, spare bedrooms, and storage spaces under the stairs in search of the perfect items to bring along for evaluation.

While one or two items might turn out to be of immense value, usually unbeknownst to the owner, most would be worthless, or even worse, fakes.

Mrs. Lloyd, who had searched her home on Rosemary Lane from top to bottom looking for that rare treasure, hoped her items would fall into the former category.

"Now, come along Florence," she said picking up her

cardboard box and opening their front door. "We want to get to the Hall early so we don't have to queue for hours. I've heard people sometimes have to wait up to four hours to be seen by an appraiser!"

Florence locked the door behind them and the two women set off for the town square where a shuttle bus service had been organized to ferry the Antiques attendees back and forth to Ty Brith Hall.

"What's that you've got there, Florence?" Mrs. Lloyd asked as they turned the corner into the square and joined the small queue waiting in front of the post office. She tipped her head at the large plastic bag from the local supermarket Florence carried.

"Oh, just a few pieces of paper I thought might be worth a bob or two," Florence replied.

"We live in hope, don't we?" said Mrs. Lloyd. She sighed. "Oh, dear, I do hope I made the right decision to bring this silver tea set. I'm thinking now I should have stuck with my original plan to bring the Carlton Ware that belonged to Arthur's aunt."

"Well, the teapot is a very pretty piece," said Florence. "And Arthur's aunt would be happy to know you've had so much pleasure out of her things all these years."

"Yes, but that's not really the point today, is it?" grumbled Mrs. Lloyd. "It's not about how much we use or like these things; it's all about how much they're worth."

At that moment the bus arrived and they climbed on board and found seats just in front of the local rector, Thomas Evans, and his wife, Bronwyn. Sitting on Bronwyn's lap and looking around cheerfully was her cairn terrier, Robbie, who went everywhere with her. If Robbie wasn't welcome, Bronwyn stayed home.

Mrs. Lloyd turned around in her seat. "And, what are you

bringing, Bronwyn?" asked Mrs. Lloyd. "Besides your Robbie, that is." Her husband laughed as Bronwyn replied, "We've got some rather nice jewellery that belonged to Thomas's grandmother," she said. "It might be art deco; I've always thought it much too nice to wear or at least, I don't go to the kinds of places or events that call for this kind of jewellery. How about you?"

"I've brought a silver tea set," said Mrs. Lloyd.

"It's interesting that many of the objects now considered antiques don't really fit into today's lifestyle," observed Florence. "Fancy jewellery, tea sets . . . things that relatively ordinary people would have used a generation or two ago seem so out of place today. I doubt many young women getting married today want a silver tea set." Bronwyn looked thoughtful and Thomas seemed about to say something, when Mrs. Lloyd spoke.

"Now I'm wondering if it would have been better to bring the set of Carlton Ware dishes. Or maybe I should have brought both." She sighed. "I wonder if they let you bring more than one item."

"I think so," said Thomas, "but you'd have to queue twice to get a second ticket. Apparently when we get there we go to the reception desk and someone gives us a ticket and tells us which appraiser we're meant to see. The appraiser will tell you about your item and give you a valuation. But," and he exchanged a smile with Bronwyn, "here's the exciting part. If the appraiser thinks the item is interesting enough for you to appear on camera, he'll hold off on the appraisal and ask you to come back so he can tell you all about your item on camera. That way, they get a more natural reaction."

Bronwyn rubbed Robbie's chest and then addressed a question to Florence.

"And you, Florence? Did you bring anything or are you just along for support?"

"Oh, she's brought some old bits of paper she got from somewhere," replied Mrs. Lloyd before Florence could reply.

"Sketches," said Florence, making a mental note to remind Mrs. Lloyd once again when they were alone that she was perfectly capable of answering for herself and in future to not speak for her. She'd told her this several times, for all the good it did.

They settled back in their seats for the rest of the short ride and the bus soon turned off onto the winding road that led up to Ty Brith Hall.

Situated above the market town of Llanelen, with stunning views over the whole valley, Ty Brith Hall had been in the Gruffydd family since the 1950s. On the death of his father a couple of years ago, Emyr Gruffydd had inherited the property, along with a sizeable estate in Cornwall. With all the comforts and features of a well-loved country house, Ty Brith Hall had hosted many special events, but nothing quite on this scale. An *Antiques Cymru* day could attract up to five hundred participants; Penny and Emyr hoped about half that many people would turn up but the show's organizers were prepared for a big crowd.

Penny and Emyr watched the arrival of the first busload of hopeful attendees from the elegant front steps of the Hall. The gates had opened at nine thirty and a steady stream of people, many clutching boxes or toting carrier bags, poured in, checking in at the registration desk and being directed to the appointed appraiser.

Penny looked up at the sky that had deepened to a brighter, more reassuring shade of blue with white clouds drifting in over the hilltops. "At least we've got a beautiful day for it," she said.

Emyr smiled and discreetly raised a finger in a gesture that wasn't quite pointing. "Look, there's Mrs. Lloyd, just approaching the desk. She's brought a box of something." Mrs. Lloyd took her ticket and headed off to the appraiser who looked after silver. Florence approached the desk and was given a ticket and directed to the art appraiser.

"I think I'll wander over and join Florence," said Penny. "I'd like to see what she's up to. She keeps everything close to her chest, that one, but whatever she's brought, I've got a feeling it'll be interesting. I'll catch up with you up later, but just send me a text if you need me."

On the way to the art appraisal, Penny passed a table where a woman was evaluating a quilt. Peering from behind a row of spectators she recognized Catrin Bellis as the quilt's owner. The quilt hung from a large metal frame, keeping it well off the ground, and displaying it so everyone could see its bright, beautiful pattern.

"What can you tell me about this quilt?" the appraiser asked.

"I don't know how old it is," Catrin replied, "but it's been in my family for a long time. The initials embroidered on the underside of it are JB, so I think that stands for my great-grandmother, Jane Bellis, who might have made it."

The appraiser, a woman in her fifties with carefully lacquered hair, nodded and then continued. "The colours are beautiful," she said, "and still bright. We find with a lot of these quilts that unfortunately they've been kept in a sunny bedroom and over time become very faded."

"It was on my mother's bed," Catrin said, "and she kept the blinds closed."

"I see." The woman stood beside the quilt and held it with one hand. A small frown flitted across her face and she squeezed the quilt in several places and then examined the side seam more closely. She let go of the quilt and said something in such a low voice to Catrin that Penny, who was a little distance away, couldn't catch it. She then resumed her appraisal in a normal speaking voice for the benefit of those who had gathered around.

"I would say this is an early twentieth-century quilt, pre–World War I. Definitely handmade, and by someone who had a talent but not too much experience. A young woman, perhaps, and this could very well be her first effort. It has a lovely freshness and is in remarkably good condition. You say it's been in your family?"

Catrin nodded. "As long as I can remember."

"I would place a value on this quilt of about three hundred pounds."

Catrin smiled, hoping her disappointment did not show. "Thank you very much," she said as brightly as she could manage. The appraiser helped her fold the quilt and wrap it up in the plastic dry cleaner's bag. Catrin retreated from the appraiser's table as the next person stepped up with an article to be evaluated, and when she spotted Penny, headed over to her.

"Three hundred pounds the appraiser said it was worth," Catrin said. "I'd hoped it would be worth more."

"There will be a lot of disappointed people here today, I'm afraid," said Penny. "But three hundred pounds isn't so very bad, is it?"

"I guess not," muttered Catrin.

"Are you going to wander around for a bit and see what the others have brought?" Penny asked.

"No, it's a bit awkward with this bundle and besides, I've got to get home. There's a woman coming to see the room. I've decided to rent out my parents' old bedroom while I decide what to do about the house. Renting out the room will bring in some extra money and the woman will be a bit of company for me in the evenings. If it all works out, of course. Still got a bit of last minute cleaning and tidying up to do. Naturally, I want the place to look its best."

"Oh, right," said Penny. "Well, good luck. I'm sure you'll find someone suitable."

Catrin got off the *Antiques Cymru* shuttle bus in the town square, and, carrying her wrapped up quilt in both arms, walked home. It was almost lunchtime. What a terrible waste of time the morning had been. All that queuing, and then to be told the quilt had so little value. She hoped the woman who had answered her ad in the newsagent's window would take the room. She hated the idea of sharing her kitchen and bathroom with a stranger, but really, what was the alternative? She'd been thinking everything through for weeks and this was the best idea she could come up with. Her little part-time job didn't bring in enough income. Still, maybe it wouldn't be so bad. Mrs. Lloyd, after all, took in a lodger, and by all accounts that arrangement had worked out just fine. And Mrs. Lloyd didn't even need the money.

At the thought of the bathroom, she picked up her pace. She'd have to make sure it was sparkling when she showed it to the woman. She checked her watch. Time was getting a little tight. She didn't like to eat in a hurry, so decided to skip lunch and get on with the tidying up and cleaning.

A few moments later she reached her grey, pebble-dashed house and bunching the quilt under one arm to get her key out of her coat pocket, let herself in. She glanced at the carpet in the sitting room and decided she'd better run the Hoover over it. Catching sight of a couple of things that did not belong in the sitting room, she set the quilt on a chair, scooped up the out-of-place items, and took them upstairs with her.

She sprayed the tub with foaming bubbles and leaving them to work their cleaning magic, she pulled off her yellow rubber gloves and laid them over the sink and went downstairs to lay out a tray so she and her potential lodger could get to know each other better over a cup of tea. She filled the kettle and set it to one side. When she realized she had no biscuits to offer the woman, she sighed and then shrugged. Tea would have to do. She surveyed the kitchen, so familiar to her, trying to see it as a stranger would. Of course it hadn't been modernized in decades, but she hoped the woman would think it was at least clean and functional. She'd spent ages scrubbing away the grease left from years of frying meat. Meat! Should she tell the woman the kitchen was vegetarian? She'd see how things went and then they could discuss it.

About halfway upstairs to finish cleaning the bathroom a knock on the door stopped her. Oh, damn, the woman was early. She plastered what she hoped was a welcoming smile on her face, walked down the stairs, and flung open the front door.

"Hello, Catrin."

She took a step back, raising a hand to her chest.

"Oh, it's you," said Catrin. "Well, you'd better come in, then."

A few minutes later, as the carriage clock that had been her parents' silver wedding anniversary gift chimed the three-quarter hour, Catrin Bellis realized she had just made the worst mistake of her life.

Nine

The grounds of Ty Brith Hall were filling up; the number of people was expected to peak sometime around lunchtime. Penny battled her way around long lines forming in front of evaluators' tables and through large groups of spectators until she reached the table designated for fine art. She saw Florence waiting in the queue, with one or two people ahead of her.

"Hello, Florence," Penny said. "Thought I'd see how you're getting on."

"Well, I haven't really got on, yet," said Florence. "But the line seems to be moving quickly, so it shouldn't be much longer." She peered anxiously at Penny. "I must admit, I'm a little nervous," she said. "I don't think I'm wasting the evaluator's time. I'm sure they must be worth something . . ." Her voice trailed off as she realized it was her turn.

"Would you like me to come with you?" Penny asked.

"Yes, if you've got time, I'd appreciate that," Florence replied.

The appraiser smiled at both women, his dark blue eyes lingering just a little longer on Penny. "Hello, I'm Michael Quinn," he said in a soft Irish accent. He was tall and slim with dark hair lightly flecked with grey. He appeared to be in his late forties, with a casual air of authority about him that Penny found intriguing.

"Who's brought what for me today?" he asked, interrupting her appraisal of him.

"I've brought you some sketches," said Florence, handing him the ticket she'd been given at the reception desk.

He took it from her, flashed a businesslike smile, and said, "Right, well then, let's lay them out on the table and see what you've got."

Florence pulled a large brown envelope out of her carrier bag and withdrew the contents. "I'll put these out first. There's another envelope with some others."

She set down about a dozen sheets of stiff sketching paper, covered in pen and ink drawings. Quinn drew in his breath, covered his mouth with his hand and then gently ran it over his chin as his eyes roamed greedily over the drawings. "There's more?" he asked. "You mentioned you had something else."

"Oh, yes," said Florence, reaching for her carrier bag. "They're in here." She fumbled with her bag. "Penny, if you wouldn't mind gathering these ones up, I'll just . . ." Her hands shook as she opened her bag and while Penny scooped up the drawings on the table, Florence laid out ten more. These were also pen and ink, but bolder and more defined as if coming from a more confident hand.

Quinn blinked, took a deep breath, and picked one up. After examining it for a moment, addressed Florence. "Thank you. Can you tell me how or where you got them?"

Florence answered his question and they spoke for a few more minutes.

"All right, then, Florence," he said. "I'd like to have you back for an on-camera evaluation." Quinn waved to a man standing nearby wearing a purple sash. "Here's one of our stewards. If you'll go with him, he'll take you to the holding area where you can get a nice cup of tea and a biscuit and they'll explain the next steps to you. Is that all right with you?" He turned his attention to Penny and spoke in a lowered voice. "Are you with her? I think it would be a good idea if she had someone with her during the evaluation."

"I'm helping organize the event today," Penny said, introducing herself. "I'd be glad to stay with her."

"Good. I'm just going to confer with one or two of my colleagues and do a bit of research. We'll see you back here, later, then." He gave Penny one last warm smile before disappearing into the crowd and she turned her attention to Florence.

"Someone else I know had his clock brought in, so I'm heading over to," she checked the appraiser categories on her clipboard, "Clocks, Watches, and Scientific Instruments to see how he's doing." As the steward approached to escort Florence to a holding area, she added, "I'll find you later."

After a quick word with a segment producer, she found Haydn Williams sitting on his own beside his longcase clock and looking a little forlorn. He'd been notified a few days ago that he had been selected for filming and the *Antiques Cymru* crew had arrived at his farmhouse yesterday to dismantle the clock and transport it safely to the site.

"Hello, Haydn," said Penny. "The producer tells me they've scheduled your interview next. They're aiming to have the interview end just before the hour so the clock can strike."

A few moments later Daniel Casey got the signal from the segment director and filming of the appraisal began.

"What we have here," he began, "is a beautiful example of an iconic longcase clock made in this very town. Let's just take an overview of the clock and then we'll look at some of the details that can help us date it.

"The clock is about seven feet high and its case is made of oak, probably felled in what is now the Gydwyr Forest that overlooks the town and then brought down by horse and cart. The case would probably have been made by a local cabinetmaker, the same fellow who made coffins for the locals.

"The wooden part of the clock at the top that covers the dial is called the hood, and it slides out so the mechanical parts can be serviced." He raised his hands, about a foot apart, and gestured at the top of the clock. "This hood is especially fine. It's got some lovely shaped cresting, a column on each side and then on top, three brass finials. The centre finial features an eagle, which was once a symbol of the town.

"Now, let's take a closer look at the dial."

He pointed to the name JOHN OWEN engraved in capital letters at the top of the clock's face. "This clock is undoubtedly the work of John Owen, a master eighteenth-century clockmaker.

"Now for the dial. The centre section is matted brass. They stopped matting the faces of these clocks about 1770, so we know this clock is earlier than that." He also pointed out the sunflower engraving on the centre section, the small lines between two circles to mark the minutes, and the size of the clock face. "So from all these elements taken together, we can date this clock at 1765.

"The mechanism is still in good working order—and this is of critical importance—the mechanism is original to this clock. Every piece of this clock is original and it all belongs together. Sometimes we see a beautiful case but it's fitted with another mechanism. But not here. It's all original and everything is as it should be. It was made to a very high standard and perfectly preserved."

He turned to Haydn. "Have you ever had it valued?"

Haydn shook his head.

"Well, on a good day, with the right people in the room, I would place an auction value on this clock of twelve thousand pounds. It's a beautiful piece of local history. Thank you so much for letting us have a look at it today."

Haydn blinked, struggled to say something, and finally came up with, "I'm gobsmacked." He stayed very still for a moment as he'd been instructed to do. A soft, whirring sound came from the clock and then somewhere inside it, a small hammer struck a bell once, announcing it was one o'clock.

Ten

Several of Florence's sketches had been arranged on a vertical display board. She sat at one end and art appraiser Michael Quinn stood at the other. He gave her a reassuring glance, looked to the director for the signal to begin, and then asked his first question.

"Now can you tell me a little about how you came to have this artwork?"

"Well," said Florence, "back in the 1960s I took up my first and only job as a secretary at the Liverpool College of Art. I was only seventeen, so they gave me all the dogsbody-type tasks. Sometimes I would get sent to the classrooms or studios at the end of the day to have a tidy round, and I would see these sketches in the bin. I just liked them, so I took them. I admired the work the students were doing."

"You certainly had a very good eye," said Michael. "You

chose the best of the best." He cleared his throat lightly, took a deep breath, and continued. "In fact, what we have here is early work by two of the school's most famous students. Let's start with this one." Holding a small baton in long, elegant fingers, he pointed to a sketch for the benefit of the camera. "It's a pen and ink drawing of a couple in a park. And it's an early work by Stuart Sutcliffe. Stuart Sutcliffe was born in Scotland but brought up in Liverpool, and he went to the Liverpool College of Art, where, in 1957 he met another student, called," he looked at Florence, who responded, "John Lennon."

"That's right. And Stuart became the bass player in John's new band; they recruited a couple more musicians, and went to Germany, where, sadly, Stuart died in 1962, aged only twenty-one."

He touched a few more sketches with his baton. "This is a major find. Each one will have to be authenticated, but because of the provenance, in my mind I'm confident these rare drawings are Stuart Sutcliffe originals. Do you have any idea how much they would be worth?"

Florence shook her head.

"You've never had them evaluated?"

"No, I've never even shown them to anyone before today."

"Well, I discussed this with my colleagues and we feel a conservative estimate would be between seventeen hundred fifty and two thousand pounds." Florence's face broke into a rare, polite smile. "Oh, that's very nice, thank you."

"Oh, sorry, I don't think I made myself clear. Each. That's about two thousand pounds each. And how many do you have?"

"Eleven."

"So we can place an estimated value of twenty to twenty-two thousand pounds on these. But at auction, they could go for much more than that. That's a conservative estimate I've given you."

Florence gasped. "I'm in shock," she said. "I don't know what to say." She swallowed and looked to Penny for reassurance, then turned back to the evaluator. "Are you serious?"

"Oh, yes," smiled Michael Quinn. "We don't joke about things like this."

He gave her a moment for the number to sink in while she collected herself, and then continued. "But that isn't all you've brought, is it?"

Florence shook her head.

Michael pointed to another drawing. "This one. Can you tell me who it's by?"

Florence nodded. "John Lennon."

"And you've got how many of them?"

"Eight."

"Eight previously unseen works by John Lennon. Eight! Again, we would need to get them authenticated, but if they are real, which my colleagues and I believe they are, we believe at auction they could go for about ten thousand pounds. Each. A total of eighty thousand pounds."

Florence shook her head and choked back tears. "I thought they might work out to a few hundred pounds each, but never in my wildest dreams as much as that. Oh, my word. I can't quite take it all in."

Michael smiled at her. "I could hardly contain myself when you pulled those out of the bag," he said. "I couldn't believe what I was seeing. This is the type of find we dream of discovering here on *Antiques Cymru*. Thank you so much for bringing them in." He laughed. "I don't think I'll be able to get to sleep tonight."

"You and me both," replied Florence.

Florence remained seated until the filming was over. And then, as the appraiser approached, Penny joined the two, a beaming smile lighting up her face. "I knew it was going to be good news," she said, "but I didn't know it would be that good. I'm so happy for you, Florence. You must be thrilled."

Florence, however, was not smiling.

"I dread to think how Evelyn's going to take it," she said.

"Let's not worry about her right now," Penny said. "Just enjoy this very special moment."

They thanked the appraiser and moved off to find Mrs. Lloyd, who had been standing in the cluster of spectators, which had grown rapidly as word rippled through the crowd that something big was happening at the art appraisal stand.

"Well, I've always said you were a dark horse, Florence," she said. "But I never expected this! Why didn't you tell me what you had? You must have suspected the John Lennon stuff would be worth something."

"Oh, I did, Evelyn. I just didn't know how much."

"Well, what are you going to do now?"

"I'm going to ask Penny what she thinks I should do. But right now, I'm hungry and I want to go home." She clutched the brown envelope containing the sketches to her chest. "I feel a little light headed, I must admit. This has been a bit of a shock and it's going to take me some time to take it all in." She stopped walking, trying to catch her ragged breath as Mrs. Lloyd walked on ahead.

"Look, Florence," said Penny, "now that we know just how valuable these drawings are, would you like me to ask Emyr to lock them up in his safe room until you can make arrangements for a safety deposit box at the bank?" Penny asked. "At least that way you won't have to worry about them getting stolen until you can arrange proper insurance for them."

"I hadn't thought about the insurance," Florence said. "I think it would be a good idea if they were locked up for safe-keeping," Florence handed her the envelope.

Penny put a gentle hand on Florence's arm. "Just a quick word before you go. I want to give you something to think about."

Penny explained what she had in mind and a couple of minutes later Florence caught up with Evelyn Lloyd marching toward the shuttle bus, the silver tea service rattling in the box she held stiffly under her arm.

Eleven

Mrs. Lloyd was uncharacteristically quiet on the ride into town.

They got off the bus at the town square and began the short walk home. "I know you haven't had a chance to think this through," Mrs. Lloyd said, "and forgive me for being direct, but will you be moving out?"

"I don't want to, Evelyn, if you want me to stay."

"I do," she said. "So that's settled then." She paused to smile at her friend, and then a look of terror spread across her face.

"Oh, dear Lord, Florence," she said. "Where's your envelope? You haven't left it on the bus have you? Oh, we must hurry to try to catch it before it starts the journey back to the Hall."

"It's all right, Evelyn. You can relax. I haven't left it on the bus. I left it with Penny. She's going to see that Emyr locks it in the strong room up at the Hall until I can make more secure arrangements. A safety deposit box at the bank, or something like that. And insurance coverage."

Mrs. Lloyd put a hand over her heart to slow her breathing. "Yes, we must see to the insurance. Oh, that's a good idea to leave them with Emyr. They'll be perfectly safe with him. And anyway, you never know who might have overheard that appraisal and everybody knows where we live. Somebody might have realized we are two elderly, defenceless ladies living on our own and come in the night, attacking us in our beds, trying to steal your artwork."

"They still might," said Florence. "How are they to know the artwork isn't on the premises?"

"Oh, dear God, Florence. Do you think that's a possibility? We'll have to barricade the door tonight or I won't sleep a wink. Every little noise and I'll be wondering if that's someone on the stairs coming for me."

"Well, he'd be more likely to come for me," said Florence. "I'm the one who owns the art."

"Yes, but he won't know what room you're in, will he?"

Florence laughed. "Look, here's a suggestion. We go home, take our shoes off, put the kettle on, and have a think about what to do for the best over a nice cup of tea."

"That sounds like a good plan, Florence. Have we got any of those nice biscuits I like so much? You know, the shortbread ones shaped like a little shell. Or better yet, the little round ones with the scalloped edges and the jam in them. And maybe we'll want something stronger than tea. A glass of sherry might be in order, by way of celebration. Things like this don't happen every day."

As she finished speaking they turned into Thyme Close, the quiet little street that led to Rosemary Lane. They had just reached the halfway point when from behind them came a woman's scream. It was a primal sound, echoing a primitive fear that spoke of unimaginable terror. After exchanging a frightened glance, they looked behind them as a woman came running toward them, her arms outstretched. She reached them a moment later and pointed back at a house.

"In there," she gasped. "Oh, my God. Call the police."

Mrs. Lloyd pulled her phone out of her handbag and pressed 999.

"What should I tell them?" she said to the woman. "Has there been an accident?"

"Worse than that," the woman wailed. "There's a dead woman in there and I think someone killed her."

She started to shake and sob.

"You've had a terrible shock," Florence said to the distraught woman as Mrs. Lloyd spoke to the police on the telephone.

"I wonder if the police would mind if I took her home and gave her a cup of tea. You could wait here until they arrive," Florence said to Mrs. Lloyd when she had ended the call.

"Me!" Mrs. Lloyd exclaimed. "What if the killer comes back and finds me alone in the street? He might think I witnessed something and kill me to keep me silent. Happens all the time. And anyway, I wasn't able to tell the police which house it is. I said we'd just be here and this lady would show them."

She turned to the woman. "Which house was it? I don't think you said."

The woman looked at a piece of paper in her hand. "Number thirty-five. The lady's name is Catrin Bellis. I was just there to see about renting a room off her. I certainly didn't expect to find a dead body."

"Of course you didn't," said Florence soothingly.

"Oh, right," said Mrs. Lloyd. "Well, Miss, er, I'm sorry but I don't know your name."

"Oh, it's Jean. Jean Bryson." Before either woman could say any more, the rising and falling wail of sirens indicated the imminent arrival of the police. "Well, I guess that settles it," said Mrs. Lloyd. "We'd all better just stay where we are until the police get here."

A moment later, the first police car pulled up. A uniformed officer stepped out of the driver's side, followed by a tall, handsome man in his fifties wearing a well-tailored suit.

"Oh, Inspector Davies," said Mrs. Lloyd. "Thank God you're here. This lady said she'd just been into number thirty-five and discovered a dead body." Mrs. Lloyd pointed to the modest pebble-dashed house with a tiny garden.

The inspector tipped his head at the uniformed officer who then opened the boot of the car, pulled out a roll of blue and white barricade tape, and entered number thirty-five. He emerged a few minutes later and began cordoning off the front of the property. The officer then stood outside the door, hands clasped in front of him, and looked straight ahead as he waited for DCI Gareth Davies to wrap up his conversation with the three women.

"Inspector, this lady's had a terrible shock and we wondered if it would be all right if we took her home with us and gave her a nice cup of tea. You could then interview her there when you're ready. You know where we live. Just at the end of the close, and then into Rosemary Lane," said Florence.

Davies agreed, and after taking Jean Bryson's details, he headed to number thirty-five for what he expected to be his last case before he retired in a few weeks time. A moment later another police car arrived, driven by a woman officer and followed by a white scene of crime van and an ambulance. Davies, the woman officer, and the first of the forensic technicians ducked under the crime scene tape as the uniformed officer lifted it for them. Before entering the house they pulled on shoe covers and donned white protective overalls.

By now, a small crowd had started to gather. The three women, not wishing to be part of it, turned and walked the short distance to Mrs. Lloyd's sturdy charcoal grey stone house with its slate roof.

Florence unlocked the door and stood aside as the other two entered. "Now just leave your coat there, Jean," said Mrs. Lloyd, "and Florence will bring us our tea in a minute. We were talking about having tea, anyway, just before we met you, so before you say anything, this is no trouble at all."

Mrs. Lloyd's sitting room was comfortable and although it might have seemed old-fashioned to some, it was furnished in a tasteful, *Country Life* kind of way. The walls were painted a pale yellow, the sofa was a Wedgewood blue, and a couple of comfortable wing chairs in a floral pattern flanked each side of the slate fireplace. Magazines and library books were neatly stacked on side tables and a few photographs in sliver frames added a personal touch, as did the bouquet of fresh flowers in a crystal vase on a walnut table in front of the window. The room had a pleasant, clean smell of furniture polish.

Mrs. Lloyd waved her visitor to one of the wing chairs. Jean lowered herself gingerly into it, then perched on the edge, knees together and turned a little to one side. She lifted the hem of her purple plaid pleated skirt and tugged it downward and adjusted the sleeve of her lavender-coloured blouse.

The room was silent except for the oddly comforting ticking of a carriage clock on the mantelpiece.

Mrs. Lloyd breathed a small sigh of relief when Florence arrived with a laden tea tray that she placed with experienced precision on the largest of a series of three nesting tables.

"Well, now, Jean, how do you take your tea?" asked Florence, pouring a cup. "They always say you need some sugar at a time like this, so you'd better have some. Milk?" Jean nodded and Florence handed the cup to her. She accepted it with a trembling hand and then looked around for a place to set it. Mrs. Lloyd brought over the smallest of the nesting tables and placed it beside her chair.

"You can put it here," she said, taking the cup from her and setting it on the table. Florence placed a small plate with two biscuits on it beside the cup, then poured tea for herself and Mrs. Lloyd.

"You know, Jean, I hope you don't mind my mentioning this, but I think I've seen you someplace before, and just recently, too, but I can't quite place you. Something about you seems familiar," said Florence.

"I've just started a new position with the library," Jean replied, "so it could be that's where you've seen me. I noticed you have a few library books." She gestured at the little stack of books on the side table.

"Oh, well, I expect that'll be it, then," said Mrs. Lloyd. "Florence is a great patron of the library, but me, I prefer my magazines. I have subscriptions."

They sipped their tea and Jean nibbled at a biscuit. The silence stretched on and even Mrs. Lloyd, usually never at a loss for words, seemed unsure how to break it. And then Jean spoke.

"Yes, anyway, I recently started a new position at the library. I live in the Junction and I've been coming to work on the bus, but they're too unreliable and too infrequent. Plus, they take so long, when you add in the bus time, a half-day job becomes a full-day job, if you know what I mean. By the time you get ready and factor in wait times."

Mrs. Lloyd nodded. "Indeed I do know what you mean. I was the postmistress here in Llanelen for many years and my husband owned the green grocer. We always walked to work. It's by far the best way."

"Exactly," said Jean. "So I saw the advertisement in the newsagent's window for a room to let and I thought that might do me while I looked around for something more permanent. This is a pretty little town and I quite like it. I had come round to see if the room would suit me, and that's when I, well, you know the rest."

"Actually," said Mrs. Lloyd, leaning forward with an ingratiating smile, "we don't know the rest but we'd love to hear about it, if you're up to telling us, that is. Wouldn't we, Florence? Now I've had an idea. What if you told us everything you can remember and Florence here writes it all down, and when the police come, you'll have already done it, so you won't have to go through it all again with them?"

Jean looked confused.

"Oh, I don't know about that, Evelyn," said Florence. "We are not trained interviewers and I'm sure the police would want to ask their own questions."

"Well, maybe so," snapped Mrs. Lloyd, "but at least it would be a start. And Jean here can tell us what she saw before she forgets anything."

"Oh, I don't think that's very likely," said Jean. "I keep going over everything in my mind. I can't stop thinking about it." She scrubbed at her eyes with clenched fists. "In fact, I wish I could erase what I saw from my memory."

"If it would help you to talk about it, you'll find me a very good listener," encouraged Mrs. Lloyd, with a sympathetic smile.

"But if you'd rather not talk about it, that's all right, too, of course," said Florence.

"Well, the buses being what they are, I arrived at the house a few minutes late and I hoped that wouldn't give a bad impression to the lady," said Jean. "In fact, I saw you," she looked from one to the other, "walking down the street just as I arrived. You must have just passed the house. And when I went to knock on the door, I was rather surprised it wasn't closed properly. So I thought, well, she's expecting me, so she's left it open for me, so I pushed it open and went in."

"That's an important clue," said Mrs. Lloyd. "Write that down, Florence. The door was slightly open so she went in."

"I never agreed to write anything down," muttered Florence, pretending to reach for her little notebook.

"Go on," said Mrs. Lloyd eagerly. "The door was open slightly, so you went in. And then you probably called out, 'Hello? Is anybody home?'"

"I don't think you're supposed to tell the witness what she probably did," Florence said to Mrs. Lloyd. "It's called 'leading' the witness, I believe."

Mrs. Lloyd shot her a dark look with an accompanying little noise of disapproval and then turned back to Jean.

"Go on," she repeated. "Tell us what happened next. After you called out, 'Hello? Is anybody home?'"

Jean let out a little howl and her shoulders began to shake. She covered her eyes with her hands as if trying to block out the image of what she had seen.

"She was lying on the floor in the sitting room. I'm pretty

sure she'd been hit with something. Her head . . ." Jean raised her right hand to the side of her head. "Just here. It was covered in blood. I'd never seen anything like it. It's like something you see on telly but never expect to experience in real life."

Mrs. Lloyd nodded wisely. "Was the room disturbed in any way?" she asked. "Lamps knocked over, that sort of thing?"

"No," said Jean slowly. "I don't think it was." She took a sip of tea, savoured it for a moment, and then drained the cup. "Oh, that's such good tea," she said. "I didn't realize how much I needed that."

"Very restorative," agreed Mrs. Lloyd.

Recently promoted Detective Inspector Bethan Morgan slowly descended the stairs in Catrin's home. When she reached the bottom, she waited in the small entranceway for DCI Davies to join her. "Anything?" he asked.

"Nothing up there seems disturbed. Found a few financial records in a drawer. Boxes of what looks like keepsakes in the smaller bedroom. The bigger bedroom looks as if nobody lives in it. Cupboards are empty."

"Hmm, could be a robbery gone bad, I suppose. Well, unless you can think of anything else, I think we've done all we can do here until the pathologist arrives. He said he wouldn't be long. We'll leave the rest of it to forensics and hope they come up with some good leads."

He opened the front door and spoke to the uniformed officer. "The pathologist's on his way. Show him in when he arrives." He closed the door and returned to the sitting room.

"What does this room say to you?" he asked Bethan. "Does

it look like the room where a fairly young woman would live? She wasn't that much older than you. Would you do up a room like this?"

Bethan shook her head. "No. It's her parents' room. Maybe even her grandparents'. It hasn't changed much since the seventies, I'd say."

The door opened and the pathologist poked his head around the doorway.

"Ah, Gareth, what have you got for me today?"

Davies gestured at the woman's body on the floor. "Fortunately, this is a good scene. As far as we know, nothing's been moved or touched."

The pathologist bent over the body. "Well, I can tell you that this lady was at the *Antiques Cymru* show earlier today."

"Really?" said Bethan. "You can tell that just by looking at her? How do you know that?"

The pathologist laughed. "I'm not Sherlock Holmes. I know because I saw her there. My wife made me take her to the show, and I have to say I was rather enjoying it. Until I got your phone call, of course."

He examined the head wound, and then peered at the raised slate hearth of the old fireplace. "You'll want your forensics people to take a close look at that," he said. "She may have fallen and hit her head on it when she went down."

He lifted the victim's head slightly and made a little tutting noise.

"Well, I won't be able to tell you too much more until I've done a proper postmortem, but it looks as if she was struck with something first, and then, if she hit her head on something as unforgiving as that hearth, it certainly wouldn't have worked in her favour."

Davies's eyes slid over to the set of brass fireplace tools on the hearth.

"We'll want those bagged and sent to the lab," he said.

The pathologist sat back on his haunches, his gloved hands between his knees, and looked up at Davies. "Right. I've seen enough. We can move her out now and let your people take over."

He stood up and pulled off his gloves. Giving Davies a sly grin, he said, "If she was struck with one of those tools, in all my years doing this job, I've never actually known anyone killed with a poker. Have you?"

Davies shook his head. "Bit of a cliché, really, isn't it?"

The three stepped outside and peeled off their protective clothing. As he handed it over to the uniformed officer Davies said to him, "If you give me your crime scene log, we'll sign out." He checked his watch. He scribbled a signature on the clipboard, thanked the pathologist, and then turned to Bethan.

"Right. Time now to see if our key witness is up to speaking to us." The two walked in silence toward the end of the close to pick up the path that cut through to Rosemary Lane.

"What a shame," said Bethan. "So awful to see a life end like that. You never get used to it, do you?"

"No," said Davies, "you don't. But the best thing we can do for her now is find out who did this. Do we know who she is?"

"I have an idea from the bank statements, but they weren't in a woman's name, and judging from the dates, they were probably her father's. I expect Mrs. Lloyd will know who she is. And if she doesn't, then Penny's bound to."

"Penny?" His voice sounded a little sharper than he meant it to. He and Penny had been close a while back and although she'd indicated that for her, the relationship was now over, the torch he carried burned brightly and he expected it would for some time.

"Yes, Penny. The woman's had a manicure recently and her hair's been professionally coloured and styled. Probably at Penny's salon."

"Of course." He grinned at her. "We'll make a detective out of you, yet."

A few minutes later Florence showed them into the sitting room where Jean Bryson had finished her second cup of tea and was looking composed.

"I've just brewed another pot," Florence said. "I'll get a couple of extra cups, shall I?"

Davies gave her a grateful nod and turned his attention to his key witness. "Now then, I'm sure these ladies have been taking good care of you. Do you feel up to answering a few questions? Let's start by you telling me your name."

"That's Jean Bryson," said Mrs. Lloyd, "and we've already started the questioning for you, Inspector. And Florence has written down the answers. 'Taking a statement,' I believe it's called."

"Very thoughtful of you, Mrs. Lloyd," said Davies, "but we prefer to take our statements ourselves. We have our own ways of doing things, you see. We're peculiar like that." Bethan smiled into her notebook. "In fact, Miss Bryson, we'd like to drive you home and we'll take your statement when you're in the comfort and safety of your own home. You'll be more relaxed there, I'm sure."

Seeing Mrs. Lloyd's disappointment, Bethan said to her, "There is something you might be able to tell us. Who lived in that house?"

"Catrin Bellis. She lived there with her parents. They both

died fairly recently and she'd decided to rent out one of the bedrooms. That's how this lady came to find the body."

"Did she have any sisters or brothers?" Bethan asked. "Do you know who her next of kin would be? Anyone we should contact?"

"I believe she was an only child, but I'm pretty sure she has a cousin," Mrs. Lloyd said. "He'd be a relative, but whether he's her closest relative I don't know."

"Do you know his name?"

She thought for a moment, and then shook her head slowly. "No, sorry. I expect it'll come to me, but off the top of my head, no, I can't think of it."

Bethan turned her attention to Jean Bryson. "And you had arrived to view the room but had not met the victim before, is that right?"

"That's correct."

"And you two," Bethan looked from Mrs. Lloyd to Florence, "just happened to be passing by, were you?"

"We were on our way home from the Antiques show," Mrs. Lloyd said. "The bus dropped us off in the town square and we had just passed the house when we heard Jean's screams and turned to see her running up the street toward us, in obvious distress, so we rang the police and when you lot arrived, we offered to bring her here."

"And very kind of you that was, too," said Jean.

"And you didn't see anybody in the street, walking or driving in either direction?"

"We weren't really paying attention," said Florence, "but all the streets are practically deserted today, because everyone in town is up at the Hall at the Antiques show."

"That's right," agreed Mrs. Lloyd.

Davies stood up. "Well, let's leave it there for now."

"Time to get Miss Bryson home. But if you do remember anything else, no matter how trivial it might seem to you, give me or Bethan a ring. Give the ladies one of your shiny new cards, Bethan," he said with a faint smile.

Florence saw the police officers out and said a quiet goodbye to Jean Bryson.

"I hope you won't have too many bad thoughts, for too long," she said, adding she hoped to see her soon at the library. She closed the door quietly and returned to the sitting room. She started gathering up the tea things but Mrs. Lloyd asked her to stop for a moment and sit down.

"This has been quite an eventful day," she said. "You discovered you've got some sketches worth a small fortune and someone else discovered a body."

"Very nicely summed up," said Florence. "That's exactly the size of it."

"I don't know what to make of this. Why would someone want to kill Catrin? What's she ever done to anybody?"

"I don't know," said Florence. "I expect you could say that about a lot of murders and yet they keep happening, don't they?"

"Well, we'll get to the bottom of it," said Mrs. Lloyd. "This is our murder, Florence. We'll show that Penny Brannigan she's not the only amateur sleuth around here. We were first on the scene of the crime and we interviewed the most important witness before the police, even. We've got a huge head start. This is quite a coup for us, Florence."

The rattling of the tea cups as she gathered them up and set them on her tray was Florence's way of telling Mrs. Lloyd exactly what she thought of that idea.

Twelve

I t's been a hugely exciting day," said the executive producer
as he thanked the *Antiques Cymru* team. "Definitely one of
those rare and special days that far exceeded our expectations.
We had some wonderful surprises, but probably the biggest find
of the day was the John Lennon sketches. Something I never
would have thought possible, and yet, there they were. That's
going to make a brilliant segment. It'll make the national news
for sure, so keep it under your bonnets for now. Thank you all,
everybody. Now let's get packed up as quickly as we can so we
can all be off home." The crew began de-rigging the set, taking down signage, rolling up cables, and replacing everything
into their shipping boxes ready for loading onto the transport
vehicles. They had done this many times and worked efficiently,
tidying up as they went. The appraisers, too, were packing up
their laptops, reference books, and notes.

Penny and Emyr stood to one side, watching as the last of the gear was carried out. Emyr's black Lab Trixxi wandered around sniffing boxes and just generally trying to be helpful. Michael Quinn, the art appraiser, gave her a friendly pat and then walked her over to Emyr and Penny.

"Thank you for hosting us today," he said. "We all enjoyed ourselves very much, and for me, personally, it was especially rewarding." He gave Penny a broad, friendly grin which she returned.

"That was really something, wasn't it, when Florence pulled those sketches out of that tatty envelope," she said.

Michael laughed. "We see the most amazing things. We had one woman bring in a very valuable ceramic bowl. Said she kept it in the laundry room and used it to collect all the bits and pieces she pulled out of the kids' pockets before she put their clothes in the washing machine." He tucked his hands in the pockets of his trousers and assumed a comfortable, casual stance. "Interested in art, are you?"

"I am," said Penny. "I'm a watercolour artist and belong to a local sketching group. We enjoy our rambles and *plein-air* painting."

"Oh, that's great," said Michael.

"And you?" asked Penny. "What do you do when you're not appraising sketches and drawings?"

"Oh, I teach art at Bangor University," he said.

"Any particular period?"

"I'm a bit of a generalist. I like Irish artists of the twentieth century, but I'm also partial to the Hudson River School."

"Oh, I love that, too!" exclaimed Penny. "The way they capture the light. Have you seen the collection at the Met in New York? Wonderful."

"I did see it a couple of years ago. Made a special point of it." The two chatted together for a few minutes until Emyr caught Penny's eye.

"Penny, I've got something on this evening," he said, "so if you'd like me to run you into town, we'll need to be on our way."

"Oh, I'd be happy to give her a lift," said Michael easily. "I'm going that way. It's no bother."

"Well, if you're sure," said Penny. "It would save Emyr having to make a special trip. I'll just make sure I've got everything."

A few minutes later they were on their way, chatting easily, on the drive into town.

"If you're not in a hurry, could I buy you a drink?" asked Michael as they entered Llanelen. "Yes, I'd like that," said Penny. "It's been a long day and we've earned one."

He parked outside the Leek and Lily and held the pub door open for her. Although there weren't many people in, Penny and Michael were immediately struck by how quiet it was. The usual pub conversation din was muted as people either drank silently or spoke in soft voices. The atmosphere was subdued and somber. Penny and Michael exchanged a quick, questioning glance and then approached the bar together.

"It's awfully quiet," said Penny to the woman behind the counter.

"We've had a bit of a shock," she said. "What can I get you?"

"A white wine for me, please," said Penny. "Mine's a small Irish whisky, no ice," said Michael. The barmaid turned her back while she poured a glass of wine and dispensed a measure of whisky then set the glasses down on the bar. "That'll be six pounds thirty, please."

"What kind of a shock? What's happened?" asked Penny as Michael held out a ten-pound note.

"There's been a murder." She moved to the cash register, rang in the sale, and returned with Michael's change. "Catrin Bellis's been killed," she said as she dropped the coins into his hand.

"Oh, no," gasped Penny. "How awful! I saw her just this morning." She turned to Michael. "She was at the Antiques show getting a quilt appraised."

As the barmaid drifted away to serve another customer Penny picked up a napkin from the bar and placed it under the base of her glass.

Michael gestured at an empty table with a questioning eyebrow and Penny led the way, sidling round the table to sit on the upholstered banquette. She'd expected Michael to take the chair on the other side of the table, but he slid in beside her. She shifted down a little to put a bit of space between them and they turned toward each other.

"So you knew her did you?" asked Michael, when they were seated.

"Yes, we saw a lot of her lately at our Spa. My friend Victoria and I co-own the Llanelen Spa."

"Do you really?" said Michael. "That big old building by the river? I've admired it many times. It was derelict for years but I always thought there was something really handsome about it and hoped the right people would come along to restore it. I was really pleased when the sign went up that a renovation was underway."

He raised his glass to her. "Well, cheers. Well done, you."

"You must come in and see what we've done with it, then," said Penny. "I'd be happy to show you around." She wondered if she should ask if he had a wife or girlfriend who might also like a tour. As if sensing what she was thinking, Michael spoke.

"Look, just to get this out of the way so we know where we stand, I was very happily married but my wife died quite suddenly two years ago."

"Oh, I'm sorry," said Penny.

"And you?" asked Michael. "Is there anyone special in your life I should know about?"

"No," said Penny. "Not now. There was someone but we called time on it a little while ago. I think both of us had hoped it might turn into something more, but it just seemed to have run its course." She shrugged. "I should probably call him, though, and tell him that Catrin was at the *Antiques Cymru*."

Michael fixed his bright blue eyes on her over the rim of his glass as he took a small sip of whisky. "And why would you have to tell him that?"

"Because he's a senior police detective and he's probably investigating this case. The police always like to piece together how the victim spent the last twenty-four hours of their life."

"I see. Do you need to phone him now? I can step away, if you'd like a bit of privacy."

"No, I'll leave it until I get home." Penny fingered the stem of her wine glass, wiping away the condensation. "Speaking of home, do you live in Bangor?"

"I do. Not too far from the university."

"A bit of a drive then, from Llanelen."

"Not too bad. I come here fairly often. The fellow who runs Snowdonia Antiques is a good mate."

"Oh, right. It's just that I was wondering . . . you see we have a small sketching club and we like to bring in special guest speakers every now and then. Artists or photographers who have accomplished something and it would be great if you'd consider being one of our speakers. You could talk about the

Hudson River School, as I'm sure most of our members aren't all that familiar with it."

"But you were," said Michael. "Why is that?"

"Oh, I have a degree in art history," said Penny.

"And your accent is Canadian, yes?"

"Good for you. Yes, it is. Most British people think it's an American accent and I know it's hard to tell the difference." Michael laughed. "I know you're Irish, not British, but you know what I mean," Penny ended.

"I do know what you mean and at least you'll not mistake my accent for anything British."

"Your accent is positively charming."

"Is there a soul in the world who doesn't like an Irish accent?" he said, exaggerating it.

As the din around them rose, he leaned forward and lowered his head so he could hear her response. He smelled faintly and subtly of luxury soap, with an expensive scent. He smiled then sat back and made soft eye contact and in that moment she felt a magnetic pull toward him. She wiped her hands on the napkin and leaned back against the banquette.

As they finished their drinks Michael asked her if she had a favourite restaurant nearby and if so, could he take her to dinner.

"I think I'd rather go home," said Penny. "It's been a very long day. I was at the Hall by seven thirty this morning and, to be honest, I'm exhausted. I can feel myself starting to fade. And you must be exhausted, too."

"Fair enough," said Michael.

"But it's a lovely offer," said Penny, "and I hope we can do it another time. I'd like to hear more about your work at the university."

"Then let me give you my number and you can text me."

"Great! I will." She entered his number in her phone and then gave him an open, encouraging smile, which he returned.

Penny basked in his presence for a few more minutes as they finished their drinks. They had just about reached the door when a group of men entered, Haydn Williams among them.

"Excuse me a moment," Penny said to Michael. "I see someone I know and I just want a word in case he might have heard something about Catrin." She stood to one side to let the men pass. They found their seats and one of them went to the bar to get the drinks in. From their casual banter and genial smiles it was apparent they hadn't heard about the murder, and Penny decided she didn't want to be the one to tell them.

Michael raised an eyebrow and she shook her head.

"It didn't feel like the right time."

"Well, let's go. Tell me where you live and I'll drive you home."

Penny directed him to her cottage and he switched off the engine. They sat facing straight ahead in a closed silence wrapped in tension as Penny wondered if he would try to kiss her. She hesitated and then said, "I hope you don't mind, but I'm tired and I can't stop thinking about Catrin. Not the right time to invite you in." She smiled at him and reached for the door handle. "Thanks for the lift and the drink."

"No problem," said Michael. "I hope we can get together again soon."

"I'd like that," said Penny.

As Michael reversed his car and drove off she let herself into the cottage. Her grey cat, Harrison, came running to her and wound himself around her legs. She bent down to pat him, scooped him up, and nuzzled his neck. He purred loudly as she held him and carried him into the kitchen. She set him down on the kitchen floor and reached into the cupboard for his dinner.

When he'd been fed, she made herself a cup of tea, then settled herself into a comfortable chair and rang DCI Gareth Davies. He had just returned to Llanelen, and said he'd be with her in about twenty minutes.

Thirteen

*P*enny gave her sitting room a quick tidy up. Finally, a car's headlights shining on the window announced his arrival. She opened the door and offered him a coffee.

"So you saw Catrin at *Antiques Cymru*," he said when they were seated. "What time would this have been?"

"Late morning. Eleven thirtyish, I suppose."

"Was she with anybody?"

"No," said Penny. "She was on her own. She had a quilt that was being appraised when I walked by, so I stopped to watch. I think it was valued around three or four hundred pounds. Can't really remember the amount, but not a lot. I think she was disappointed it wasn't more. The appraiser didn't spend too long with her, and didn't choose it for filming."

"Quilt? What kind of quilt? What did it look like?"

"It was handmade and had a pattern of turquoise triangles on a white background. It looked like it would be really pretty on a summer bed."

"And you didn't see her after she finished with the appraiser?"

Penny shook her head. "Just briefly. I think I asked her if she was going to stay and watch some of the appraisals but she said no, because she had the bulky quilt to carry around. And she said she had to get home because someone was coming to view a room. She'd decided to let out a room, apparently. She said it was for a bit of company, but I got the feeling it was more about money."

Davies took a sip of coffee. "Yes, the poor woman who came to view the room found the body. Awful shock for her."

"I wonder what will happen to the house," said Penny. "Catrin lived there with her parents, and was an only child. Maybe she made a will. I hope she did. I have no idea who her nearest relative would be."

"We think it might be a cousin," said Davies. "But we haven't established that yet. In fact, we haven't even found someone who can identify the body."

"I expect someone will turn up," said Penny. "There's bound to be an aunt or uncle or cousin nearby. Her father was a local butcher, I believe. Sold the business not long before he died, and then his wife died soon after him."

She stifled a yawn.

"Do you have any idea yet why she was killed? She seemed like such an innocuous person. Why would anyone want to kill her?"

"It could have been a robbery gone bad, I suppose. She might have let someone into the house who then tried to rob her and panicked."

"You do hear about people being killed for a ridiculously small sum," said Penny. "But I can't imagine she had much money. She'd recently started working at the chemist on the makeup counter and from what I hear, was very good at it. Women liked her."

"People will kill to get a few pounds to buy drugs," agreed Davies. "But I don't think that's what this was. In that kind of scenario, there are signs of a struggle. There's an argument and a fight. In this case, there's none of that, and it looks to me as if there was something personal about it. I think she knew her killer." He shrugged. "When you've been looking at murder as long as I have, you just get a sense of it. I expect this will be my last case."

"Oh, you've made your retirement decision, then?"

"Yes, this just feels like the right time to go, so I'm planning to pack it in by the end of July. Not sure what I'll do after that, but it'll be good not to have to face any more late nights." He looked at his watch. "Speaking of which. I'm sure you're tired, too. It's been a long day for all of us."

"I was just saying that to someone," said Penny, "and yes, I am rather tired. It's a nice bath and then bed for me, I think."

"Oh, that reminds me. Bed. What you said earlier. I'll have to check with Bethan. I didn't go upstairs in Catrin's house so Bethan might have seen the quilt, but I didn't see it downstairs." He pressed a number on his phone, spoke for a few minutes, then ended the call.

"Interesting. She said there was no quilt upstairs. We'll have to go back to the house tomorrow and have a look for it."

"Is it important, do you think?"

He stood up. "I don't know. But it's important that we find out what happened to it."

91

He pressed a button on his phone. "I'm sorry to be making these calls," he held up the phone in an apologetic gesture, "but you know we have to do these things sometimes as a matter of urgency." He waited a moment, and then spoke. "Yes, it's DCI Davies here. I want all the rubbish bins searched between Ty Brith Hall and Thyme Close, just off Rosemary Lane. You're looking for a handmade quilt. It's a turquoise pattern on a white background." He looked at Penny for confirmation and she nodded. "Need it done tonight. I don't want anyone to have a chance to pick through the bins and I don't want the bins cleared. Right. Thanks."

"There was a little shuttle bus between Ty Brith and the town square," said Penny. "She probably took that so I doubt anything would turn up between the Hall and the town square."

"Well, there won't be that many bins," said Davies, "so we'll get them all checked just in case. You never know."

"No, I guess you don't."

After a gentle good-bye, which Penny found was getting easier and less awkward, Davies was on his way.

Exhausted, Penny made her way upstairs and ran herself a bath. She usually showered in the morning, but there were times, like tonight, when a soothing lemon-verbena scented soak was the only thing she wanted. And then she'd go downstairs and fix herself something to eat. A poached egg on toast, maybe. Something light and unfussy.

She stretched out in the bath, her head resting on a soft towel placed on the back of the tub. She closed her eyes and let the warm water work its magic. When the water started to feel just a little too cool, she stirred, gave herself a quick wash and rinse, and climbed out. She toweled herself off, slipped on a terry cloth dressing gown, and went downstairs. She scooped up her phone on the way through to the kitchen. One text message: Michael. He hoped she was having a good evening and could he take her sketching tomorrow? She smiled to herself. Yes, he certainly could.

Fourteen

*I*s there anything lovelier than a Sunday morning in May, Penny asked herself, as she opened the back door to let Harrison out. She stood for a moment breathing in the warm, softly scented air as he scampered onto his favourite spot on the stone wall. Leaving him there to enjoy the sun's warmth, she went upstairs to get dressed. She took her time choosing what to wear, sliding clothes hangers along the rail, dissatisfied with just about everything available to her. I must do a clear out for the charity shop and get some decent clothes, she thought, after finally selecting a pair of comfortable jeans and a blue and white striped Breton top that she would pair with a bright turquoise jacket and a hot pink scarf. A trim woman in her early fifties, with red hair worn in a chic, blunt-cut bob, Penny studied her stylish silhouette in the full-length mirror and decided she looked appropriate for what the day was likely to bring. Michael had suggested an afternoon walk with time to sketch, then dinner in a country pub. She went downstairs and caught up with the local news on her laptop while she munched her way through a bowl of cereal and sipped a coffee.

Haydn Williams had returned home from church that Sunday morning in a troubled frame of mind. The murder of Catrin Bellis had shocked and saddened the townsfolk, and those attending church had been unusually attentive during the service. Haydn, who was filling in that morning for his cousin who usually played the church organ, had chosen solemn, peaceful music for the congregation's exit. He played for a few more minutes to a nearly empty church, stopping only when Bronwyn Evans, the rector's wife, began walking up and down between the rows of pews, replacing hymn books in their little wooden racks and gathering up abandoned church notices. When the rector returned from the outside step where he had been wishing departing parishioners a good morning, he and Haydn had had a few words about the funeral service for Catrin.

"I believe there's a relative somewhere," the rector said.

"Yes, there is," replied Haydn. "You didn't know?"

The rector looked puzzled. "No. What didn't I know?"

"Evan Hughes is her cousin. He's a mate of mine. I can talk to him about the funeral if you like."

"Oh, I'd forgotten that. Well, if you would speak to him that would be very helpful," replied the relieved rector. "I guess we can't really set the date until we know when the coroner is likely to release the body." He shook his head. "Murder is always such an inconvenience with all that legal formality and red tape. You just never know where you are."

When he got home, Haydn changed out of the suit he wore to church into his working clothes, gathered up Kip, and headed out to check on the ewes. As they strode across the fields his thoughts returned to Catrin. She'd been a lovely lass. His cheeks began to burn as he remembered the one time he'd walked her home from school and her mother had sent him away, pulling Catrin into the house and closing the door gently but firmly in his face.

Michael picked Penny up just before one o'clock and after loading her sketching gear into his car, they set off for Gwydyr Forest, a centuries-old, beautifully preserved landscape of rivers and lakes, trees and mountains that ranges across the eastern flank of Snowdonia National Park. Wooded hillsides rise steeply from the valley floor, providing a dramatic backdrop to the town of Llanelen.

He parked the car by Llyn Sarnau, a reedy, shallow lake, and lifted out the sketching stool. Penny gathered up her satchel filled with art tools and they began the trek along a forestry path, gradually climbing higher until they were looking over a peaceful scene of an open field dotted with ewes and lambs, with direct views to Moel Siabod, a mountain in the Snowdon range with an impressive, pointy profile. A sprinkle of patchy snow still capped the highest mountaintops and in the afternoon light the ancient peaks shimmered a rich, dark purple. A light, steady breeze blew fluffy white cloud formations through a bright blue sky.

Penny surveyed the landscape, breathing in the beauty of it.

"This looks perfect. The light's just right," she said. "I'll just find a flat piece of ground and get started." Michael set the stool down for her, then stretched out beside her on the grass, leaning back on his hands with this legs crossed. He remained still for a few minutes, his face upturned to the sun. After a while he got to his feet, brushing bits of grass off his trousers. "Just going to wander a little farther on down the path and stretch my legs," he said. "If we're anywhere near a mast, I might try to make a couple of phone calls."

Penny glanced at him, gave him a brief, preoccupied smile, and returned to her work. She kept her head down, focused on the easel in front of her, and looked up just as he returned to her side, letting out a little exclamation of surprise. "What's that?" he said, pointing across the valley. "Definitely not a sheep. It looks like a ghost."

A white dot moved slowly across the landscape. Penny picked up the small pair of binoculars that she sometimes wore around her neck when sketching. She got to her feet, raised the binoculars to her eyes, and adjusted the focus. Her body moved slowly to the right as she scanned the slow moving figure below. She lowered the binoculars and handed them to Michael.

"I'm pretty sure that's Dilys, of all people, and if I'm not mistaken, she's somehow got hold of the missing quilt that the police are looking for. Let's see if we can catch her up." Michael sized up the situation, then slung the folding stool over his shoulder and picked up Penny's satchel.

"You can tell me all about her on the way," he said as they charged off. "We'll drop this lot off in the car, then try to catch her on the other side of the lake. She's walking pretty slowly and if we head in that direction," he pointed to the east, "our trajectories should just about cross."

After a quick stop at his car, they headed down the path that led round the lake.

"Who is she?" Michael asked.

"She's a local character. She comes and goes, scouring the hedgerows and fields for plants. She's a bit of a naturalist, you might say. Knows everything there is to know about roots, berries, leaves, and twigs and what have you.

"I haven't seen her for ages and thought she'd left the area for good, but apparently not. She has these recipes and formulas for botanicals, and in fact, the hand cream that's so popular at our Spa is made from one of her formulas. My partner and I bought the licensing rights from her and it's a big seller. And a little while ago she somehow knew I wasn't sleeping very well and gave me something for it. And surprisingly, it worked."

"Is she a little, er, how shall I put this, eccentric?"

Penny laughed. "More than a little, I'd say, and that's probably the least of it." They were getting closer to her now and Dilys looked in their direction. Penny was afraid she'd try to run if she thought they were chasing her, so waved in what she hoped was a friendly gesture. Dilys stopped and stared, allowing Michael and Penny to get closer to her.

Her long grey hair was tied back with a piece of raffia and draped over her overcoat was a white quilt with a turquoise pattern that she wore around her shoulders like a bulky shawl. She carried an old-fashioned trug basket filled with small plants.

When they reached her, Dilys squinted at Penny.

"It's you, is it? The woman who likes my hand cream."

"Yes, Dilys, it's me, Penny." She lifted a hand in the direction of her companion. "And this is my friend Michael. We were out walking and sketching and saw you."

"You come from up there." She pointed to the spot where

Penny and Michael had been. "Why are you come down here to talk to me?"

"Well, Dilys, I want to ask you about that quilt you've got round your shoulders."

"It's mine. I found it. I didn't steal it."

"No one's saying you did. Tell me, where did you find it?"

Dilys's lips thinned and her eyes narrowed as she shifted her weight from one foot to the other. She bent over slowly and set down the basket.

"It's a beautiful day," said Penny. "Aren't you hot with that quilt around your shoulders? Would you like me to hold it for you?"

"No, I would not," said Dilys, taking a step back and clutching the quilt closer to her with dark green fingerless gloves flecked with mud and bits of dried leaves. "I'm all right just as I am. You won't take this off Dilys. I told you. I found it and it's mine. Now you let me be."

Penny took a deep breath. "All right, Dilys. I'm going to be honest with you. The thing is, you see, the lady that owned that quilt has been killed and the police want to examine that quilt because it belonged to her. It could be an important clue. They'd like to know where you got it. They want to talk to you. Will you help them find out what happened to the lady? Where are you staying now? Maybe they could come round for a little chat. It would really help them if you told them what you know."

"Where I'm staying is for me to know and them to find out, then, isn't it, if they want to talk to me all that bad?"

She gave Penny a defiant nod, then narrowed her eyes slightly as she subjected Michael to an all-encompassing once over. He took a step back and raised an eyebrow at Penny who shot him back an imploring look.

"Dilys, can we give you a drive anywhere? We were thinking about going somewhere for tea. If you need something to eat, we can get you a sandwich."

"No, I thank you, just the same. I'm not hungry and I prefer to walk." She retrieved her basket, hooked it over her arm, and took several steps in the direction of the lake before turning back to give them one last curdling look. She was just close enough for them to make out the wisp of a taunting smile playing at the corner of her lips.

"Short of ripping the thing off her back, I don't think there's much else we can do," said Michael in a low voice.

"I'd better call the police right now, while we still know where she is," said Penny.

They headed away from Dilys in the direction of Michael's car as Penny fiddled with her phone. "No luck," she said. "It's often difficult to get a signal out here. I don't know if it's because of the mountains or there just aren't enough masts around, but I'll have to try later. Damn. By the time I get in touch with the police, she could be anywhere. She covers miles every day with her foraging."

They plodded on in silence until Michael spoke. "She's a very strange creature, when you see her up close. She seems more than eccentric. Do you think she's a little, er . . . ?"

"Doolally? Away with the fairies?"

Michael smiled. "Yes, if you want to put it like that."

"We've never been able to work that out," admitted Penny. "She certainly comes across like that. And yet there's also something about her that strikes me as sly and cunning. What the

Scottish call canny. She's probably a bit of all of it. They often go together, don't they?" He didn't reply and they trudged on in silence.

"I think we should find that tea you mentioned," he said a few minutes later. "Or even better, a pub. I don't know about you, but I could do with a drink."

Penny slowed down, her mind exploding with fireworks of conflicting thoughts and ideas shooting off in all directions. She glanced after Dilys's steadily diminishing figure and reached a decision. I can't let this man I barely know get between me and the right thing to do, she thought.

"Michael, I'm very sorry, but I've got to go after her. I haven't really thought this through, but it looks to me as if someone might have taken Catrin's quilt from the house. And then for some reason they threw it away or dumped it where Dilys found it. How else could she have got hold of it? Why would they do that? Whatever happened, I think that quilt is critical to finding out what happened to Catrin, and I can't let it just disappear. And besides, the police are looking for it."

Michael hesitated just long enough for Penny to reassure him that if he didn't want to come with her, she understood perfectly.

"Well, if you're going after her, I'm coming with you," he replied.

"We'd better get after her, then," said Penny. "We've given her enough of a head start."

They set off at a steady pace. Dilys had crossed the road and darted up a natural footpath flanked on both sides by scrawny larch trees, their new, needle-like leaves a bright green, and luxurious Scots pines, the fresh growth at the end of their branches overhanging the path.

"How old do you think she is, by the way?" Michael asked.

"In her early seventies, I would guess. Or maybe she just looks older than she is. Or maybe she's older than she looks. There's no telling with her."

"Well, there we are, then. How far or fast can she walk?"

"Oh, you'd be surprised. Prepare yourself. Farther and faster than you might think. We're in her world now."

Fifteen

There are so many paths in this forest, we'll have a job keeping her in our sights," Penny panted after about ten minutes of steady uphill walking on the rough dirt path bordered by large rocks. "We could easily lose her."

"We could," said Michael, "and we could easily get lost ourselves. That's starting to worry me. I have no idea what direction we're going in, or where we are."

"I think this path leads to several small lakes, and hopefully when we reach them, we can pick up enough reception to ring the police. We only have to follow her until we can let the police know where she is."

"We aren't very well prepared for this, are we?" said Michael. "We've got nothing to eat and no water."

They continued to pick their way along the rocky path,

managing to keep Dilys's quilt-covered back in view. Finally, her pace slackened and they began to gain on her.

"What are we actually going to do?" said Michael. "Are we just going to watch where she goes or do we want to catch up with her?"

"Just keep her in view," said Penny. "She knows we're following her and if she changes her mind about talking to us, she'll stop." She tried her phone again. "No signal yet. Hopefully when we get out in the open we'll be able to get through." She slipped the phone back into her jacket pocket and they plowed on. The path was part of an extensive network used by mountain bikers, with an occasional steep drop. Some sections were easy going, others more strenuous. Occasional smaller paths converged or crossed the path they were on.

Dilys was now walking much more slowly and Penny and Michael were glad of the chance to slacken their pace. Although some daylight remained, the sun was starting to slant across the sky, indicating the afternoon was slipping away, The earlier blue sky had changed to a glowering grey. Michael frowned at it. "I hope it won't rain. We haven't got any waterproofs and I really don't fancy getting back to the car soaking wet. If we can even find the car, that is."

"It can't be much farther," Penny said. "We'll reach one of the lakes in a few minutes, I'm sure."

And then, they emerged from the protective cover of the forest canopy into an open area. Spread out below them was a small lake. They paused for a moment to admire it, but when they turned, Dilys had vanished.

"Oh, no," wailed Penny. "She can't have. Not after all this."

"She can't have gone far," said Michael. "If we hurry, we should be able to spot her."

And then Penny saw it. Slung over a stone wall, abandoned, was the quilt.

They hurried toward it looking in all directions, but Dilys had vanished like a puff of chimney smoke borne away on an autumn breeze.

"Well, at least we've got the quilt," said Penny. "Let's see if we can get any reception here." She reached into her jacket pocket and a questioning look of astonishment flashed across her face. She tried the other pocket, then plunged her hands into the pockets of her jeans, then searched every pocket again. "My phone," she wailed. "I've lost it. It must have fallen out of my pocket somewhere on the trail." She shot him a desperate look. "Have you got yours?" Michael shook his head. "Left it in the car, I'm afraid."

"Well, let's get the quilt, and then head back. The last thing we want is to be up here after dark. We'll leave Dilys for the police to sort out. She's their problem now; they can deal with her," said Penny as they approached the stone wall. With a quick coordinating glance at each other they each took one end and raised the quilt off the wall in a smooth gesture, being careful not to snag it on the rough stone. When it was free, they laid it gently on the grass. It would drape over the sides of a single bed, but barely cover the top of a double bed.

Penny felt the seams and discovered that a side seam had been torn open near the top.

"This is interesting," she said. "When the evaluator was examining the quilt she ran her hand along here and then had a puzzled look on her face. She said something to Catrin but I wasn't close enough to hear what she said. I wonder if there was something in here."

"Well, never mind that now. Let's fold it up and get going," said Michael. "It'll take us at least an hour to get back to the car and it'll be darker on the path than it is out here because of the tree cover. We'll have to hope there'll be enough light for us to spot your phone." He swallowed and held his hand to his throat. "I really wish we had some water. I'm parched."

"So am I," said Penny. She looked around one last time for Dilys, but there was no trace of her. The late afternoon light was intensifying and thinning at the same time, signaling the rapid approach of dusk.

"We're almost at the golden hour of light just before sunset," Penny remarked. "We've got about sixty minutes left. And you're so right. It's time we got out of here."

Sixteen

With Michael carrying the bundled up quilt, they re-traced their steps along the rugged mountain bike path that had brought them to the lakeside clearing. Michael had been right; it was darker under the canopy of trees. They picked their way carefully along, mindful of the occasional steep drop and sharp rocks that bordered the path.

"We should reach the car soon," said Michael. "Almost there. We'll have earned a really good dinner."

The last mellow rays of a sinking sun filtered through the tree branches, bathing them in a soft, dying light. Penny's skin glowed with a warm radiance and Michael reached out and took her hand. And then, the tranquility of the moment was broken by loud shouts coming from behind them.

"Oi, oi, out the way," yelled the first of two youths on speed-ing mountain bikes. Michael managed to push Penny over the rocks and into the safety of the foliage flanking the path as the first of the bikes flew past them, its helmeted rider standing on the pedals and leaning over the handlebars. But he was not so lucky with the second bike that hit him as it careened past. Penny caught a glimpse of the scowling face on the biker as he struggled to keep his balance, but he managed to recover and the cyclists disappeared, without stopping or looking back.

"Oh, no," cried Penny as Michael lay on the path, bleeding from his head. She put her arm around him and helped him sit up.

"That's a nasty cut you've got there and we've got nothing to put on it. Can I help you up?"

He rubbed his left leg. "Just give me a minute," he said. "I'm feeling a bit dizzy."

Penny waited. A few minutes later he reached for her hand and she tried to help him up. He winced as a look of pain flashed across his face and he sank back to a crumpled sitting position.

"I don't think I can walk," he groaned. "I've done something to my leg."

"I don't know what to do," said Penny. "I don't want to leave you here, but the best thing for me to do might be to get to your car as quickly as I can and find your phone so I can call for help before dark."

Michael looked at the sky. The golden haze had now darkened to a deep, smoky violet. "I'm not sure you could get there before dark and without a torch, I think it's too risky. You could easily get lost if you somehow got off the main path. At least if we stay together, I wouldn't have to worry about you."

"Oh, what a mess I've landed us in," moaned Penny. "I'll bet you're desperately wishing you'd never agreed to come. We've got nothing to eat, no water, no light, no warm clothes, and it's too late for anyone else to come along now." She made a tight fist. "Those damn, inconsiderate kids! He must have known he'd hit you and then to just ride off without even bothering to stop and ask if you're okay. The kids could have organized some help for us!"

"I think we're just going to have to make the best of it until morning," said Michael. "Let me think. Give me a few minutes and then I'll see if I can hobble off the path. We'll find a sheltered spot, and you'll have to pull down some pine boughs so we've got something to keep us off the cold ground." He lifted the quilt. "And we've got this, so it could be worse."

They didn't speak for a few minutes and then Penny struggled to her feet. "I'd better get those pine branches sorted while the last of the light remains. It's going to be dark in a few minutes."

She stumbled over a rock on the edge of the path as she headed off into forest, holding onto trees for support.

"Be careful!" called Michael. "We don't want you down, too. And don't go far."

As the last of the light drained from the sky, the birds fell silent and the wind dropped. The tree branches no longer sighed about his head and the stillness was at once comforting and frightening.

The sound of snapping branches, accompanied by the occasional light grunt, reassured him that Penny was nearby. He was sitting upright, his feet stretched out in front of him, wishing there was something he could lean against. His leg was starting to throb and although he had done his best to hide his discomfort from Penny, he was now in real pain and worried that his leg was broken. For the first time, acute awareness of the dangerous situation they were in began to creep into his thoughts.

From somewhere not too far off he heard the hooting of an owl as it began its nocturnal hunting. We forget, he thought, how really dark a forest is at night, with no lights. He looked up at the sky. Stars were starting to become visible, small and twinkling against a black velvet backdrop. He realized how tired he was and how desperately he needed to lie down.

Penny emerged from the woods and stood over him. "Can I help you up now?" she asked. "Give me the quilt." She took it from him and reached down for his hand. He shifted his weight slightly, groaned softly, and then took a deep breath as he reached for her hand. His face contorted into a grimace as she pulled him up a few inches but realizing how badly he was hurting, she lowered him to the ground.

"It's no good is it?" she said. "You're in too much pain."

"You're going to have to lift me up, I'm afraid," he said. "Do you think you can?" She set the quilt down and bent over, then grasping him under both arms, struggling against his weight, managed to haul him to his feet. He stood there unsteadily, all his weight on his right leg. She tucked his right arm over her shoulder. "Can you hop?" she asked. "It's not far. We have to do this. Let's do it."

They limped and lurched to the pine boughs Penny had laid out and Michael lowered himself into them. "I think my left leg is broken," he said. "In the morning you'll have to leave me and go for help."

"At first light," Penny said. She returned to the path to fetch the quilt and put it over him. "I think I should take your boots off," she said. He moaned slightly as she moved his left leg. She took off her own boots and then, being careful not to touch him, she slid under the other half of the quilt. They lay back to

112

back, listening in awkward silence to the night sounds of the forest that surrounded them.

"It's very odd, Dilys turning up again like this," Penny said finally. "Her brother used to be the head gardener up at the Hall—you know, where the *Antiques Cymru* show was held. He died in a fire up there, oh, must be eighteen months ago now, and Emyr—that's the owner—let her stay on for a bit in her brother's old cottage. But the cottages have all been done up now as holiday lets, so I have no idea where she's living."

"Does she live rough?" Michael asked. "If this is what living rough feels like, I can't imagine anyone doing it."

"I wish I knew where she is right now," Penny said. "She could find us some safe water and then go for help."

"When you go for help," Michael said, "you'll have to tie something to a tree near the path so they can find me. I don't know if I'll be able to get back to the path. My leg's in a pretty bad way."

"I'm so sorry," Penny said. "I feel terrible that this happened."

"Don't apologize. You've nothing to be sorry for. It wasn't your fault. Things happen." He let out a long sigh. "It could be a long night and I think the best thing we can do is try to get some sleep."

"Do you think you'll be able to sleep through the pain?" Penny asked.

"I hope so."

Penny ran her hand down the edge of the quilt and slid her hand in the empty pocket created when the seam had been split open. She wiggled her fingers around but felt nothing except a bit of batting. This quilt has a story to tell, she thought.

"Are you warm enough?" she asked. He made a little murmuring noise by way of an answer and not long after, rather to her surprise, and despite the hardness of the ground beneath her, Penny felt herself drifting off to sleep.

It was still dark when she awoke, stiff, sore, and wondering where she was. As it all started to come back to her, Dilys, Michael's injury, the cyclists, the loss of her phone, she struggled to sit up. Without her phone she had no way of telling the time, but the birds had started their dawn chorus so daylight would be coming soon. Michael's breathing was quiet and regular. She lay back and waited for the light, planning what she had to do and envisioning herself doing it. She should have got Michael's car key off him last night so she wouldn't have to wake him now. She'd have to get into his car and find his phone to call for help. How would she describe this place so rescuers could find him? He'd asked her to tie something to a tree on the trail to mark where he was. Thank God she was wearing a scarf. She wondered how soon after sunrise hikers or bikers might be out on the trails.

The blackness began almost imperceptibly to fade to dark grey until she could just begin to make out shapes. A tree trunk here, a branch there. As the sky lightened into dawn and a pale pink filtered between the tree branches, Penny touched Michael on the shoulder. He moaned and tried to turn over.

"Michael, I'm leaving now to find help. Give me your car keys."

He shifted to one side so he could reach into his pocket and handed the keys to her.

"Good luck," he whispered. "Sorry, I'm so parched I can barely speak. Come back soon, with water if you can."

"No matter what happens, you mustn't move," said Penny as she laced up her hiking boots. "I'll be back as soon as I can with help but you need to stay here."

"I don't think you need to worry about that. I couldn't leave even if I wanted to." His eyes remained closed and his breathing was ragged. She gave him what she hoped was a reassuring, encouraging pat on the shoulder.

Brushing the low overhead branches out of her way, she headed for the trail. She pulled off her scarf and tied it to a tree to mark the spot where rescuers would find Michael just off the path. With a bit of luck and the wind at her back, she reckoned she could be at the parking lot within half an hour as the path sloped downhill. The cool, early morning air invigorated her and she set off at a brisk pace, driven by hunger and a rising sense of fear for Michael's safety.

Forty minutes later the parking spot beside the lake came into view. One lone car remained. Clutching Michael's automatic car door opener she pressed the button. At the chirp of the door unlocking she wrenched open the passenger door and dove inside. The phone wasn't in view. She ran round to the driver side and checked the pocket inside the door. There it was. Oh, dear God, let there be battery power, she prayed. As she picked it up, it flickered to life. Fortunately, it was a basic, old-fashioned phone that didn't need a password. She entered a familiar number.

"Bethan, listen, it's me Penny. I need your help. The mountain bike trail above Lake Sarnau that leads up to the little lakes. A man is injured. Broken leg, I think. Can't walk. We need mountain rescue. Probably the air ambulance."

She listened for a moment. "I know it's early and it's a long story. I'm at the lake where the cars are parked. He's farther up the trail. Should I wait here so I can lead you to him or should I go back and wait with him? Here? Okay. And bring food and water. He's badly dehydrated. Please come as quickly as you can. He's not doing well. How long will it take you to get here?"

At least thirty minutes Bethan estimated. That's thirty reassuring minutes, Penny thought. What Bethan really means is it could be up to sixty very long minutes with nothing to do, unless Michael has a book or magazine stashed somewhere. She opened the boot. Empty, except for her sketching materials. She pulled out her satchel, opened the door to the backseat, and sat sideways on it, with her feet on the ground and began to sketch. But within minutes she put the pencil down, stood up, checked the time, and walked some way down the road. She walked back to Michael's car, sat in the front passenger seat, and checked her watch again.

Finally, after what seemed an endless wait, the sound of approaching vehicles alerted her to the arrival of a police car and ambulance. She climbed out of the car, remembered to lock the door and waving, ran toward the response vehicles. As the police car got closer she could make out Bethan in the driver's seat, with DCI Gareth Davies seated beside her.

Bethan parked the car and got out. Without saying anything, she handed Penny an egg and bacon sandwich, coffee, and a bottle of water. Penny opened the bottle and drank gratefully. A paramedic wrapped a blanket around her shoulders.

"I've got more food for our injured hiker," Bethan said. "If you can point us in the right direction, and the way is straightforward, the paramedics suggest that you wait here for the mountain rescue team so you can direct them where to go. We'll go on ahead with the paramedics to assess the situation and do what we can to make him comfortable or begin treatment if necessary, but we won't be able to bring him down until mountain rescue arrives."

Penny directed them to the path, told them to stay on it, and to look for her scarf, a loose weave Indian cotton in graduated colours of orange to hot pink, tied to a tree. And just off the path at that point, to their right, they should find Michael waiting for them. "Oh, and please keep your eyes open for my phone," she added. "I dropped it somewhere up there."

The police officers and paramedics set off and the rescue mission began.

She went back to the sketch. She wished she'd been able to do this last night when the face of the biker that had hit Michael was still fresh in her memory, but this morning was better than not at all.

Seventeen

.

"*I* don't think I've ever been so happy to brush my teeth and take a shower," Penny said to her friend and business partner Victoria Hopkirk that afternoon. "Poor Michael. He's going to be all right, but he will be laid up for a bit with that leg."

"And you're sure you're all right?" Victoria asked. "It must have been quite an ordeal. Were you frightened?"

"Not for me, no, but I was for Michael. He got worse as the night went on and with nothing to take for the pain, he was in a lot of discomfort but he tried to keep that from me. He really put on a brave face. I can't tell you how relieved I was when the police and paramedics arrived."

"And the police must have been really pleased to recover that quilt," said Victoria.

"Oh, they were," agreed Penny. "Almost as glad as I was that Bethan found my phone. I was just thinking about Michael and so focused on him I forgot to tell Bethan we had it, so they were amazed to find poor Michael huddled under it. The paramedics said he'd have been much worse off without it. At least he was warm. It's been sent for forensic testing by now, I expect."

"About the quilt," said Victoria. "And you and Michael spending the night together. Under it." She hesitated and Penny gave her a slow look of surprise.

"Certainly not! With Michael in the pain he was in? But it did make for a bit of an awkward moment when Gareth and I met up again in the parking lot when it was all over."

"Oh, I'll bet. But he accepts that it's over between the two of you, doesn't he?"

"I think so. I hope so. He asked a few questions on the way home about what we were doing up there. I told him we were sketching and walking and saw Dilys and followed her."

"But that must have been really uncomfortable for the two of you up there all night."

"It certainly was." Penny covered her mouth as she yawned. "Sorry. I'm dead tired."

"I expect you are. Just one more thing, though. I want to hear all about Dilys turning up again and with that quilt, of all things. I wonder where she's staying now. She might have another product or two we'd be interested in."

"The police are definitely going to want to know where to find her. Or more importantly, they'll want to know where she found the quilt and how it got from Catrin's house to wherever she found it."

"Could Catrin have dumped it on her way home from the Antiques show, disappointed, maybe, that it wasn't worth what she thought it was?"

"She could have, I suppose, but that doesn't seem very likely to me. Even if it wasn't terribly valuable, it was pretty and it had been in her family for years, so I don't see her doing that," said Penny.

"Yeah, doesn't sound right to me, either," agreed Victoria.

"For what it's worth, here's what I think could have happened. Whoever killed her took the quilt, slashed it open to get something hidden inside, and then that person dumped it. He'd got what he wanted, and didn't need the quilt anymore."

"What makes you think something was hidden inside?" Victoria asked.

"When the appraiser at the show was evaluating the quilt she ran her hand down the side, and then said something to Catrin that I couldn't catch. But someone in the audience standing closer than I was could have heard it. And then the next time I see the quilt, the seam was ripped open. I think there was something in there and someone took it."

"It does sound suspicious," Victoria said slowly. "But maybe Catrin slit the quilt open herself when she got home."

Penny stifled a yawn. "That's possible, I guess. Sorry. I'm going up for a nap and then I'm going to call Michael and see if he needs me to bring him anything in hospital."

"You like him, I take it."

"Yes, I think I do. He's interesting and I'd like to get to know him better. And I do find him attractive. But we got off to a pretty bad start. I feel terrible about what happened to him. We'd all feel better if some good can come out of his terrible ordeal, so be sure to keep your ears open and if you hear anything about Dilys, let me know."

Victoria stood up. "I'll be on my way, then, and let you get some proper rest. Do you need me to get anything for you? Milk, in case you want a cup of tea when you wake up?"

"No, I'm all right for that sort of thing, thanks, but there is something you could do, if you don't mind," said Penny. "Would you ring Emyr and see if he knows where Dilys is staying?"

"Right. I'll give you a call at teatime if I learn anything. You should be up and about by then. Enjoy your nap. I'll see myself out."

A few minutes later Penny tumbled into bed. After the night spent on hard, cold ground, she luxuriated in the feeling of stretching out between smooth, clean sheets. How much we take for granted, she thought as she drifted off to sleep. And just as her eyes closed, she was jolted back into wakefulness by the image of the boy on the mountain bike bearing down on Michael, the look of fear and pain on his face as the bike hit him and the sight of the teenage boy riding off, knowing he'd hit someone, and not even bothering to look back. And then, finally overcome by exhaustion, she fell asleep.

She awoke a couple of hours later, somewhat disoriented from a deep sleep in the afternoon, but after a coffee, felt decidedly better. She wondered how Michael was doing but hesitated to ring him. If she called the ward to ask how he was doing, the nurse would ask her if she was a relative and then probably refuse to give her any information. She couldn't ring his mobile—assuming there was still a charge on it—because patients were allowed to use their mobiles only in designated areas of the hospital.

And then she thought of the best solution. She rang the hospital and asked to speak to the ward where he was located. When someone at the nursing station responded, she asked if she could leave a message for him. "Tell him I called to see how he's doing," she said, "and that I'm coming to see him tomorrow morning. Ask him to text me, if he can, if there's anything he'd like me to bring." She thanked the woman and rang off. If he wanted something, like his phone charger, she'd work out a way to get it.

She had just finished the call and was thinking about supper when Victoria rang. She'd spoken to Emyr, who'd said that he had no idea where Dilys was living, but he'd seen her around, carrying her trug basket filled with plants. From the dark soil clinging to their roots, he thought she was going to replant them somewhere. That might mean she'd found herself a little cottage or at least someplace where she could garden.

Penny thanked her, then told her she'd be taking a bit of time off in the morning to visit Michael in hospital.

Eighteen

The next morning Penny caught the bus to the local hospital. The journey involved two changes, with waiting, so it was midmorning by the time she arrived.

Michael was sitting up in bed, his left leg propped on a couple of pillows. He smiled sheepishly at her.

"I wasn't sure what to bring you," Penny said, "so I brought you good old fruit and flowers."

"Oh, very kind," said Michael. "Have a seat."

"How are you feeling?" asked Penny.

"Not too bad."

"And your leg?"

"Actually, it was my hip they were most concerned about because I landed on it but it's not broken. They've just got the leg propped up to take some of the weight off it. My leg's badly bruised and I'll be a bit sore for a few days, but it could have been much worse. And they said the cut on my head didn't need stitching. They tell me I need to rest the leg and hip for a day or two before putting weight on it. The good news is I can go home tomorrow."

"Do you need me to bring you anything?" Penny asked.

"No, I'll make do with what I've got here," he said. "But my car. I'm a bit worried about it. What happened to it, do you know?"

"I handed over the keys and a police officer drove it to one of their lock ups where it'll be safe. It couldn't stay up there by the lake—could have been vandalized or stolen—so when you're ready to collect it, you just have to show your registration papers at any police station and they'll release it to you and tell you where you can pick it up."

Michael nodded. His face looked a little thinner and his blue eyes seemed a little duller.

"Michael," Penny began, "there's something I want to ask you, if you feel up to talking about it. How did you get to be an *Antiques Cymru* appraiser?"

"Not sure really, I think you just establish yourself as an expert in a certain field, maybe through publishing papers, or by reputation, and they ask you. They source their experts locally, as local people would be more likely to be familiar with the items people are bringing."

"If I wanted to get hold of a certain appraiser, how would I do that?"

"You could start by asking me. Maybe I know him. Who do you want to speak to?"

"It's a her."

126

"Ah," said Michael. "And would she be an expert on fabrics and textiles? Quilts perhaps?"

Penny smiled. "She would."

"That would be Julia Ormerod. I don't have her number, but I'm sure I can get it. I'll call someone from the show who'll know. Hand me my phone." He pressed the button but nothing happened. "Of course. The battery needs charging."

"I wonder if anyone at the nurses' station has the same type of phone and a charger we could use," said Penny. "Shall I see?"

"Is it that urgent?" asked Michael. "I can get the number for you tomorrow. Of course I can't give out her number without getting her approval first."

"Oh, that's fine," said Penny. "About tomorrow, when you go home. Would you like me to come here and go home with you and help you get settled in?"

"I've been thinking about that," said Michael, "and I'll tell you what I'd like. As I've not got much food in, and no car, and I won't be able to drive for a few days, I wondered if you'd be kind enough to come round to mine later in the day, and bring an evening meal for us. I hope that isn't asking too much, but really, there's no one I'd rather ask. And it doesn't have to be fancy. Something simple like scrambled eggs would do nicely."

"Oh, that's no problem at all," said Penny. "I'd be happy to do that." She learned forward. "Have the police been round to talk to you? I gave them a sketch of the face of the biker that hit you, as best as I could remember it. I hope it will help catch him, although I've no idea what he could be charged with."

Michael nodded briefly, then closed his eyes.

"Well," said Penny, "you're tired and I'd better get off to

work. I'll see you tomorrow for dinner. I'm glad you're feeling a little better."

He smiled his thanks.

Bronwyn Evans liked to keep lunch light and simple. She set a plate of salad and a small piece of cold salmon in front of her husband, Thomas, the rector. He leaned forward slightly, peered at it, and then looked at his wife.

"Is this meant to be my lunch?" he asked mildly.

"It is," she replied. "We need to eat a healthier diet. I get some exercise every day walking Robbie, but you, well, not so much. I noticed on Sunday when you were greeting the parishioners that seen from the side you aren't as flat as you used to be."

"No, I guess I'm not," he said, picking up his fork. "Well, thank you, my dear, for preparing this delicious looking lunch with my best interests in mind."

Bronwyn laughed. "Oh, Thomas, was there ever a more diplomatic man than you?" They ate for a few moments in silence, and then Thomas set down his fork. His wife raised a questioning eyebrow. "Not hungry?" she asked.

"No, not really," he replied.

"I know you, Thomas Evans, and when you're not hungry, you're troubled. Can you tell me what is worrying you?" Bronwyn asked.

"It's the funeral for Catrin Bellis. No one has contacted me yet to make arrangements. I'm not sure what kind of funeral she would have wished, but I do know her parents would have wanted her to have one. I'll ring Haydn this afternoon and ask if he's heard anything. And if he hasn't, I'll suggest that he speak to Evan Hughes and ask him to get in touch with me,"

Thomas said. He mulled that over for a moment, then picked up his fork and resumed eating.

"Do you suppose I could have a piece of bread and butter with this?" he asked.

Haydn Williams put the phone down and returned to the large oak table in the middle of his farmhouse kitchen. Kip gazed lovingly at him from his basket, and went back to sleep. The rector was asking if he'd heard anything about funeral plans for Catrin Bellis and he'd had to reply that, no, he hadn't. But he might see Evan Hughes in the pub later and if so, he'd have a word.

Nineteen

Michael Quinn lived in a well-kept, three-storey pebble-dashed house within the shadow of Bangor University. The house was painted a light cream, with Wedgwood blue window frames and door and a slate house sign that said RHOS-GOCH. Red roses clung to trellises on each side of the door.

Penny knocked and a moment later Michael, leaning on a cane, opened the door and stood to one side so she could enter.

"Good to see you," he said as he closed the door.

"How are you?" Penny asked. "Better today?"

"A little," he said, "but not really, if you know what I mean. The bruising on my leg is really coming up today, and it's not a pretty sight, let me tell you."

She made a little noise of concerned commiseration and he gestured toward an open doorway.

"Please, go through."

The sitting room was bright, comfortable, and tastefully furnished. A sage green sofa with lemon yellow and white patterned decorative pillows sat against the wall facing the window that overlooked the street, behind a coffee table with several expensive-looking art books. Bookcases on either side of the fireplace displayed ornamental objects. Prints and original paintings, that Penny longed to take a closer look at, hung on pale green walls. The overall impression was one of a carefully chosen, magazine-perfect look that was decidedly feminine.

As if reading her thoughts, Michael remarked, "This was all done by my late wife and I haven't had the inclination to change it. Just used to it, I guess. Easier to live with it."

"If you like it, then why change it?" said Penny.

"It's just that sometimes I think I could move on better if there weren't so many reminders of her everywhere," Michael said.

"Do you have any children?"

"A son. Lives in Dublin."

"Well, it looks very nice," said Penny. "Tasteful."

"I'm sorry. I should have offered you something to drink. What can I get you?"

Penny gestured at the bags she'd brought. "There's a bottle of Chardonnay in there. I'd love a glass of that but why don't I get it?" She picked up the bags. "Shall we take these through to the kitchen?" Michael limped ahead of her, and pulled a corkscrew out of a self-closing drawer. He opened the bottle and pointed to a cupboard. "Glasses in there," he said.

Penny removed two glasses and set them on the worktop. When they were filled, Penny and Michael clinked glasses and she took a sip. "Now," she said, "I've brought some smoked salmon and lovely brown bread from the bakery, and you mentioned scrambled eggs, so let's get started."

He sat at the little table and they chatted while she prepared the meal. About fifteen minutes later she snipped fresh dill over the creamy scrambled eggs and set a lemon quarter beside each serving of smoked salmon. Michael sliced the bread and put out fresh butter.

"Looks delicious," he said. "I thought we could eat in the conservatory." He led the way to a glass-enclosed room at the back of the house, filled with flowering plants. French doors led to the garden beyond.

Penny set the plates of scrambled eggs on the table and returned to the kitchen for the wine glasses and cutlery while Michael lowered himself gingerly into a chair.

"Cheers," he said. "Thank you so much for this."

"It's the least I can do," said Penny. "You wouldn't have been injured if we hadn't gone after Dilys."

Michael nodded. "I might think twice before doing that again."

He reached into his pocket. "I got the number you wanted. Julia Ormerod. The woman who evaluated the quilt. She said she'd be happy to talk to you."

Penny took the piece of paper he offered her and glanced at it. "Wonderful. Thank you."

She took a sip of wine. "You know I'm surprised our paths haven't crossed before. I thought I knew everyone around here who was involved in the art world."

"I confine myself pretty much to the university," said Michael. "To be honest, I was surprised when the show's producer contacted me, but apparently the person they'd lined up had to drop out, and because I was local, they asked me to step in. Which, of course, I was happy to do. Saturday was my first day with that particular show, actually, although I've done similar ones."

"You seemed very comfortable in the role," said Penny.

"That comes from teaching university students," said Michael. "If you can hold your own in front of them, you can talk to anyone. And I was comfortable with the process and with what people were bringing me. And they have lots of behind-the-scenes resources, if you're not sure about something—you can look it up yourself or a researcher is available to help."

"You must have been stunned when you saw Florence's John Lennon drawings."

"Stunned! It was beyond belief. It's the most exciting thing that's ever happened to me. Artistically speaking, of course."

"I suggested to Florence that since they've been stowed away in her cupboard all these years, she should choose one Stuart Sutcliffe and one John Lennon, get them framed, and enjoy them. And send the rest to auction."

"That's a good idea. They'll sell for more and attract more buyers if they're sold as a lot. Sometimes people hang on to things like that and release them one at a time. The right collector will pay many times over the odds to acquire all of them at one time."

"Tell me about Julia Ormerod," said Penny.

"I just met her on the day, but apparently she's an expert in quilts, fabrics, tapestries, costumes, wall hangings, silk wall papers, that sort of thing," said Michael. He smiled at her. "You're dying to ring her, aren't you? Well, let's try to speak to her after dinner."

"While she was evaluating the quilt she said something to

Catrin that I don't think was meant for others to hear. I'm very curious to know what that was."

"Then I'm curious to hear what she has to say, too."

Penny threw him a grateful smile.

Over dinner, Penny told Michael about the Stretch and Sketch Club.

"So it's drawing, with ramble benefits," said Michael.

Penny's little ripple of laughter made him smile.

"Now, I don't know if you'll feel up to this," said Penny, "but the opening of the new exhibit at the Llanelen Museum is tomorrow night. Would you be interested in coming?"

Michael winced as he shifted in his chair to take the weight off his left hip. "I think it's a bit early for me to be undertaking social engagements," he said. "But believe me, there's nothing I like more than an opening."

Easy conversation, punctuated by smiles and laughter, accompanied their meal. After a light dessert of lemon mousse, Michael made coffee and set out cups and spoons on a tray.

"I'm still a little unsteady, so probably best if you carry it through to the sitting room," he said.

When they were seated and coffee poured, Michael smiled at her. "Go on, then."

Penny dialed Julia Ormerod, asked a few questions, and listened intently.

"Well?" said Michael when the call was over.

"Julia said while she was examining the quilt she felt something inside, something that wasn't part of the batting. She checked the seam and it looked original, so she thinks whatever was in the quilt was sewn in when the quilt was made, not put in later. But when we got hold of the quilt the side seam had been ripped open. There wasn't anything there, was there?"

135

Michael shook his head. "No, definitely not."

"So it would be interesting to know if the quilt was intact when Dilys got hold of it, or had whatever was inside already been taken out."

"Did Julia have any idea what this thing might be?"

"She said it was small, about two inches by two inches, and a little stiff. It didn't feel like jewellery, or some kind of keepsake like that."

Michael thought for a moment. "I'd like to know what it was," he said.

"And I'd like to know who else knew it was there," said Penny.

Twenty

The Llanelen Museum is a long, low, whitewashed building situated across from the rectory and adjacent to the churchyard. In the seventeenth century it was designated as an almshouse, providing simple meals and basic shelter to elderly ex-servicemen. When the last of the servicemen died in the 1930s, the building was repurposed as a museum. The tiny bedrooms upstairs, sparsely furnished with a narrow bed, wooden chair and table, could still be viewed as part of the museum experience.

The large space downstairs, formerly the almshouse dining room, kitchen, and sitting room, was used for displays, organized by Alwynne Gwilt, president of the Llanelen Historical Society and museum curator. She was also a good friend of Penny from the Stretch and Sketch Club and had asked Penny to help out at the opening of the newest exhibit.

Like many communities across Britain, Llanelen was remembering its role in World War I.

Throughout 2014, the centenary of the start of the war, the exhibit entitled The Run Up to War had featured photographs taken during the spring and summer of 1914 in the town and on neighbouring farms. Several of the horses shown in the black and white photographs had been sent to join the war effort.

The new exhibit about to open, Llanelen at War, was scheduled to run until the following June. The museum would then close for two weeks while the next exhibit, The Battle of Mametz Wood, was set up for a July opening.

Florence Semble, Mrs. Lloyd's companion, who was acquiring quite a reputation for her excellent catering skills, had agreed to look after the light refreshments for the opening reception.

"Alwynne would like you to circulate and make sure everyone has a drink," she said to Penny, who had volunteered to help. "I could use you for a few minutes, though, to plate these little quiches and sandwiches." She pointed to several large boxes. "After you've washed your hands, if you don't mind."

"Oh, happy to," said Penny.

Just before seven Florence surveyed the table of food, crossing off items on a hand-written check list. She nodded. "It's all there," she said. "The party can start." Just as she finished speaking Mrs. Lloyd, almost always the first to arrive at any event, pushed open the door and Penny and Florence exchanged amused looks.

"Alwynne's been working on this exhibit for over a year," Mrs. Lloyd said. "I sent along photos and letters from Arthur's relatives." She shook her head. "Looking back on it now, what a terrible thing that war was. So many young lives lost, and needlessly, if you ask me."

Alwynne herself entered from her small office at the back of the building. A pleasant-looking woman with short, grey hair and a friendly open expression, she had taken on the museum role about the same time her husband retired. She loved him dearly, but found spending all day, every day with him, too much. She was glad to have the museum and the sketching club as excuses to get out of the house, especially on those mornings when he announced he planned to do some baking. She somehow always managed to slip out of the house just as he was tying on his apron.

"Oh, thank you so much for doing this, Penny," she said. "We're going to have a short meet and greet, with refreshments, for about half an hour, and then the mayor herself will say a few words." She turned to Florence. "And if people want tea or coffee rather than wine . . . ?"

"Right over here," said Florence, pointing to a corner of the table. "I'm just brewing up now."

The room began to fill and Penny moved easily through the small crowd, chatting and smiling. But as the crowd din filled her ears, she felt herself withdrawing into herself and wandered slowly down the tables looking at the exhibits. Each one had been carefully labeled. Alwynne does a beautiful job, she thought. She looked at the photographs. A whole regiment, some soldiers on horseback, caught her eye.

She bent over for a closer look.

"Those were the Llanelen boys who joined the Royal Welch Fusiliers," said a familiar voice behind her. She turned to see her friends the rector Thomas Evans and his wife, Bronwyn.

"The boys all went to war together," he added. "With their friends and neighbours. Of course a lot of the boys from this area were farm lads, who'd probably never been out of the valley."

"So sad when you think of it," said Bronwyn. They moved down the display until they came to a studio photograph of three young men. The man in the centre was seated, his peaked hat resting on his knee, looking self-consciously at the camera. He was flanked by two men, standing stiffly in their new uniforms, holding their caps at their sides. The man on the right of the picture rested his hand on the left shoulder of the seated soldier. In the regimental large-group photos you couldn't distinguish facial details but in this one, three earnest, young faces from a different time gazed back at her, their expressions serious and apprehensive, as if they knew they were on the brink of something momentous.

Something about one of the standing subjects looked vaguely but distantly familiar. Something in the tilt of his head, the friendly look in his eyes that she'd seen recently. She pointed at the photo.

"Do we know who they are?" she asked. "I don't see a card beside this photograph."

"We can ask Alwynne," Bronwyn said. "She's right over there." She took a few steps toward her but before she could speak to her, the door opened, letting in a burst of evening air, followed by a robust woman in a bright blue suit with a large, heavy, gold chain around her neck. "Oh, my, it's the mayor herself," said Bronwyn. "Thomas is introducing her, so we'll continue our talk after the formalities are over." The couple crossed the room, and joined Alwynne, who introduced them to the mayor. A few minutes later the official part of the program got underway.

Penny remained where she was, stealing the occasional glance at the photograph in the glass case. Who were you in life, she wondered. What happened to you? Did you make it home? Or were your bodies left behind, in some corner of a foreign field that is forever Wales?

Shortly after finishing her brief remarks, the mayor, trailed by her small entourage of husband and assistant, made a sweep around the room, smiling and shaking hands with as many guests as she could. Her stiff, lacquered hair remained in place as she nodded graciously at everyone before giving a little wave and then leaving through the door held open by her assistant.

Alwynne breathed a small sigh of relief, and gratefully accepted the glass of wine Florence handed to her. Penny caught her eye and Alwynne joined her.

"This photo," said Penny, pointing to the three young soldiers in their Royal Welch Fusilier's uniforms. "What can you tell me about it? Who are they, do you know?"

"Well, I'm not exactly sure who's who, but the photo is on loan to us by Haydn Williams, so I assume that one of them is an ancestor of his," Alwynne replied. "I wanted to ask him about it, but you know what he's like. Always off with that dog of his, or just a bit vague."

"Yes, he can be a little difficult to pin down."

"I'll try to find out from him what he knows about it. I expect the men would all have been friends, probably since childhood. The community was so much smaller back then and very tightly knit."

"It doesn't matter, really; I'm just curious. When you see old photographs, sometimes you get drawn in and want to know the story behind them, don't you?" asked Penny.

"You certainly do," agreed Alwynne. "And anyway, I really should have their names so I can display them properly on an exhibit card. To be fair, I should have done that before the exhibit opened. But it may not be too difficult to find out who they were. In the old days, people used to write names and dates on the backs of photos. Always in ink, and always in that distinctive style of handwriting that's a little difficult to decipher now."

Penny handed her empty wine glass to Florence who had begun collecting them. Mrs. Lloyd was deep in conversation with a tall man whose back was to Penny, but from the way Mrs. Lloyd was smiling and nodding enthusiastically, she seemed to be enjoying what he had to say.

"I tell you what, Alwynne," said Penny, turning back to her friend. "A while back, Haydn invited me up to the farm to sketch the spring lambs. Why don't I fix up a date with him soon and we can go together? We can ask him about the photo."

"Good idea. I'll bring the photo with me and we can take it out of the frame when he's there."

"Let's go as soon as we can. Are you free in the next day or two? If it's convenient for him, that is. Those lambs are getting bigger every day."

Alwynne smiled. "You're very keen. Can you take the time off work?"

"Oh, I always take off a bit of time in May, to make up for all the extra days I work in June."

Alwynne raised an eyebrow.

"Weddings. Every woman in the wedding party wants a manicure. And a lot of the out-of-town guests want them, too. Keeps us busy."

Twenty-one

"Now Florence," said Mrs. Lloyd the next morning, "I bumped into Brad Driscoll at the museum party last night and had a few words with him."

"Oh, yes? I saw you talking to someone but didn't know his name. Who's Brad Driscoll when he's at home?" said Florence, buttering her toast.

"He's my insurance agent. I was telling him about you and your valuable artwork and your need for insurance coverage on it. Naturally, he was very interested."

"Of course he was."

"But I didn't tell him too much about the actual artwork because to be honest, I don't know that much about it. I thought I'd leave that up to you when you meet him. He's going to explain to you all about the appraisal process and what's involved with insuring your property." Mrs. Lloyd paused to take a sip of her coffee. "Where is your artwork, by the way? Is it still locked up in Emyr's vault?"

"According to Penny, it's a safe room. There's a whole room right off the old butler's pantry where things can be locked up. The family used to keep the silver and other valuables in there. The room is actually temperature and humidity controlled, so it's as good a place as any to store artwork. Much better there than at the back of my wardrobe where it's been for decades."

Mrs. Lloyd nodded. "Right. Well, the thing is, he's coming over this evening, Brad Driscoll is. After dinner."

"Fine," Florence said.

"There's another thing, Florence." Something in the change in the tone of Mrs. Lloyd's voice made Florence set down her coffee cup and give Mrs. Lloyd her full attention.

"I've been thinking about this murder, Florence," Mrs. Lloyd began. "And the more I think about it, the more I know who did it."

Florence sighed. "I was rather hoping you'd forgotten about that by now," she said.

"Forgotten! How could I forget about it when the most important witness was sat right here in our drawing room, telling us everything she knew about it!"

Mrs. Lloyd leaned forward. "Well?" she said.

"Well, what?"

"Aren't you going to ask me who did it?"

Florence gave a little sigh. "Oh, very well. Who did it, Evelyn?"

"Why Brad Driscoll, of course!"

"And why would he do that?"

"Because he was having an affair with Catrin Bellis and she threatened to tell his wife. His wife was a friend of hers from their school days. It's the oldest story in the book, Florence, the eternal love triangle. Happens all the time. And someone always gets hurt. And usually it's the other woman."

"Well, hurt maybe. But killed? And what proof do you have of this may I ask?"

"I saw them together, didn't I? Catrin and Brad. On several occasions. Walking in the street and chatting together nice as you please in the town square."

"Yes, but that doesn't mean they're having an affair, and it certainly doesn't mean that he killed her."

"Oh, I can tell, Florence. I could tell from the look in his eyes when I was talking to him last night. I pretended to hang on his every word, but he didn't fool me. Not for an instant. When you work in the post office for as long as I did, you get so you can read people, and believe me, I could read him like a book."

Florence thought for a moment.

"All right, then, Evelyn. What about this? If you think Catrin died because she was caught up in a tragic love triangle, how do you know it wasn't the wife who killed her? She might have burst into the house and said something like, 'I know you're having an affair with my husband and it's got to stop.' And Catrin said, 'But we love each other and he's going to leave you and we're running off to Tunbridge Wells together.' And the wife, whatever her name is . . .'"

"Tegwen," said Mrs. Lloyd, her eyes shining. "She's called Tegwen."

"Right. So Tegwen says something like, 'You'll never have him.'"

Mrs. Lloyd poured herself a rare second cup of coffee.

"I like the way you're thinking now, Florence," she said. "You're starting to think like a detective. But there's just one thing wrong with your argument. A flaw in your logic, we might say."

"What's wrong with my thinking?" asked Florence, widening her eyes.

"It's like this, Florence, I was a married woman before my poor Arthur passed on, whereas you have never been married. If you had been married, Florence, you'd know that this isn't how Tegwen would respond. She'd be much more likely to say, 'Having an affair, is he? I'll bloody kill him with my bare hands.' So in that case, you see, Brad Driscoll would be the victim, not Catrin Bellis. So that's why he's the killer, not her," Mrs. Lloyd finished triumphantly. "You're just not thinking clearly."

The beginnings of a faint smile played in the corners of Florence's lips.

"I think it's you who's not thinking clearly, Evelyn. If you think this man is a murderer, why on earth would you invite him into our home so you can question him? Once he works out that we're onto him, what's to stop him from murdering us?"

"Oh, that will never happen," Mrs. Lloyd reassured her.

"And how can you be so sure?" Florence demanded.

"Well, he can't murder both of us at the same time, can he? So while he's busy murdering you, I would run out into the street and call for help."

"Oh, very comforting," said Florence dabbing her eyes while she tried to control her shaking shoulders.

Florence showed Brad Driscoll into the sitting room. He was smartly dressed in a suit and tie and carried a leather portfolio case under his arm. After declining her offer of coffee, he unzipped his portfolio case and took out several documents and a brochure. He handed the brochure to Florence explaining it contained information on how the company he represented could protect her fine art investment.

"Now tell me what kind of art it is and how much you think it's worth," he said. "Wow," he commented when Florence finished describing the *Antiques Cymru* appraisal.

"And where is this art at present?" he asked. "I ask because I wouldn't like to think it's uninsured on these premises."

"It's locked up in a secure location," said Florence.

"Right. Very good. Well, you will need to have it appraised for insurance purposes." He shuffled some papers and then addressed Mrs. Lloyd. "The art is covered up to ten thousand pounds under your home policy, so I think we'll put a rider on your policy with immediate effect insuring the work for one hundred thousand pounds, in the event of fire, theft, damage. There's appraised value and insured value, which is always more. Of course, it's irreplaceable." He handed Florence a few papers. "Please review those and if you are in agreement, you can drop into my office to sign them. Here's my card with the address on it." He clipped his business card to a corner of the papers and handed everything to Florence. She didn't look at them, but sat stiffly with them on her knee.

"Thank you," she said, and waited. Mrs. Lloyd had told her that she would take the lead on the questioning of Brad Driscoll and Florence was more than happy to let her get on with it.

He checked his watch and began arranging his papers. "Now, any other insurance needs I can help you with? Planning a trip? Life insurance? Do you have any questions?"

"That was a terrible thing that happened to Catrin Bellis," Mrs. Lloyd blurted out after a moment's silence. Driscoll raised his eyes from his briefcase. "Yes," he agreed. "It certainly was."

"And she and your wife were great friends, I understand," Mrs. Lloyd continued.

"Yes, they were. We all went to school together, so we were friends for a long time."

"That's interesting," said Mrs. Lloyd. "I always think there's something very special about a school friendship that lasts a lifetime."

"Yes, there is," said Driscoll getting to his feet. "Well, if there's nothing else, I'll be on my way."

"Oh, but are you quite sure you wouldn't like a cup of coffee before you go?" asked Mrs. Lloyd rising from her chair. "It really wouldn't be any trouble at all, would it, Florence?"

"No trouble at all," smiled Florence. "But perhaps Mr. Driscoll hasn't even been home yet and he's anxious for his dinner."

"Yes, that's exactly it," said Driscoll a little too eagerly. He made for the front door, which Florence opened for him.

"Good night," she said, then closed the door quietly behind him and returned to the sitting room.

Mrs. Lloyd glowered at her. "Well, how do you think that went, Evelyn?" Florence asked.

Mrs. Lloyd sighed. "I was just starting to get someplace and then he realized I was on to him, and he couldn't get out of here fast enough. I thought it best to let him go, as you never know what might have happened."

"No," said Florence. "You don't. But that talk of coffee's rather put me in mind to have one myself. Would you like one?"

Mrs. Lloyd, deep in thought, didn't reply.

Twenty-two

The next afternoon Penny and Alwynne waved good-bye to Alwynne's husband as he drove off, leaving them with their sketching paraphernalia at Haydn Williams's farmhouse gate. They walked down a short path that had recently been a dark brown soup of thick, lumpy mud but was now hard and rutted. Ahead of them was a two-storey grey stone farmhouse, with outbuildings and sheds built of similar stone off to the right. The sheds, open sided and empty now except for piles of sweet smelling straw, had housed ewes and their newborn lambs from early April until just a few days ago. A dark green Land Rover spattered with mud was parked beside the nearest shed alongside an equally muddy quad bike.

The farmhouse door opened and Kip, Haydn's black and white Border collie bounded out, tail wagging furiously, to give them a boisterous welcome.

Haydn was right behind him. "Come in, come in," he said, smiling broadly. "Glad you've come to see the lambs. They're about a month old, and as playful as can be but they won't be small much longer. And they won't be here much longer, either," he added.

"You're not selling them already, surely?" asked Penny.

"No, no. Nothing like that. The flock'll soon be ready to be moved to the high pastures for summer grazing. Why don't you come in for a moment and then I'll show you the way to the field. It's not far."

The women set down their stools and easels by the door and entered a kitchen that smelled faintly of wet dog and heavily of a fellow living on his own who enjoyed a hearty fry up. A man dressed in same style of farming clothes as Haydn stood up and smiled as they entered. Haydn made a simple introduction. "This is Evan Hughes," he said, then introduced each of the women.

"Evan's a friend of mine. Farms farther on down the road. He's kindly been helping me repair a boundary wall that was damaged in that February storm so we can keep the sheep enclosed when we move them. And we've been discussing the funeral arrangements for Catrin Bellis. He's, er, was I guess I should say, her cousin."

A tall man with dark wavy hair stuck to the sides of his head by a flat cap, Evan held out a rough, work-hardened hand to Penny. His grip was surprisingly gentle as he shook her hand, appraising her with dark brown eyes.

"I'm very sorry for your loss," Penny said. "Catrin's closest relative, were you?"

"Aye," said Evan. "She had no brothers or sisters. Only child, she was."

"Well, we don't want to keep you from your wall mending, Haydn, but I brought the photo you loaned us for the exhibit and I wondered if you would tell us what you can about who's in it. I really would like to do a proper exhibit card and to do that, I need to know the names of the three men," said Alwynne.

As she was speaking, Evan stood up. "Just going out for a smoke," he said to no one in particular.

"Well, why don't you do your sketching now and then when you're done come back here and we'll look at the photo over a cup of tea," said Haydn. "And you're not holding us up. We're done with the stone wall for today. Come on, then. I'll show you the way."

As they passed Evan in the farmyard he twisted a cigarette butt under the toe of his boot. He gave them a little wave as they continued on their way to the field of ewes and their spring lambs.

Haydn raised a dirty hand and pointed. "If you go round this way, there's a path that'll take you higher up so you look down into the field. But don't go in the field with them. The ewes get nervous and besides, there'll be a lot of sheep muck in there."

Penny and Alwynne thanked him and walked on until they reached a small field not far from the house. A stream ran through it, clear and cold, and several stunted rowan trees beside a dry stone wall provided what shade they could.

"Oh!" exclaimed Penny when she saw the sheep. "I was expecting just the regular white ones but these will make for a much more interesting picture. I like them!"

They exchanged quick grins as they set up their gear on the side of the gently sloping hill where Haydn had suggested. Not far below them, a small flock of ewes and their spring lambs, several of them black, stopped their grazing to study the new-comers. The ewes soon lost interest and lowered their heads to return to their task but three adventurous lambs, including a black one, approached the stone wall to get a better look at the newcomers. Penny reached for the camera she kept in her sketching kit.

"So adorable. I love their little faces," Alwynne said.

"I wonder what kind they are. What breed, I mean."

"Oh, they're Welsh Mountain, I believe," replied Alwynne. "Haydn entered one or two in last year's agricultural show and he told me all about them. Very hardy and perfect for a life in these hills. Mostly white, but every now and then a black one pops up."

Penny continued to photograph the lambs as they regarded her with curious, intense looks. She took a few steps closer to the stone wall, but they turned away, flicked their tails, and in endearing little bounds, returned to the safety of their mothers' sides.

She returned to her collapsible stool, pulled out her sketch-book, set it on her knee, and began to pencil in the lambs' faces.

"So Evan is Catrin's closest relative," said Alwynne as she unscrewed the top of a water bottle and took a swig.

"Apparently. Do you know him?" Penny asked.

"Not really. At least, not very well. I see him at church on Sundays every now and then with his family. His father is, or he used to be, the churchwarden."

Penny frowned as she examined the tip of her 2B pencil and then scrabbled around in her bag for a pencil sharpener. "What does a churchwarden do, exactly?" she asked as she twisted the pencil and blew the shavings on the ground.

"Oh, he's responsible for making sure the building is looked after. The roof doesn't leak, the doors are unlocked on Sunday morning, everything is tidied up after the service . . . that sort of thing. But Bronwyn could tell you more about it than I can."

As she finished speaking the farmhouse door opened and the two women turned their heads as Evan stepped out into the farmyard. He turned as if to say something to Haydn, raised a hand in a brief gesture, and began walking to the Land Rover. When the kitchen door closed, he stopped, pulled out his phone, studied it for a moment, then lifted his eyes to where Penny and Alwynne were seated, then once again checked his phone. Alywnne waved to him and he returned the gesture, then continued to his vehicle and a few minutes later drove off down the lane, through the gate, and disappeared.

Artistic peacefulness settled over them as they sketched, immersed in their work, oblivious to the world around them and each other, connected only to the scene in front of them. One of the ewes wandered over to the stream for a drink and Penny decided to use this as the focal point of a picture. The splashing sound of the little brook and the occasional baaing of lambs and ewes calling to one another broke the stillness. Although they weren't close to the sheep, the wind carried a faint smell of farmyard animals that was strong enough to remind them where they were but not strong enough to be unpleasant. The women remained in deep concentration for about forty minutes, until Alwynne checked the time and glanced up at the sky.

"We should start to pack up, Penny," she said. "The best of the afternoon light is gone. When we've just about finished talking to Haydn, I'll ring Himself and let him know it's time to come and pick us up."

Penny made a soft sound of acknowledgement, sighed, took

a critical look at her work, and began to put her art supplies back in the wooden case she used to transport them. "I've got three good sketches to be going on with," she said. "So I'm happy with that." She showed Alwynne her sketches. "How did you do?"

"I did four, but mine aren't as detailed as yours. I like what you did with the ewe at the stream, the way she was taking a drink, and then looked up as if something caught her attention. I focused on the lambs." She placed her sketches in her case. "Interesting, isn't it, how we can both look at the same scene but see such different things."

The women walked back to the farmhouse, knocked on the door, and entered. Haydn was seated at the table, a glass of whisky in front of him. He asked the women if they'd like a drink and when they declined, he offered tea.

"Why don't I make it," said Penny, "while you and Alwynne get on with the photograph." She filled the kettle, plugged it in, and remained standing leaning against the cluttered work-top facing them.

Alwynne pulled the photo from her bag. "Would you mind if we took the photo out of the frame so we can see if there's any writing on the back?"

Without replying, Haydn took the photo from her. "That's my great-grandfather," he said, pointing to the man standing on the right. "If you wait here a moment, I can get you his full name." He disappeared into a nearby room and returned with the family Bible. Alwynne's face lit up when she saw it. "Oh, these are a wonderful resource for tracing family history," she said. "Bless those dear women who took the trouble to write down the names and birthdates of their family members."

Haydn pushed some dirty cups and spoons on the table to one side and was about to set the Bible on the table when Alwynne sprang forward. "Let's put a cloth down," she said, "in case anything's been spilled. Even one drop of tea could stain the cover."

Haydn looked about helplessly. "Have you got a towel perhaps, Haydn?" Alwynne asked.

A look of relief came over his face. "Oh, yes, there's a clean towel in the drawer in the dresser. I was saving it for Kip. I'll get it." He handed the Bible to Alwynne while Penny cleared the dirty glasses and mugs off the table and deposited them in the sink and then wiped down the table with a not-too-clean cloth. Haydn spread the towel on the clean area and set the Bible on it. He turned to the pages where his family genealogy was recorded.

"Right. This is me, this is my father, my grandfather, and my great-grandfather," he said, running his finger up the row of names.

"This man," he pointed to the man on the right of the photo, "is Wilfred John Williams. He was born in 1890, and he married in 1912, so he must have been, let's see . . ."

"Twenty-two," said Alwynne. "That might seem a little young to us today, but that's about the age men got married back then." She scrabbled around in her handbag and pulled out an unopened envelope.

"Now, it says here in 1913, their child was born, a boy that was, so he would have been my grandfather," Haydn continued. "And then in the next entry, Wilfred John Williams dies on July 10, 1916, aged twenty-six." Alwynne jotted down the dates on the back of the envelope. "And that's all there is here about him," Haydn said quietly.

157

"It's always moving, learning about your family members who went before you," Alwynne said.

"It just struck me that my grandfather was only three years old when his da died," said Haydn. "I never knew that before."

Alwynne gave him a quiet moment and then spoke. "Shall we see what it says on the back of the photo?" She examined the frame. "I'm going to need a knife or small screwdriver to pry up these little nails that are holding the back on." Haydn fetched a knife and she inserted it carefully under a nail and gently prised upward. When all four tacks were loosened, she slid the back off and eased the photograph out of its frame.

She turned it over as Penny set a couple of mugs of tea on the table and the three of them moved in for a closer look. No names or date were written on the back, but there was an oval stamp in faded ink. T R HAMMOND, ROSE HILL, CONWAY, NORTH WALES it read.

"The town was spelled Conway, then," Alwynne remarked. "I'm disappointed there aren't any names on the back. That's too bad."

She picked up the photo and scanned it closely. "From the cap badge, I'm pretty sure they were in the Royal Welch Fusiliers," she said. "It was a fine old regiment, even then, and most of the boys from North Wales who joined up enlisted with them. I saw a recruiting advertisement once that said something like, 'Why enlist with an English regiment when you can join a Welsh one?'" With a small sigh, she replaced the photo in the frame, bending the tacks back into place as carefully as she'd removed them. "Well, thank you, Haydn. We can name your great-grandfather now in our display, and we'll keep digging until we discover the identities of the other two. I expect they were all friends who joined up at the same time."

"What about the photo?" Haydn asked. "Why was it taken in a Conwy studio?"

"It's a practice that I think started during the American Civil War. Wherever men were preparing to go off to war, professional photographers would show up, set up little makeshift studios—often in tents—and offer to take their photographs."

"Something they could leave behind for their wives and girlfriends," said Penny. "Exactly," said Alwynne, "and their mothers, too, of course. Many of the photographs were signed by the soldiers. 'To Nellie, my own sweetheart,' is one I saw. Conwy was a staging area for some the of Royal Welch regiments, so these young men might have reported there for basic training and decided to have their photograph taken. And again, because these three had their photo taken together, rather than as individuals, that's another reason I think there was a special bond among them."

"My great-grandfather never came home," said Haydn. "I wonder what happened to the other two."

"We'll see what we can find out about them," said Alwynne, as she wrapped the photo in its protective covering and tucked it gently in her satchel. "By any chance, did your great-grandfather Wilfred write any letters home that your family kept? The soldiers often mentioned their closest comrades in their letters, especially if the families knew one another, as would probably be the case here. It's likely that Wilfred's parents would have known who these other two young men were, so he would have let his parents know how his chums were doing. That way, parents shared the news of their children."

She paused. "You'd be surprised how many heartbreaking letters from soldiers I've read that started, 'Dearest Mother . . .'"

Haydn shook his head. "No," he said, drawing the word out.

"I've never seen any letters from him. But wait, there might be something." He retrieved something from a drawer in the Welsh dresser and returned with a piece of paper that he held out to Alwynne.

"That antiques fellow found this in the clock when he was here for the appraisal. Look at the date in the corner."

Penny leaned over Alwynne's shoulder to look at the map. In the lower left corner was printed 7/00.

"Now I lived here in 2000," said Haydn, "and this had nothing to do with me, so I'm thinking it must mean July 1900."

Alwynne checked the dates she'd written on back of the envelope. "Wilfred would have been ten years old at the time." She and Penny exchanged a puzzled glance and then examined the map again. "The drawing is definitely child-like," said Penny, "but there is perspective and scale. This could have been made by Wilfred or one of his friends. But it's only half a map. I wonder what happened to the other half."

Some hours later, after a lovely dinner with Alwynne and her husband, Penny walked the last stretch of road that would take her home. Although they'd wanted to drive her, she'd insisted on walking as the evening was fine and she wanted the exercise and time to think.

A pale quarter moon, partially obscured by fast moving clouds, was just starting to rise as she turned down her lane.

As she approached the path in front of her cottage something stirred on the other side of the hedgerow that flanked the road. Her heart beat faster as she called out, "Who's there?" When there was no response, she thought perhaps she had disturbed a nocturnal creature setting off on its night hunt. And then a dim figure emerged from the deepening shadows and walked toward her.

"I've brought you something," the apparition said. A moment later she revealed herself, reaching out to Penny with an outstretched arm.

"For God's sake, Dilys, what are you playing at? You practically gave me a heart attack, lying in wait and creeping up on me like that."

"I'm sorry. I didn't mean to startle you. But I figured you had to come home some time."

As they turned up the path to Penny's cottage the motion detection sensors came alive, bathing the area in a bright white light. Although the evening was warm for mid-May, Dilys was wearing a long grey cloak which she pulled tightly around her slim body. She held out a cloth bag to Penny. "Here. I brought you this. For your friend."

"What is it?" Penny asked.

"Dried comfrey. You should make a warm compress with it and apply it to your gentleman friend's bruises. It will speed the healing."

Penny took the bag from her.

"And how do I make this warm compress, exactly?"

"You pour two cups of boiling water over a small handful of the comfrey leaves and let the mixture sit for ten minutes, then strain. Soak a gauze pad or a washcloth in the solution and apply it to the bruise for an hour."

"How do you know about his leg?" Penny asked.

"I heard all about what happened to the two of you on my travels," Dilys replied. "People talk up and down the valley, you know. And they seem to like talking about you."

Why is that, I wonder, thought Penny.

"What were you doing up at Lake Sarnau?" asked Penny. "Looking for something, were you?"

"I was gathering hemp agrimony, if you must know. Butterflies love it, so I've planted some outside my little cottage." She nodded at Penny. "Yes, I have a place of my own now."

"Where is it?" Penny asked.

"I'm not telling you that. You'll only send the police round and Dilys doesn't want to talk to them."

"Well, they want to talk to you. They want to know more about that quilt you found."

"I've got nothing to say to them."

"Well, I'm sorry to hear that because I think you are in a very good position to help them find out who killed the lady who owned the quilt."

"I've been thinking about that," said Dilys. "It troubles me. I'm sorry she died."

"Well, why won't you help the police then?"

"I said I wouldn't talk to them. But I will talk to you, and you can tell them. I know you're friendly with them, although maybe not as friendly as you used to be."

Penny smiled to herself. Not much got past Dilys.

"Do you want to come in the cottage and have a cup of tea?" she asked.

"I wouldn't mind sitting down. I've walked a fair distance today. My feet are feeling it."

Penny opened the door and invited Dilys in. "We'll sit in the kitchen, I think," said Penny.

When Dilys was seated with her hands wrapped around a warming cup of tea, Penny took the chair opposite her and set down a pad of paper and a pen in front of her. "Two things, then, Dilys. First. Where did you get the quilt?"

"I didn't steal it, if that's what you're thinking." Her grey eyes, set wide apart, gave her a perpetually curious look.

"No, that's not what I'm thinking. I think you found it and you couldn't resist its pretty colours."

"I liked the pattern. It reminded me of the dress on a doll I had when I was a girl."

"So just tell me where you found it. And I'm going to write down your answer."

"I found it in Evelyn Lloyd's front garden." Penny hesitated a moment, then wrote that down. "What time did you find it?"

"I don't remember."

"This is important. Try to remember." Penny looked at Dilys's wrist. She wasn't wearing a watch. "How do you tell time, by the way?"

"I don't really need to. I know when it's morning, I know when it's afternoon. That's good enough for me."

"Well, approximately what time was it, then?"

"It was approximately afternoon." Realizing that was the best answer she was likely to get, Penny moved on.

"Now then. Here comes question two. When we picked up the quilt, the side seam had been split open. Did you do that or was the quilt like that when you got it?"

Dilys did not hesitate. "It was like that. I wondered why. I thought there must have been something valuable hidden in there that somebody wanted."

"One last question," said Penny. Dilys took a sip of tea and puckered her lips slightly. "That's awful tea, your store bought stuff. Why do you waste your money on it when beautiful herbal teas are all around you, just for the picking."

"Because I don't have your expertise in wild plants," said Penny. "I'd probably brew up something lethal. And anyway,

I like that tea. Now what I'd like to know is why did you leave the quilt on the wall for us to pick up?"

"You said two questions and I answered two," said Dilys with a mournful, put-upon sigh. "But I'll answer that question anyway. I left it for you so you would leave me alone. I'm old and I don't like being chased. And I thought if the quilt was all that important to you, well, you could have it."

"Oh, it's important, all right," said Penny. "We just don't know how important yet."

Dilys finally gave up on the tea, setting down the cup.

"I'll be on my way now."

"It's getting late, Dilys," said Penny. "Will you be all right to walk home?"

"Of course I will, but thank you for your concern."

She stood up, wrapped her cloak around her, and headed for the door. "But what if I need to speak to you again?" Penny asked. "How will I find you?"

"If you need me, I'll find you," said Dilys. Penny opened the door and Dilys vanished into the night.

And just as in that awful instant when you realize you don't have your keys at the very moment the door locks behind you, just as she closed the door Penny thought of the all-important question she didn't ask.

Twenty-three

*D*etective Inspector Bethan Morgan examined the lab report and then closed the file. She rested her head on her hand while she mulled over what she had just read. Fiber samples taken from the quilt that Penny and Michael had recovered from Dilys matched fibers found under the finger-nails of the dead woman, Catrin Bellis. Had some kind of strug-gle taken place over the quilt, or had she clutched at it, trying to save herself when she went down?

Bethan sighed and not for the first time thought, be careful what you wish for. This was her first investigation in her new role as a detective inspector, and although she'd thought this was what she wanted, now she wasn't so sure. Investigations had always seemed to move ahead so smoothly and logically under the direction of her boss, DCI Gareth Davies. But now, with his retirement approaching, he'd been taken off this case and the reins had been handed over to her. He would be available if she asked for his advice, he said, but he had every confidence in her ability to lead this investigation to a satisfactory conclusion. She asked herself what he would do at this point. He'd probably do what he called churn the file. He'd reread everything because the answer, he always said, is in the file somewhere. It might be a chance remark made during a house to house, a piece of DNA from a criminal in this file that needs to be matched up with the victim in another file, or it could be something ordinary but out of place—someone who should have been somewhere but wasn't, a door that shouldn't have been locked, but was.

And the other thing he did when he wasn't sure where the case was going was stick pins in a map. Somehow, the visual representation of a crime in a geographic way helped him tie things together. She picked up the phone and requested a large map of the area.

When the police constable brought one in, they pulled all the notices off the bulletin board in the office Bethan had recently been assigned and hung the map. Then she picked up the little box of coloured pins and began to stick them in.

Catrin Bellis was here, at Ty Brith Hall, at the Antiques show. Bethan pushed in a yellow pin. Then she made her way home, here, where her body was found. Bethan stuck in a red pin. Now what?

Well, something else Davies would do is return to the scene, absorb the atmosphere, and think. And try to listen to what the walls could tell him, if only they could talk. She stood up, slipped on her jacket, and walked through the station, almost empty at this time of day.

The police officer outside Catrin Bellis's home was gone, but the crime scene tape remained. She ducked under it, then let herself into the house. The forensics team had finished their work and the quiet, still house had a mournful feel to it, as if it knew the emptiness was permanent.

Bethan sat on the sofa and eyed the slate hearth where Catrin's body was found. What happened here, she asked the silent room. Before the walls could answer, her phone rang. She checked the number. Penny. She listened for a moment.

"She did? Look, I'm at Catrin's house on Thyme Close. Can you meet me here? No, it's okay. Forensics have finished. Ten minutes? Fine."

I wonder what will happen to this house, Bethan thought. She examined the sideboard in the little dining area, opening and closing drawers. Old-fashioned table linen, with embroidered flowers in the corner, clean and pressed, lay waiting to be brought out for a meal that would never happen. A faded colour photograph of a wee girl in her mother's arms stood on the sideboard. She picked up the photo and examined it. The little girl with the tousled curls in the smocked dress squinted at the camera while the mother offered a forced smile on command of the photographer.

She went upstairs. The stairs creaked under her feet as if protesting her presence. We don't want you here, the house seemed to say. We're waiting for our girl to come home.

Bethan pushed open the door to Catrin's room. It was neat and orderly, the bed made, clothes hung up. A school girl's desk, now used as a dressing table, was covered with makeup, a few packets still unopened. She pulled out a few drawers and turned over the contents.

At the sound of a knock on the door, she went downstairs and let Penny in.

"So Dilys came to see you," said Bethan. Penny nodded. Bethan got out her notebook and pointed at the sitting room. "We might as well be comfortable."

When they were seated, Penny summarized the gist of the conversation. "She found the quilt in Mrs. Lloyd's front garden."

Pen poised, Bethan smiled. "We've already done a door to door, but we didn't think to ask if anyone saw someone carrying a quilt. Mrs. Lloyd's front garden is round the corner and what, a three-minute walk from here? Five minutes at most?"

Penny nodded. "And Dilys said the side seam was ripped open when she found it. She said she didn't want to talk to the police. I'm really sorry, but I think you're going to have to talk to her, anyway, because I forgot to ask the most important question of all."

"Did she see anyone between here and there?"

"That's exactly what I didn't ask her."

Penny gazed around the room. Muted light filtered through the space where the curtains didn't quite meet, not because they hadn't been fitted to the window, but because someone hadn't closed them properly. Already, in just a few days, a light film of dust was starting to appear on the furniture.

"What do you think happened here?" asked Penny.

"We're still piecing things together. There was no forced entry, so she knew her attacker, or at least opened the door to someone she apparently had no reason to fear.

"And speaking of attacker, we weren't sure at first that she had been attacked. She died of head trauma—we thought she could have fallen for some reason and hit her head on the hearth. But the postmortem results indicated a different kind of head wound. DCI Davies asked for the fireplace tools to be examined forensically and although they'd had been wiped, traces of blood belonging to the victim were found on the poker."

"The poker? Really?"

Bethan nodded and Penny groaned.

"That's really such an awful way to die. What a shame."

"That's what I thought. It looks as if it was a spur of the moment kind of crime. I think whoever killed her wanted whatever was in that quilt."

The two women sat in silence.

"About DCI Davies," Penny said after a moment, "how is he doing?"

"Oh, he's fine, I guess," Bethan replied. "I think he was hoping his life in retirement would be different, that you'd be a big part of it, but he understands how you feel."

"I hope so," said Penny. "The thing is, it's early days yet, but I've met someone. I really like him."

"I wondered about that," said Bethan. "It's that fellow who was injured on the trail, isn't it?"

"It is. Michael Quinn, he's called." She said his name as if it felt like melted chocolate on her lips.

"Well, I hope it works out for you," said Bethan. "What do you think of this house, by the way?"

"This house? In what way?"

"As a property. It'll have to be sold."

"Oh, a property for you, you mean? Well, I don't know. I haven't really seen it."

"Why don't you take a quick look around? I'd be curious to know what you think." Penny stood up. "May I open the curtain?" Bethan nodded. "Probably a good idea. The forensics people close them sometimes when they're testing for blood stains or spatter."

Penny pulled the curtains open, flooding the sitting room with light. Everything from the patterned carpet to the old-fashioned, heavy furniture to the flowered wallpaper seemed a dreary brown, with no splashes of colour to relieve the drabness. "You have to try to see beyond the furniture and wallpaper," said Penny. "With new paint and light furniture it could be a lovely little room. I'll look at the kitchen now."

She returned a few minutes later. "I don't think much has changed in there since the 1970s. Definitely needs a new kitchen. But the back door leads to a pretty garden."

"I haven't seen the garden yet," said Bethan. "Have a look upstairs, and then we'll check out the garden together."

Penny disappeared up the steep, narrow stairs. She glanced at Catrin's room on the left, then entered the larger bedroom. It had two windows, one that overlooked the front garden and another that looked onto the neighbouring house. The slightly musty smell reminded her of her aunt and uncle's bedroom from many years ago, but they had had twin beds. You never see twin beds nowadays, she thought, but for some reason, when she was growing up, they were quite popular with married couples. Here again, the predominant colour was brown, relieved only by colourful bedding. This, she thought, was likely Catrin's touch in preparing the room for a potential lodger. It's too bad the lodging arrangement never came about. Perhaps the two women might have got on well together, had some fun, even, and brought a little life into the unending gloom of this abandoned place.

She opened the closet door. The trouble with these older houses, as she knew from her own cottage, was that they were built at a time when people owned fewer things, including clothes. There was never enough storage room in these old properties.

The closet was empty. She opened a drawer in the larger chest of drawers and it, too, was empty. Catrin must have cleared out the room ready for her new tenant.

She then crossed the little hall, if you could call it that, and entered Catrin's bedroom. The sloping ceiling made the sparsely furnished room look even smaller than it was; a single bed was pushed up against one wall and the flowery curtains were pulled back. On the school girl desk now used as a dressing table, surrounded by makeup, an old-fashioned silver-backed hand mirror and hairbrush seemed forlornly out of place. Her mother's, thought Penny. She admired the filigree work on the back of the mirror then picked it up and peered at her face. Thinking that the harsh light and the close up mirror were cruelly unforgiving to a fiftyish face, she replaced it and picked up the next item, a folded scarf in rich colours of deep greens and blues in a distinctive small floral pattern. She shook it open. Not a headscarf, but an accessory to be knotted around the wearer's neck or tucked into a collar. She knew exactly what it was but checked its little tag anyway: LIBERTY OF LONDON in sewn, not stamped, gold letters. Nice, thought Penny. Also her mother's, probably. She'd never seen Catrin wearing a neck scarf.

A quick look in the lavatory, with its peach-coloured fix-tures and green linoleum floor, told her everything she needed to know.

"Well?" said Bethan when Penny rejoined her.

"Definitely new bathroom and kitchen. The bedrooms are so small, it might be an idea to make them into one decent-size room and have the whole upstairs as your bedroom with an en suite. Of course, that means you don't have a guest room, but if you were living here on your own, it might work."

Bethan nodded and smiled. "Well, something to think about."

"If you were to buy this house, with everyone in the family deceased, who would you buy it from?" Penny asked.

"Whoever inherits it," said Bethan. "And that would be her closest relative who we've learned is her cousin, Evan Hughes."

"I guess you've checked out his alibi," said Penny.

"He says he was at the antiques show. We're still checking out CCTV coverage to try to verify that. It seems everybody in town was at the antiques show and yet we know at least two people who weren't. Catrin and whoever killed her." She stood up. "Let's take a look at the garden."

They stopped off in the kitchen long enough for Penny to suggest what a brand-new kitchen could look like. Bethan then opened the back door that gave onto a small garden and the two stepped out. At one time, the garden had been well cared for, but it was overdue for spring maintenance. Weeds were threatening to overrun the flower beds along each side of a wooden fence and had just about filled in the vegetable patch in the sunny spot at the end of the garden. A small glass house stood in one corner.

"Anyone who bothers to put up a glass house is really into gardening," observed Bethan.

"I don't think it would take much to knock this garden back into shape," said Penny. "It's well laid out and it hasn't had enough time to get really wild. I suspect that the parents were keen gardeners but Catrin couldn't be bothered." They peered through the panes of glass streaked with dirt and bird droppings. Clay flower pots, some of them stacked and others tipped on their sides, a trowel, and a few seed packets were strewn about on a narrow wooden worktable. A battered cardboard box had been shoved roughly under the worktop.

Because the glass house was too small to accommodate both of them, Penny stepped aside to allow Bethan to enter. She pulled out the box and peered into it, then pulled it closer to the door. Penny leaned in to get a better look. The box was filled with items that looked as if they had been set aside as donations to the charity shop. A jumble of men's ties, smaller boxes, a couple of books, picture frames, and on the very top, a long narrow leather case.

Bethan picked it up, and slid the clasp open, and unfolded it. It contained a pale blue leather apron, with insignia. She tipped the case toward Penny.

"It's a Masonic apron," Penny said. "I haven't seen one of those since I was a girl. My uncle was in the Masons but he was always very secretive about it."

Bethan rooted around in the box, flipping pages of the books, turning things over.

"I think I know what that box is all about," said Penny. "Catrin cleared out her parents' room to get it ready for her perspective tenant and she didn't know what to do with some of the stuff. It's a problem. You don't really want it, but you can't really throw it out, either. I mean, what do you do with Masonic stuff?"

"Take it to the Masons' place and see if someone else can use it?"

Penny shrugged. "Well, I guess all this is her cousin's problem now. He'll have to clear out all the personal possessions and then decide what to do with the property."

Bethan rummaged through the contents of the box one last time and then straightened up. "Well, I don't think there's anything more to see here," she said.

"Wait a minute," said Penny. "That photo you've just brought to the top of the box. May I see it, please?"

Three familiar faces, this time on a grey and white postcard, looked back at her, almost as if they had been waiting for her to discover them. "This photo," she said, "Alwynne and I are trying to find out the names of the soldiers." She squeezed her way into the glass house and Bethan took a step back.

Penny put the photo on the worktop, image down.

"Do you think it would be all right if I removed the photo from the frame, just so I can see if there are any names written on the back?" she said. Bethan scanned the implements on the worktop and held out a spoon, handle toward Penny, that had been used to fill the clay pots with potting soil. Penny pried up the tacks that held the photo in place and then removed it.

"Yes!" she said. Written on the back was *Herbert Bellis, before he left for the front. 1914.* "The problem is," said Penny, "it doesn't say which one is Herbert. Oh, well, maybe Alwynne's learned something more by now and she can work that out." She glanced at Bethan before putting the photo back together. "I guess Herbert would have been Catrin's great-grandfather. Her father's grandfather."

Bethan set the photo back in the box and took off her jacket.

"This glass house is getting hot."

Penny immediately stepped outside and Bethan followed.

As she took one last look around the garden a break in the wooden fence caught her eye. Her head turned toward the back door and then she looked at Bethan.

"Was the back door unlocked when you found Catrin's body?" she said.

"I'm not sure," Bethan replied. "I'll have to check the case notes."

"I think it was," Penny said. "And the reason nobody saw anyone on Thyme Close, out the front, is because the assailant left by the back door, and escaped through this little gate. You can barely notice it in the fence. It's been cleverly concealed. The passageway there leads to Rosemary Lane. And look," she said, pointing, "you can see the roof of Mrs. Lloyd's house from here. I think whoever killed Catrin grabbed the quilt, ripped it open to take what whatever was inside it, then dumped it in Mrs. Lloyd's front garden."

Her eyes wandered over the windows of the houses that backed onto the passageway. "You need to do your door to door along here. Someone could have seen this person out one of those windows."

She took a step toward the fence.

"Don't take another step," said Bethan, punching numbers into her phone.

"I need forensics back at the Catrin Bellis house on Thyme Close," she said. "Yes. Right now."

Twenty-four

"*B*ethan was beside herself," Penny said to Victoria Hop-kirk, her friend and business partner, later that day. "She realized that the gate had been mentioned in the initial report by one of the first officers on the scene and she'd skimmed over it. She just didn't make the connection."

"Oh, poor her," said Victoria. "I can understand how that can happen, though. I'm sure she's overwhelmed trying to run her first case and impress everyone."

She handed Penny a telephone message.

"Heather Hughes rang about the arrangements for her daughter's wedding. She wants you to drop by the house for a consultation." She pointed at the slip of paper. "And did I mention you're to bring bottles of bridal nail polish so she can choose?"

"Wait," said Penny. "So who can choose?"

Victoria shrugged. "Heather?"

"Oh, here we go," said Penny. "It's not so much bridezilla as mother of the bridezilla. Honestly, the grief the mothers give us. They had their day. Why can't they just let their daughters have theirs?" She sighed. "And when am I supposed to do this?"

"Today, of course," said Victoria. "I'll drive you. We'll leave in about an hour."

"This is not something we normally do," protested Penny. "If we made a house call for every bride, we'd be doing nothing else."

"I know," said Victoria, soothingly. "But Heather Hughes is a good customer, she has influence, and with the wedding season getting underway, we need to keep her happy. So I agreed to do an in-house consultation to work out the details of how we'll take care of the wedding party. Besides, she's hurt her hand and can't drive. And let me do the talking. I'll work out what we need to charge."

"Let's try to get the manicures and pedicures done the day before."

"Of course. And you'll have Eirlys to help you."

Eirlys, Penny's capable, trustworthy young assistant, had joined the Spa right out of school and Penny didn't know what she would do without her.

"So there's no way I can get out of this, I guess?" said Penny. "I'm tired and I was rather hoping to see Michael tonight although we don't have any special plans."

Victoria shook her head. "Sorry, no."

"Well, I'd better gather up the samples, then."

"And you will try to be pleasant, won't you?" said Victoria.

"Do you know what's the best thing about this time of year?" Penny asked Victoria as she lowered the window on her side of the car, letting in a light breeze.

"What's that?" Victoria replied as she checked her rearview mirror and signaled a right turn.

"It's the return of colour. Everything is brighter, somehow." Penny gazed out the car window as the lush Welsh countryside sped past. The green fields were filled with lambs and their mothers; the oldest lambs were just starting to lose their newborn adorableness of a month or two ago. The trees still retained some of their spring vibrancy before settling into the darker, more mature greens of summer.

They turned off onto the road that led to the Hughes's farmhouse. A few minutes later Victoria slowed the car down as a young woman riding a horse approached them at a posting trot. She wore a black velvet riding hat, breeches, boots, and a neat hacking jacket. The women all waved at one another.

"I love that sound," said Penny. "Horses' hooves. It's so rhythmic and unmistakable. Has a lovely rural sound to it. Puts me in a better mood just hearing it. I must remember to put more horses in my paintings."

They drove along the country road flanked by hedgerows on each side until they came to the gate of the Hughes's farm. The drive up to the house was bordered on one side by a low stone wall; the other side featured a broad expanse of lawn shaded by oak trees. The driveway led to a small parking area in front of a graciously proportioned two-storey stone house.

Carrying their bags, they walked across the graveled forecourt to the glossy black front door. A flower bed graced by only white flowers spread out on both sides of the door. Pyracantha, looking like a bridal bouquet of pearls and petals, climbed on trellises, bell-shaped columbines nodded a graceful welcome to the visitors, and two white lilacs, one on each side of the door, gave off a heavenly fragrance. But soon they would all have to step aside to make way for the quiet beauty of white roses.

"Do you think we should knock on the front door or go round to the back?" Victoria asked.

"What, you mean use the tradesmen's entrance?"

But before Victoria could reply, the door was opened by a tall, slim woman. Her dark hair was scraped back in a tight ponytail, giving her face a stretched, unnatural look. The corners of her thin lips tipped downward.

"Hello, Heather," said Victoria.

"Oh, hello," she said, in a pleasant voice that contrasted with her appearance. "Please, come in." She stood to one side as Penny and Victoria entered.

"Straight down the hall to the end," she said. "The kitchen."

They entered a kitchen about the size of the entire ground floor of Penny's cottage. A comfortable sitting area for four at one end of the room featured large windows with views over grassy fields to the hills beyond.

"We've just had it done up," said Heather Hughes. "This part of the house was a building site all winter. You could barely make a cup of tea. I wondered what we'd got ourselves into, but I think it turned out all right."

"It's right off the cover of a home and garden magazine," said Victoria. "Did you get your interior designer from Chester?"

"No, I did it all myself," Heather said in a tone that seemed casually dismissive but resonated with pride in her accomplishment.

"It's beautiful," said Victoria. Pot lights in the ceiling reflected off gleaming stainless steel appliances and endless granite worktops. The walls were painted a sophisticated taupe that contrasted with the bright yellow and purple fabric of the upholstered chairs in the sitting area.

"Please have a seat. May I get you a tea or coffee?"

"I'd love a coffee, please," said Victoria.

"I'll have one, too," said Penny.

"Americano, latte, or mocha?" Heather gestured at the selection of coffees with her bandaged hand.

"Are you all right to make it with your hand?" asked Victoria. "Need any help?"

"No, it's fine, thanks," she said. "I cut my hand gardening, caught it on some thorns, I think, and it got infected. The antibiotics are helping but I did have to get a tetanus jab. It doesn't hurt; it's just a nuisance really. But the machine makes the coffee, so not a problem, but if you wouldn't mind helping me get them to the table."

The coffee machine, like something in an upmarket Italian restaurant, hissed and spurted steam like a medieval dragon. Victoria carried the finished drinks to the table and the women got down to business.

"You're probably wondering why I'm the one fussing about the girls' makeup and manicures," Heather said, "but Jessica has no interest whatsoever in that sort of thing. If it doesn't have four legs and a mane she takes no notice. She spends all her time on that horse of hers. In fact, you probably passed her in the road on your way."

"I think we did," said Victoria.

They discussed the wedding arrangements while they sipped their coffees. Penny glanced at her watch, thinking her cat, Harrison, would be getting hungry and hoping the meeting would wrap up soon. And sure enough, it wasn't long before the details were agreed, how many manicures, how many pedicures, and how many makeup applications for bride, bridesmaids, and mothers. Alberto, the Spa hairdresser, would take care of hair cuts and colours the day before, and do whatever was needed on the morning of the wedding. Victoria negotiated what she and Penny felt was a fair price, and Victoria filled in a contract that she and Heather signed.

"Just so there is a clear understanding on both sides," explained Victoria. "We want to make sure that we meet all your expectations."

Heather set the used cups in the sink before accompanying Penny and Victoria out of the kitchen.

As they entered the hallway, she smiled shyly at Penny. "Before you go, there's something I'd like you to see," she said. "It's in what we call the library." She led the way past a spacious, understated reception room of grand proportions and then turned down another hallway.

"In here," she said.

Light flooded into the room from a set of French doors that led to a terraced garden at the rear of the house and two walls were taken up with floor-to-ceiling bookshelves. The centre of the room featured two burgundy leather love seats and a comfortable chair casually arranged on a burgundy carpet that was becoming a little threadbare in the centre set on a patterned oak floor. The room was masculine but welcoming. Penny glanced at the bookshelves; almost all the books in one section were about gardening.

Several paintings hung on chains from a picture rail and

Heather gestured at a watercolour in a plain but expensive-looking frame.

Instead of showing the entire span of the three-arched Llanelen bridge, the painting showed only one arch, up close, with two swans paddling lazily beneath it down the River Conwy.

Penny's face broke into a delighted grin at the sight of one of her own paintings.

"I love your work," said Heather, almost shyly. "I thought you might like to know that this painting has found a good home. Evan bought it for me. It was the most romantic gesture he's ever done. He proposed to me on that bridge."

Penny smiled and turned away. A bouquet of pale lavender and cream roses in a crystal vase caught her eye and she paused to admire them. The stems had been trimmed so the flower heads formed an almost perfect circle.

"I can tell by your hands you're a very busy gardener," Penny said. "The flower beds at the front are lovely."

"They'll be even lovelier when the roses come into full bloom," said Heather. "The climbers put on a very good show all summer long. And the fragrance!" She breathed in heavily, and smiled as if remembering.

"I love this room," said Penny. She took a few steps in the direction of the window when a display of photographs in silver frames on a small desk caught her eye. She recognized the now familiar photograph instantly and picked it up. She held it toward Heather.

"Alwynne at the historical society is trying to identify the men in this photo," she said. "Can you tell me what you know about it?"

Heather took the photo from her. "Oh, that one," she said. "That's my great-grandfather with a couple of his fellow soldiers in World War I."

"Which one is your great-grandfather?"

"That's him, on the left. His name was Sydney and he was very fortunate in that he survived the war. He made it home."

"What was his last name?" Penny asked.

"Wynne. Didn't you know? We're the Llanelen branch of the Wynne family."

"I didn't know Heather was a Wynne. Did you?"

"No," said Victoria, "I didn't. The family may not be as prominent now as it once was, but the name still carries a lot of weight around here."

The Wynnes had maintained a powerful presence in the valley since Tudor and Stuart times. Well-educated, prosperous, and with close friends in high places throughout England and Wales, the family had prospered over centuries, building the town's church and hospital, endowing a school, and funding the very almshouses that now housed the town museum.

In the sixteenth century John Wynne built a grand manor house just outside the town and a hundred years later, another Wynne had had a lavish Renaissance garden laid out with raised walks, yew hedges, Cyprus trees, fountains, and graceful stone steps leading from one level to another.

In Victorian times, the house, built mainly of wood, had almost been destroyed by fire and by the mid-twentieth century the house had fallen into a heart-wrenching state of disrepair. But a young entrepreneurial couple with energy, commitment, and resources, had bought it and were gradually restoring it to its former glory.

And the replanted garden, after hundreds of hours of back-breaking work, was now considered one of the finest examples of a Renaissance layout in all of Wales. Watched over by its own imperious peacock, it was now open to the public and featured prominently on garden coach tours.

The Hughes's farmhouse, where a daughter of this once-great family lived, was not on the scale of the original manor, but nevertheless it was a fine country house with lovely, well-cared for gardens.

"It's rather nice that Heather is so into gardening," said Penny. "Her ancestors certainly had a gift for it."

"Of course her ancestors wouldn't have done the actual work," said Victoria. "There would have been a team of gardeners."

"Maybe so," said Penny, "but still they must have had a great love of horticulture to create that beautiful garden. Have you ever seen it? So tranquil and the peacock's delightful. I wonder if Michael's ever been there. He might like it."

Victoria focused on the road ahead and didn't reply. Dusk was closing in and she switched on the car's headlights.

Penny took out her phone. "Just going to send Michael a text," she said.

"Oh, yes?" said Victoria.

"We're having lunch out tomorrow. His hip is much better and we want to make up for the last time when everything went so horribly wrong. But we won't be doing a lot of walking. At least, I don't think we will."

"So have you been seeing much of him?"

"He isn't out and about much yet, but we're doing a lot of texting and phone calls."

"But you do like him?"

"Yes," Penny said with a soft smile. "I think I do. He's very charming."

"He is," agreed Victoria. "A real charmer. Which makes me wonder . . . he wasn't seeing anyone when you met?"

"His wife died a couple of years ago. He may have been seeing someone, but I don't think so. It is possible he wasn't, you know. Gareth wasn't seeing anyone when I met him."

"True. But Gareth's . . ." she hesitated.

"Gareth's what?" said Penny.

"Well, he's different."

They continued their journey in silence and Victoria dropped Penny off at home just before dark.

Twenty-five

"Where are we going?" Penny asked Michael as they drove along a narrow road enclosed on both sides by trimmed hedgerows.

"Here's a hint," said Michael as he downshifted in preparation for a sharp turn. "There will be bells, and they will be blue." He grinned and then turned his attention back to the road ahead. "Not long now."

"Oh, I know where we are now," said Penny. "Haydn Williams's farm is along here—we're just approaching it from a different direction."

"I don't know about that," said Michael, "but Gwinllan Clychau'r Gôg is just up here on the right. Bluebell Wood isn't very big, and we won't walk far and then I'll treat you to a really nice lunch."

After passing Haydn's farm they turned off onto a narrow dirt road that led to a small clearing.

"I'm glad I brought my camera," said Penny as she hung it around her neck. A short walk later and a vibrant carpet of bluish-purple haze welcomed them with a stunning display. A path wound through an ancient woodland of oak trees, and all around them, under a dappled canopy of recently opened leaves, were shimmering bluebells. Their sweet perfume, a combination of cooking apple and freshly mown grass, heady but at the same time delicate, filled the air, and Penny breathed it in deeply. She smiled at her companion and then took a series of photographs.

"I'm sure you've been here before," he said.

"Not to this wood, perhaps, but yes, I've seen the bluebells." She thought back to a year ago—or was it two?—when Gareth had taken her to see them. "When the bluebells come I never know if it's late spring or early summer," she said.

"It's a bit of both," he said. "The weather this time of year is unpredictable. One day it's spring, the next it's summer, and then we get a cold day and it almost feels like we're back to late winter."

"Well, at least we've got a lovely day today," said Penny.

The sun filtering through the waving tree branches above their heads cast a flickering light on the path beneath their feet. They walked on without speaking and then Michael asked, "Have you ever painted them?"

"I have," Penny replied. "Well, tried. The particular shade of violet-purple-blue is difficult to capture and the colour changes depending on the time of day and the light situation. Everything looks better under a sky full of light. That's one of the reasons I love the Hudson River School so much."

"I'd like to see your work sometime," Michael said.

"I don't know if I'm confident enough to show it to you," said Penny, "although I do sell some of my work through a local gallery. It was quite strange—Victoria and I were doing a consultation yesterday and the client said she had something to show me. It was one of my own paintings! It had been beautifully hung in a charming room and looked very well on her wall, if I do say so myself. It was at the Hughes farm, just down the road. In fact, the woods here is about halfway between the two farms. I never realized that before."

Michael looked at his watch.

"Getting hungry? I'm starting to give lunch some serious thought."

"Fine with me," said Penny. They had reached a crossroads in the path and were about to turn back when she noticed what looked like several dark grey panels. They leaned crazily and crookedly sideways and tipped back, like loose, uneven teeth. "What are those, I wonder." Michael stayed where he was as she examined them. When she got closer, she saw they were slabs of slate, wired together.

"Oh, they're part of what used to be an old slate fence," she said to Michael over her shoulder, and then bent down to take a closer look. "This one seems to have something written on it." She snapped a couple of photos and they strolled back through the bluebells, headed for lunch.

"Oh, Penny, come in," said Alwynne Gwilt later that afternoon as she held the door open and welcomed Penny into her comfortable kitchen. "Have a seat. I was so pleased when you called." She opened the refrigerator door and took out a bottle of wine, with a raised eyebrow. Penny smiled her thanks and she placed the bottle on the worktop and reached into the cupboard for two glasses.

Wine poured, she joined Penny at the table.

"Not with Michael this afternoon?" she said.

"No, we had a nice walk and lunch and then he dropped me off and headed home. He's driving to Holyhead later to meet the ferry. He's got a relative coming over from Ireland this evening."

"Did he say who this person is?"

"No, just a relative. That's all. But his son lives in Dublin, so I expect it'll be him."

"But he didn't ask you to go with him?"

Penny gave her a blank stare.

"No. Why would he? I wouldn't have expected him to. I haven't really known him long enough to meet his family. I'll see him again in a day or two, I expect."

Alwynne started to say something, and then lowered her head to avoid direct eye contact and so Penny couldn't see the lines in her forehead as a frown spread across her face.

"Anyway," said Penny brightly, "I can't wait to show you what we found today. Michael and I had a lovely walk up at Bluebell Wood before lunch and I saw an old piece of slate fencing. It had some figures scratched into it, and they looked familiar." She showed Alwynne the photo on her camera. "Do you recognize anything here? Does anything seem familiar?"

"Can't really tell on the camera view," said Alwynne, squinting at it. She then turned her face directly to Penny. "Why, what does it remind you of?"

"It puts me in mind of the map we saw at Haydn's farm. The one hidden in his clock."

"Really?" Alwynne took a sip of wine. "Well, it's possible, I suppose. If his great-grandfather Wilfred John Williams created the map, he might also have carved that on the slate. The path through the Bluebell Woods is ancient and back in his school days, young Wilfred and his friends would have walked through those woods back and forth to school. They could have carved this into the slate. It's the sort of thing boys do, for no particular reason. One of them gets a new knife for his birthday, and he wants to try it out."

"And I've learned something about the photograph," said Penny, "and something's occurred to me."

They examined the Haydn Williams family photograph of the three soldiers and Penny named them and told Alwynne what she'd learned about each one.

"I've been thinking about the way they're seated," said Penny. "And from their body language, I wonder if these two," she pointed to Wilfred John Williams whose hand rested lightly on the seated Herbert Bellis's shoulder, "weren't closer friends. It's almost as if they have an emotional bond that excludes Sydney Wynne. Three can be a difficult number, relationship-wise. One is often left out, if only just a little."

Alwynne examined the photo. "Hard to say. You may be right."

She gave Penny a questioning, half smile. "Is there something you aren't telling me?"

Penny looked taken aback. "No, I've told you everything I know."

"No, I didn't mean about this. I meant about you."

"I'm not sure I know what you mean."

"Well, you're very, oh, I don't know what the right word is, sparkly this afternoon. Bubbly. Excited. You seem very happy. Your eyes look as if they have diamonds on them."

"I did have a lovely day out with Michael," Penny said. "It's early days, of course, but who knows what might happen?"

"Well, it's good to see you looking so happy and enjoying yourself."

Twenty-six

I've brought your invitation to DCI Davies's retirement party," said Det. Insp. Bethan Morgan a few days later, standing at Penny's front door and handing her a beige envelope. Her mouth tipped down at the corners.

"Can you come in?" Penny asked. "You don't look very happy. Have you got time for a cup of tea or coffee?"

"I'd love one."

"Would it help if we talked about it? Just in very general terms, of course."

"What's making this case so difficult," said Bethan, "is that there are no real suspects. We've interviewed everybody who knew her and everyone seems to have liked this lady, if they thought about her at all. No one can give me any reason why someone would want to kill her. There's just no clear, obvious motive. She lived a quiet life. Kept herself to herself for the most part. Had very few friends. Had a part-time job that she liked and was good at. She had no enemies that we've been able to find. Usually when someone's killed it turns out suspects were practically queuing up to kill that person."

"Well, maybe it wasn't that kind of murder," said Penny.

"What do you mean 'wasn't that kind of murder'?"

"Well, maybe the person who killed her didn't hate her. Maybe hate didn't come into it at all."

"Go on."

"Well, as you know, people kill for all kinds of reasons. Somebody knows something or somebody said something. Or somebody's got something that the killer wants. Doesn't it look to you as if the killer wanted whatever was in that quilt? Why else would the killer take it from the house, rip it open, and then dump it in Mrs. Lloyd's front garden? Doesn't the fact that it was dumped tell us the killer wasn't after the quilt itself but wanted whatever was hidden in it?"

"That's about the only scenario that makes sense," admitted Bethan. "We haven't been able to come up with anything more plausible. People usually kill for very basic emotional reasons. Hate, jealousy, anger, greed . . . that sort of thing. As I said before, we haven't been able to establish a motive."

"But somebody must have had one," said Penny, "unless . . ." her voice trailed off while she contemplated a spot somewhere above Bethan's head.

"Unless what?" Bethan prompted.

"Unless you're right and there wasn't a motive. Not a motive in the usual sense, that is. What if it just happened? What if the killer had no intention of killing her—just wanted what was in the quilt, she wouldn't give it to him, they fought, and in the struggle, Catrin got killed."

"Well, that would mean that the motive was the theft of whatever was in the quilt. She had something he wanted."

Before Bethan could continue Penny excused herself and ducked into the kitchen. She returned to the sitting room a few minutes later with a cafetiere of fragrant coffee.

Bethan's shoulders relaxed as she took a reviving sip and sank back into the sofa.

"Even just talking it through with you helps," she said. "I feel as if I'm just spinning my wheels and getting nowhere. The DCI says there's always a moment in the case when things start to open up. When you crack it and everything comes spilling out. But I'm not there yet, and I don't know how to get there. I don't know what to do that I'm not already doing." Her voice had taken on a slightly plaintive pitch that made Penny laugh.

"Careful, there, Bethan," she said. "You're getting dangerously close to a whine. Inspectors aren't allowed to whine."

"Sorry. I'm so frustrated. There's just nothing to go on." She placed her mug on the coffee table beside the envelope containing the retirement party invitation and stood up. "Well, thanks for the coffee and chat. I'd best be off. I really hope you'll come to his party." She gestured at the envelope. "It should be a good night out, if nothing else."

"Of course I'll come. Oh, and there's a couple of friends of his from Sherebury that I'm sure he'd want to be invited, too, if they haven't been already. Alan Nesbitt and his wife, Dorothy Martin. I can give you their address. He's retired from the police. His rank was about as high up as you can get."

She saw Bethan out and then checked her phone. Nothing

from Michael yet today. She sent him a quick text and then picked up a book and settled in for a quiet read. After reading the same paragraph several times without it making any sense she put the book down and with a creeping sense of anxiety, checked her phone again.

Twenty-seven

I haven't heard from Michael in a couple of days." Penny placed both hands on Victoria's desk and leaned on them. "Do you think I should be worried?"

"Not if it's just been a couple of days," Victoria replied, her eyes fixed on her laptop. "You know what men are like. He's probably just got tied up at work. It'll be a conference or something."

But Penny had thought of that and checked the university Web site. No conferences or art exhibits listed.

"It's been so long since I've done this dating thing, I forget how it works," said Penny. "Am I supposed to wait to hear from him, or should I text him again?"

"Again?"

"I texted him last night."

"Then I would think the ball's in his court. If I were you,

I'd wait to hear from him. Let him come to you. And anyway, what do you mean it's been so long since you've done this dating thing? You were dating Gareth."

"Well, yes, but he was different. I was always comfortable with him. He was just . . ." She shrugged. "You know. There. Steady, solid Gareth."

Victoria stopped typing and looked at her friend. "Yes, he was. But Penny, maybe you should prepare yourself that Michael's not . . ."

Penny interrupted her. "Yeah. He's just not . . ." Almost at the doorway, she turned back and asked, "Does our photocopier do enlargements?"

"Why, you're not going to blow up a photo of Michael are you?" At the look of pained disgust that flashed across Penny's face, Victoria recoiled.

"Oh, God, Penny, I'm sorry," she said as she stood up and came round the side of her desk. "I could kick myself. I don't know what possessed me to say such a stupid thing. That was so insensitive. I'm an idiot. I'm so sorry."

"It's all right," said Penny. Victoria touched her arm. "Yes, I think we can make an enlargement. I'm not sure how, but I'll work it out. Do you want to e-mail me the photo—I'm assuming you've got a photo—and I'll sort it for you."

"Fine. Thank you." Victoria had never heard Penny sound so cool. She lowered herself into her chair and rested her head in her hands. She'd have to find a way to make it up.

A few minutes later the e-mail arrived and Victoria printed the attachment and took it to the photocopier. After she'd tried several settings, it finally cranked out a large sheet of paper with a series of little scratches that looked vaguely like ancient cave art.

Hoping Penny would accept it as a peace offering for her tasteless remark, she set it down on her desk.

"What is it?" Victoria asked.

"It's a photo of some scratchings or carvings on a slate fence post," Penny said as she picked it up. "You know, the ones that look a bit like grave markers. They're flat and wired together to make a fence."

She tipped the paper toward the window to catch the light and then walked over to it.

"It looks a little like the map I saw in Haydn's kitchen." She spread it out on her desk and clicked on the task light to shine a bright beam on it.

"What do you see here?" she asked Victoria. "Describe it to me. Talk me through it."

Victoria sat down and pulled the paper closer to her.

"I see a series of funny little drawings. If we start at the top, it looks like a . . . little bug?" She pinched her lips as she concentrated. "Then there's something that might be a sheep and a stone wall and a number one hundred." She rested her hand on the paper. "Sorry, I'm not much use. It doesn't mean anything to me. Or at least, I can't make any sense of it."

"I'm going to see if Haydn's home."

A moment later she put the phone down. "He's taking a photo of his map and will send it to you. Would you mind making an enlargement of it, too? In fact, please make two copies."

About twenty minutes later Victoria appeared in the doorway of Penny's office, waving a piece of paper. "Here it is. The background is very grey, so the figures are a little hard to see." Penny took the paper and then pulled a black marker out of her drawer. With it, she carefully outlined the small symbols, a scattering of small, child-like drawings. When she'd finished, she set the two photocopies side by side on her desk and, her head moving slightly side to side, compared them. Victoria watched, saying nothing. Finally, Penny looked up.

"Believe it or not, Haydn's map is roughly the same as the carving on the slate fence. What are the chances of that? I believe two boys made the map, tore it in half and one boy—Haydn Williams's great-grandfather—kept half and hid it in the clock and the other half of the map was given to the other boy. And if I'm not mistaken, that boy was Herbert Bellis, because we know that Herbert and Wilfred were friends. And I think his half of the map for some reason found its way into the quilt that Catrin had. Maybe they each agreed to hide their half of the map. Then, the boys carved the map into the fence on their way home from school, all those years ago."

"Could be."

"Now, Haydn's map just covers the top part of the fence, so the bottom half must be the other part of the map, the bit that was in the quilt."

"Which we don't have."

"No, we don't have it, but we do have this," she tapped the photocopy of the drawings on the slate fence. "So maybe we don't need the other half."

"We just have to work out what it all means," said Victoria. "But there seems to be a lot of leaps in your logic there. Do we have anything that proves half a map was in the quilt?"

She waited for a reply, but when none came, changed the subject and continued. "Now about Saturday morning. Jessica Hughes's wedding. You and Eirlys have to be at the farm by nine to get Jessica, her mother, and her bridesmaids ready, so let's all meet here at eight thirty and I'll drive you."

Penny didn't look up from the maps, and as she left the room, Victoria wasn't sure she'd even been listening. Just outside Penny's office she bumped into Eirlys, head down, approaching from the other direction.

"Eirlys! Watch where you're going!" Victoria said. "Where are you going, by the way?"

"Just into the supply room to look through the lost and found box. There's a lady on the phone who wants to know if we found a scarf."

"Scarves, gloves, we find them all the time," said Victoria, "although not so much now that summer's almost here."

"Not that kind of scarf. Not a winter scarf. A neck scarf with little flowers on it." She made a looping movement under her chin. "You know, the kind you put around your neck and tie."

Penny got up from her desk and stood in the doorway.

"Go on," she said. Eirlys looked at the scrap of paper in her hand. "Little flowers," she repeated. "That's all I know."

"Who's looking for this scarf?" Penny asked.

"Tegwen Driscoll. She had her hair done a while ago and thinks she might have left her scarf in the salon."

"I don't think she did," said Penny, "but go and check anyway." Eirlys was soon back, shaking her head. "Not there. I'll ring her back and tell her we don't have it."

Penny held out her hand for the piece of paper. "You can leave that with me, thanks. I'll ring her." She checked her watch. "But it'll have to wait." She glanced at Victoria. "We have to get ready for the retirement party tonight."

Twenty-eight

*D*CI Gareth Davies had been to a lot of retirement parties during his long career with the North Wales Police Service, but this would be the first and last time he'd attend his own. A few years ago, he'd have worn a suit with a tie, but now, in these more casual times, that seemed overdressed. So he chose a pair of grey trousers, a navy jacket, and a light blue checked shirt, open at the collar with no tie. In his late fifties, he was lean and fit. He watched what he ate, bicycled regularly, and spent his spare time maintaining a meticulous garden. He wasn't concerned about filling the retirement hours that would come in about three weeks.

He checked his watch. Alan Nesbitt and his wife, Dorothy Martin, should be arriving soon. He opened the door to the guest room and peered in. His weekly cleaner had left everything welcoming, a simple bouquet of carnations on the dresser and a couple of new paperback mysteries on the bedside table. Unable to ever quite leave policing behind, he and Alan, retired chief constable for the county of Belleshire, enjoyed their conversations over a pint of bitter discussing how fictional detectives almost always get the procedures wrong. He'd met the couple a few years ago through Penny, when Dorothy, an expat American, had dropped into Penny's old manicure salon and the two women from the other side of the Atlantic Ocean had struck up a friendship. Davies had hoped his relationship with Penny would end in marriage as Alan's and Dorothy's had, but he knew now this was not going to happen. He'd heard she was seeing some kind of artist fellow from Bangor, but had resisted the temptation to find out what he could about him.

A tired silver banner proclaiming HAPPY RETIREMENT! surrounded by swirls and stars that was trotted out at every retirement bash had been strung across the bar of the modest function room in the local golf club. Davies didn't need to worry about his send off being poorly attended—although the food was mediocre, everyone's invitation came with two free bar tickets. After that, guests paid for their own but the drinks were relatively inexpensive and for obvious reasons, because the attendees were mostly serving or retired police officers, plenty of free cabs were booked throughout the evening to see everyone safely home. The attendees tended to be one of two kinds: the kind who came along to say a polite good-bye and stayed just long enough for the most senior officers to note their presence and the kind who were there for a good time and would drink until the bar closed. Davies had always belonged to the first group and wondered vaguely how soon after the speeches and presentations he could make a decent escape from his own party without attracting too much attention.

As the party got underway, a blonde woman wearing a pair of tight black trousers, high heels, and a sparkly blue jacket teetered toward him, holding a glass of wine in one hand and a small clutch bag in the other.

"Hello, Gareth," she said. "How are you? Haven't seen you in ages."

"Oh, hello, ah . . ."

"It's Isla. From the evidence room?"

"Ah, the evidence room. Of course, Isla. Good of you to come this evening." She bestowed a wide smile on him and made the occasional emphatic gesture with the clutch bag as she chattered away. Every now and then he smiled down at her, occasionally lowering his head to hear her better against the increasing crowd noise as the room filled up.

With as much subtlety as he could muster, he scanned the room looking for the latest arrivals and eventually was rewarded when he spotted the woman he'd been waiting for.

"Excuse me a moment, Isla," he said. "A couple of old friends have just arrived." Penny and Victoria had been a big part of his life over the past two years and he was going to miss both of them.

"Here you are. So glad you could make it. Will you join us? We saved spots for you at our table." He smiled at Penny. "Dorothy and Alan are here. And Bethan, of course."

As he led the way to his table through the small crowd of noisy drinkers Isla glided along beside him and when he introduced her to Penny and Victoria as, "Isla from dispatch," she corrected him, "the evidence room, Gareth," and grabbed the chair beside his. Penny and Victoria found places on the other side of the table and exchanged warm greetings with Dorothy and Alan. Penny watched Isla laughing with Gareth, leaning into him, taking an occasional sip of wine as she touched his arm, and listening to him with her head lowered while she looked up at him with what she probably hoped were wide, doe-like eyes.

Penny turned to Dorothy.

"I always find it so hard to hear what anyone's saying at events like this," she said. "The background noise can be so overwhelming and on top of the music, it's hard to carry on a conversation."

"You're right," agreed Dorothy, who had been observing Penny's uneasiness with increasing concern. "Let's find a couple of comfortable chairs in the lobby where it's a bit quieter and we can have a good chat."

They settled into side-by-side wing chairs and Penny told Dorothy about the drawing on the slate fence and the piece of paper found in Haydn Williams's clock. When she got to the part about the map having been torn in half, Dorothy, who'd solved a case or two of her own, laughed.

"Oh, the number of times I've seen that," she said. "Remember, Penny, I used to be a teacher. The kids—and they were mostly boys—were forever drawing maps and tearing them in half to share with their best friend. And then the next year the friend moves away or they each find new friends, and it's all meaningless."

"Why did they draw the maps in the first place?" Penny asked.

"It'll be about something buried," replied Dorothy. "The boys were always burying something, and usually it was a pocket knife. Why, they did that, I don't know. There must be hun-

dreds of pocket knives buried across the American Midwest."
She took a small sip of wine.

"I think the other half of the map was hidden in a quilt,"
Penny said, "and the person who owned that quilt was murdered."

"Oh, dear me. How awful!"

"Now whether she was murdered for the map, or for some
other reason, I don't know," said Penny. "But I think her death
is linked somehow to the map. Because it's pretty certain that
whoever killed her, took the quilt." They chatted about the case
for a few more minutes and then Penny abruptly changed the
subject.

"Who's that woman with Gareth?"

"I don't really know," said Dorothy. "He never mentioned
her on the way over but they were having a good chat before
you arrived. I wouldn't be surprised if she's set her cap at him.
She certainly seems possessive and he seems to like the attention."

Penny frowned.

"You don't like that?" Dorothy asked gently. "But you've
moved on. Surely you don't mind if he does, too."

"I don't know what I think," muttered Penny. "I didn't think
I minded, but then seeing her simpering at him like that . . .
well, I just hope he knows what he's doing. I don't like the look
of her. Did you see the way she grabbed the spot beside him?
You'd think she was playing musical chairs." Dorothy gave her
a relaxed, fond smile and stood up. "I'd better get back to Alan,"
she said. "If I'm away from him for too long he always assumes
I've gone looking for trouble."

"I'm just going to pop into the loo," said Penny, "and I'll
see you in a few minutes."

She frowned at herself in the mirror as she passed the sinks and entered a cubicle. She had just secured the lock when the outside door opened and a moment later, over the sound of running water, voices she recognized drifted over the top of her stall.

"I don't know what to do," said Bethan. "I don't know if I should tell her or not."

"I think you should," said Victoria. "If it were me, I'd want to know. Wouldn't you?"

Penny's heart missed a beat and then began to pound as the water stopped and the air hand dryer started up. "Well, you had that thing with a married man a while back," said Bethan. "Italy, wasn't it?"

"Yes, but he was separated from his wife and the moment it looked like they were getting back together, I was out of there," said Victoria. "But the thing is, she doesn't know he's married."

No one spoke. The only sound was what Penny thought must be one of them riffling through her handbag, probably looking for a lipstick.

"What made you suspicious of him?" Victoria's question broke the silence.

"I wasn't suspicious, really. Just wanted to make sure he got his car back, that's all."

"Of course you did. So what did you do?"

"I looked up his car on the compound record. It had been claimed, all right, but he wasn't the one who retrieved it. It was picked up by one Annabelle Quinn, of the same address."

"His daughter maybe? Or sister?"

"No. Someone with identification showing the same address as the vehicle's owner is allowed to claim it, and the relationship with the owner is noted. She stated she was his wife. Everything was in order, so the vehicle was released to her."

"Oh, God," said Victoria. "Well, you've definitely got to tell Penny. She's been in agony because she hasn't heard from him and now we know why."

Penny's stomach churned as she held a hand over her mouth. She didn't know whether to reveal herself or stay where she was. Realizing she was just too numb to move, she lowered herself slowly onto the edge of the toilet seat.

"Yes, I'll tell her. Not tonight, though, because I don't want to upset her and ruin the DCI's party."

"Tomorrow," said Victoria.

"Yes, I'll call her tomorrow."

"She really liked him, you know," said Victoria. "This is going to be hard for her." The last few words were barely audible as the two moved toward the door and a moment later the sound of it opening and closing signaled they were gone.

Penny stayed where she was, her breathing heavy and difficult. Michael Quinn was married. No wonder his house looked so feminine. His wife lived there! She thought back to everything he'd said to her, and the things they'd done together. He had seemed so sincere, so relaxed, so into her. But of course he wasn't.

She could feel the heat starting to flush through her body. He'd been so smooth, so full of charm, he must have had lots of practice at this. The lies he must have told his wife.

She unlocked the door to the cubicle and head down, hurried to the lobby, hoping she wouldn't meet anyone on the way. But instead of returning to the retirement party, she made for the front entrance of the club. As she pushed open the glass door two important-looking men stepped out of a cab. She pushed past them, threw herself into the backseat, and gave the driver instructions to her cottage.

She tipped the driver and stumbled up the path to her front door. As her emotions ricocheted from anger to humiliation, from disbelief to embarrassment, she fumbled in her handbag for the key. She pushed the door open and tore off her jacket, tossing it onto the nearest chair. She rushed to the drinks tray and poured herself a large vodka, added a splash of tonic, and then dropped to the sofa. As if she were sorting through a pile of photographs she got out every memory she had of Michael Quinn and sifted through all of them. She tried to remember everything he'd said to her, searching for something that could have told her he was married. She couldn't remember anything that should have been a red flag. Not a word. And the cruel lie that his wife was dead! What kind of man says that about his wife?

The growing, tender feelings she'd had for him had evaporated, replaced by an overwhelming feeling of revulsion. His lies and dishonesty sickened her. And she hated the way her association with him made her feel about herself.

She drained her glass and was thinking about another one when the glare of headlights shining on the drawn curtain announced the arrival of a vehicle. She listened as it drove away and footsteps approached her front door, followed by knocking. She debated whether to open it, and thinking it would be Victoria, come to see what had happened to her, she sighed and opened the door.

When she saw who it was, she burst into tears.

Twenty-nine

I came to see if you're okay, but I guess not," said DCI Gareth Davies. Penny stood to one side so he could enter. He
closed the door behind him, gazed at her for a moment, then
held out his arms.

"Come here," he said. She hesitated, then let his familiar
warmth enfold her, resting her head on his chest. He embraced
her for a moment, then gently released her.

"Better now?" She nodded and led the way into the sitting
room.

"I just had a large vodka," she said. "Want one?"

"Well, maybe a small one." He steered her to the sofa. "I'll
fix them."

He handed her a drink, then sat beside her. She took a delicate sip then set the glass on the coffee table. This one didn't

taste as welcome as the first one. This one just tasted like desperation.

"Do you want to talk about it?" he asked. "Tell me what's upsetting you?"

"What have you heard?" she countered.

"Bethan and Victoria came back to the table, wondering where you'd got to. Dorothy said you'd just popped into the loo and they looked horrified. Do you want to tell me what happened?"

She shook her head. "Not really."

"But something did happen?" he pressed her.

She nodded. "But really, I don't want to talk about it," Penny said. "It was very good of you to come all the way out here to make sure I'm okay, but I'm fine. You should be at your retirement party. You'll be missed."

"Oh, Alan can hold the fort. He was a very senior officer and very well respected in police circles so our guys will be more than happy to talk to him. I'll head back in a few minutes, but I'd like you to come with me, if you feel up to it."

"What about Isla from the evidence room? Isn't she with you at the party?"

Davies looked confused. "With me? No. I barely knew who she was. She just sort of glommed on to me and came to sit at our table. I couldn't very well tell her she couldn't sit there, could I? I've got no idea what she's up to."

Penny almost laughed. Smart men could sometimes be so naïve.

"Okay, well, I'm feeling a bit better, but I don't think I'll go back with you," she said. "We've got a big wedding on tomorrow and I have to be up early for that. And anyway, I'm not sure I could face anyone right now. I think I'll just have an early night."

"Everyone's going to want to know you're okay so I'll just tell them you're feeling better but decided to call it a night, shall I? I'm surprised no one's rung you."

"My phone's switched off," Penny said. "Look, say goodbye to Dorothy and Alan for me, will you? Tell them I'm sorry and that I'll be in touch soon."

After he had gone she went upstairs and patted her puffy eyes with a wash cloth dipped in cold water to minimize the after effects of crying, although since she was home with just Harrison her cat, she wasn't too worried about her appearance. It just made her feel better. She changed into lounging pyjamas and settled on the sofa. She checked her phone for missed calls. Two from Victoria. None from Michael. She'd lost track of how many days since she'd heard from him, but now that she knew the truth, it didn't matter.

She was just thinking about going up to bed when once again headlights announced the arrival of a car. Who is it this time, she wondered. The headlights dimmed as they were switched off and then the car's motor was silenced.

She opened the door to a breathless Victoria.

"Oh, Penny," she said. "I'm so, so sorry. Bethan and I felt just terrible when we realized you must have overheard our conversation in the loo. And then you disappeared. We were just working out what to tell you."

"Well, you told me, didn't you? But honestly, it's all right. I'd rather know than not know. I just feel like such an idiot. How could I not have realized? Did you know?"

Victoria winced. "To be honest, I thought something wasn't

right and wondered if he might be married. Either that or he's just what they used to call a cad. I don't know what they call them now. A man who uses women. But look, it wasn't your fault, and I bet a lot of smart women have fallen for his Irish charm."

"It's that Irish accent. I was so taken in. I just hope Mrs. Lloyd doesn't get to hear about this."

"No, he'd better hope Mrs. Lloyd doesn't get to hear about this. You know she would be supportive of you one hundred percent. Look, I know you feel really awful right now, and you'll think it's easy for me to say this, but the thing is, you will get over this very quickly. You'll soon see that he isn't worth one more minute of your time or one more tear."

"You're probably right."

" 'Course I am! Aren't I always?" She sat down. "Anyway, listen, there've been developments you'll want to know about."

"Can I get you anything?"

"No, I've got to drive home, so I'd better not have any more to drink. I'm probably a bit over the limit as it is."

"All right. But tell me what happened."

"Well, when Gareth got back, his superior officer, I don't know his rank or what he's called, but anyway he made a little speech and presented Gareth with a watch in a really nice box. By then the party was in full swing. And then Bethan got a phone call and spoke to Gareth and then the two of them spoke to Gareth's boss, who was just getting ready to leave, I think.

"Anyway, Bethan's father's had a heart attack and he lives on his own, so she's gone off to Abergele to look after him and you'll never guess!"

"Oh, I can guess. Gareth's been reassigned to the Catrin Bellis case?"

"That's right! He's got about three weeks to go until his retirement is official, and they want it wrapped up by then but he can stay on a bit longer if he has to."

"Oh. How did he feel about that?"

"Well, he took it in his stride. I think he liked the idea of getting back in the old murder investigation harness. He's not really happy being desk bound, doing whatever it is he's been doing. Writing up crime statistics reports, I think he said."

She started to laugh. "Oh, and this bit was really funny. By the time he got back after seeing you, Isla'd had a bit too much to drink and was all over him like a rash."

Penny wasn't laughing.

Thirty

There's a reason brides choose to be married in June, Penny thought as she, Eirlys, and Victoria drove to the Hughes's farm the next morning. There's a softness about it as spring fades into the bright, early days of summer. Lush, vibrant fields in a thousand shades of green, enclosed by grey stone walls, stretched for miles around them under an atmospheric sky filled with wispy clouds.

They turned down the narrow tarmac road that led to the Hughes's farm and parked in the same spot as they had on their earlier visit. The garden that flanked the front door was now filled with white roses, fresh and beautiful in the morning light.

"Hiya," said a young woman in a pair of black jeans and a white blouse as she opened the door. Her tousled hair was piled on top of her head and held with a large red clip.

"I'm Jessica, the bride. We're supposed to go up to my room

and get me ready." Heather Hughes bustled into the foyer and stood beside her daughter, one hand resting lightly on her arm.

"Eirlys here will do Jessica's manicure and then makeup," said Victoria, "and Alberto, our hairdresser, will be here in about an hour to do everyone's hair."

The bride wasn't much older than Eirlys, who had started working at the Spa a couple of years ago right out of school. The two young women, already deep in conversation, disappeared up the stairs.

"We'll take them up a cup of tea in a few minutes," said Heather. "In the meantime, may I get you anything?"

"A coffee would be wonderful," said a slightly hung over Victoria, as Penny murmured agreement.

"Come through, then."

They found themselves once again in the stunning dream kitchen. Two women, wearing large white aprons, looked up as the group entered, and then returned to their food preparation tasks.

"We're having the wedding in the garden and the reception there, too, under the marquee," said Heather. "Thank God the weather is good. Of course, we're prepared for rain, but sun is much better."

"Who is Jessica marrying?" asked Penny as Heather handed her a coffee and turned back to the machine to make Victoria's. She took a few moments to reply as if considering what she should say.

"She's marrying a farmer called Jones from just down the road," Heather said in a low voice with a glance at the women slicing vegetables. "We think he's a bit old for her, but she insists this is what she wants. Well, of course it is. He breeds some of the finest horses in Wales. Jessica's been competing for years.

Trying now for a spot on the national equestrian team, with a view to the Olympics."

"But that's wonderful!" exclaimed Victoria.

"Yes, I suppose in a way it is," said Heather. "But it's not what her father and I would have chosen for her. We wanted her to go to university."

She handed Victoria her coffee.

"Well, I suppose we'd best get started," she said. "I thought you could do my nails in the library. It's quiet there and we won't be disturbed."

Penny gathered up the things she would need, and Victoria filled a small bowl with hot water from a special tap that dispensed water for beverages. It was hot, but with a couple of ice cubes dropped in, the water temperature was perfect.

"If you wouldn't mind, we'll just set that on a little tray so if any water is spilled it won't get on the floor," said Heather.

The room had that just-cleaned smell of old-fashioned beeswax mixed with the fragrance from a large bowl of white roses embellished with sprigs of lavender and baby's breath. The door leading to the garden stood open and a warm, gentle breeze drifted in, carrying with it the sweet scent of more flowers.

"What a beautiful bouquet!" exclaimed Penny.

"Oh, I'm glad you like it," said Heather. "I've been trying out different looks for Jessica's bridal bouquet and she decided on that one. Well, that's not her bouquet, that's in the fridge in the flower room. She also wanted a sprig of rosemary tucked into it."

Victoria retrieved a business magazine from her bag and settled in to read as Penny began work on Heather's manicure. A feminine peacefulness settled over the room; the only sound was birdsong that drifted in through the open French doors.

When the first coat of nail varnish in a dusty rose colour had been applied, Heather stood up and stretched her arms out. "I'm sorry," she said, "I'd just like to run upstairs and see how Jessica's getting on and then I've got a couple of calls to make. I'm a little worried that the cake hasn't been delivered yet and the bridesmaids should be arriving any minute. Have a wander round the garden, if you like, and whilst you're at it, you can check to see if the marquee is going up properly!"

Penny started to say something, but Heather interrupted her. "Yes, I'll be very careful with the nails. Won't touch anything. Promise." She bustled out of the room just as the doorbell rang.

"That'll be the cake, I expect," said Victoria.

"I was going to ask her if it would be all right if I went upstairs with her. I'd like to see how Eirlys is getting on, too."

"Well, catch her up," said Victoria. "She's probably just in the front hall with the cake people."

Alone in the room, Victoria wandered over to Penny's watercolour painting and admired it for a few moments, her hand resting on top of a small pile of books on a small bureau. Idly, she picked up the top book, a lavishly illustrated history of the garden at Buckingham Palace, and began flipping through it. Holding it, she strolled to the open doorway to admire the garden that stretched down to the river, with panoramic views to the hills beyond.

The room opened onto a broad terrace with a stone balustrade. She stepped onto the terrace, which ran the full length of the back of the house and from which shallow steps descended to an area featuring several beds of lavender, with gravel paths between them. A perennial border in pastel shades of pink and mauve plantings graced a stone wall that flanked one side of the sweeping lawn that sloped down toward the river.

The marquee was being set up on a broad expanse of lawn at the far end of the garden but she didn't think she had time to walk that far to check on its progress. She stepped back inside the house and turned a few more pages in the book, then replaced it on the bureau and picked up the other one: *The Elements of Organic Gardening* by the Prince of Wales. As she riffled the pages, soft footsteps in the hall suggested Penny or Heather might be back, so she put the book down just as Evan Hughes entered the room. He was wearing his farmer's clothes, but had removed his boots and was in his stocking feet. He had his work cut out for him to get cleaned up in time for his daughter's wedding, but Victoria had a feeling he'd scrub up rather well.

He glanced at the desk, and then looked at Victoria.

"Looking for my wife."

"She was seeing to the cake, so try the kitchen, maybe?" said Victoria. He made a light grunting noise of acknowledgement and disappeared. Victoria returned to the doorway and once again enjoyed the garden view. A minute or so later Penny returned. "The cake arrived but there's a problem with it, so Heather went upstairs to fetch Jessica. All hell's breaking loose in the kitchen."

"What's the matter?" asked Victoria.

"Apparently the decoration isn't exactly what Jessica was expecting, so the cake decorator is on her way over to fix it." She sat down. "And then Alberto arrived and needs to get on with Jessica's hair because he's got a full schedule of appointments lined up for this afternoon. I told Heather she should get back in here so I can finish her manicure."

"And Eirlys?" asked Victoria, preparing to leave.

"She stayed upstairs."

"Well, we have to make sure Alberto gets out of here on time. I'll let Heather know that if he can't get started on Jessica in the next ten minutes or so, he'll have to leave. We're on a schedule, too."

"Weddings, eh? Because you can never have too much stress."

"How are you feeling now?" asked Victoria after they'd dropped off Eirlys.

"Fine. I'm not the one who drank a bit too much last night. How are you feeling?"

"Felt pretty rough for a while there first thing this morning, I'll admit that," said Victoria. "But I'm okay now. What I meant was, how are you feeling now about the Michael thing?"

"I'll admit I was really attracted to him and definitely starting to fall for him," said Penny, "so I'm glad Bethan found out he was married. Makes me think, though. I bet he tries it on with a lot of the young women around the university. I didn't think profs did that sort of thing anymore."

"They shouldn't," said Victoria. "It's an abuse of a position of trust."

Penny didn't reply so Victoria continued.

"I really hate that he was so deceptive. I've been asking myself what kind of man does that?"

"I guess he was hoping for an affair," Penny shrugged. "Some men are like that, probably more than we'd like to think. There's that Web site married men go to if they're looking for an affair."

"They deserve a comeuppance," Victoria said, "and I've been thinking about that and had an idea. You're not the kind of person who would key his car or rip up his clothes and throw them in the street."

Penny laughed. "No, I'm not. And we only went out a couple of times, so that seems really extreme."

"It does. So I thought maybe we could be a little more devious. We could send his wife a gift certificate to the Spa, she'd tell him she was going to spend the morning here, and he'd be beside himself with worry that you might say something to her." She glanced at Penny. "Would you?"

"Absolutely not."

"But you were happy to know what he was like, why wouldn't his wife be?"

"Well, first, I think she already knows, because he's probably been like this for their whole marriage, however long that is, and second, I just don't want to be the one to tell her."

"So you don't like my idea?"

"No. Honestly, I just can't be bothered. And if I engage in something like that, it keeps me connected to him." She spread her fingers on both hands and intertwined them. "Like this. And besides, revenge just isn't my thing. I've already started to move on and I just want to keep moving. Sooner or later, karma will take care of him."

Thirty-one

Finally, after the retirement party the night before and the morning spent working the Hughes wedding, Penny had a chance to telephone Tegwen Driscoll and ask if she could come and see her. "It's about your scarf," Penny said.

Tegwen met her at the door with a smile and held out her hand. "Oh, thanks so much for dropping it off," she said. "Very good of you. It's a favourite of mine. I misplaced it a little while ago and couldn't think where I'd left it, and it finally occurred to me I must have left it at your Spa."

"I don't have it, I'm afraid," said Penny. "But I think I know where it is."

"You'd better come in, then."

A deep frown creased Tegwen's face as she showed Penny in. She did not invite her into the sitting room, but stood in the hall, arms folded. "Well?" she said.

"Are the colours green and blue in your scarf?" Penny asked. Tegwen nodded. "And who made it?" Penny asked.

"It's a Liberty."

"Then I can tell you where it is. It's in Catrin Bellis's bedroom."

"And how do you know that?"

"I saw it there recently when I went through the house with a police officer, and if you want it back, you're going to have to contact them. I can tell you who to speak to."

Tegwen's shoulders slumped and she waved a hand in the direction of the sitting room.

"I don't have much time because the girls will be back soon and I don't want them to know anything about this," Tegwen said.

"About what?"

Tegwen clasped her hands in her lap and rubbed them lightly together.

"I thought Catrin was having an affair with Brad. I asked her about it a little while ago and she got very huffy. Denied it. And then I didn't really hear from her again, so I thought the reason she was binning me was because of Brad. That she couldn't keep on seeing him, and be friends with his wife, too, at the same time. That would be too, I don't know there's a word for it. Not dishonest, but sounds a bit like that."

"Duplicitous?"

"That's it. I saw it in a self-help book."

"You know, Tegwen, I don't know if your husband is or was having an affair, and I really hope not. I know how devastating that would be. But if, and it's a big if, I don't think it was with Catrin. And I hope you'll let go of these thoughts about her, because it's not fair to her reputation or memory, and it poisons all the years of a wonderful friendship that you two shared."

"I never thought of it that way." Her eyes began to fill with tears and she clasped her hands together in her lap and rocked slightly forward. "And so I haven't been able to grieve her death properly."

They remained silent for a moment, and then Penny spoke.

"So tell me. You went to see her. When did you go?"

"Friday evening. The night before the Antiques show. After dinner. We talked for a little bit and I confronted her again about Brad. And again, she denied it. She was quite cold about it, as if she couldn't understand why I was so upset. I wanted to believe her but someone told me she'd seen Brad talking to Catrin in the town square and then he's out that evening saying he's with a client and a bit flustered and in a really bad mood when he gets home."

"So you assumed he was with her?"

Tegwen nodded.

"I was always so afraid he'd leave me for her. It's been a big cloud hanging over our marriage. He always preferred her but her parents wouldn't let him court her, as we used to say, so he settled for me." She scoffed. "Can you imagine? Living a whole marriage feeling like second best? And then when her parents died and she started to come out of her shell, and transformed herself into a really nice-looking woman, well . . ."

"Your feelings of jealousy intensified."

Tegwen nodded. "Yeah. I couldn't shake the feeling that there was something going on between them. Maybe I'll never know, for sure. And now it's too late."

"Too late for what?"

"I want so badly to tell her how sorry I am and I can't. Because she's not here anymore."

Before Penny could respond, the front door opened and a youthful, girlish voice called out.

"Mum, we're home and we've got Lili with us!" Laughing and chattering, the three girls clattered up the stairs. Their footsteps faded away at the sound of a closing door.

Tegwen sighed and reached for a tissue. "I'd better pull myself together. They'll be wanting a snack soon."

Thirty-two

*H*i, it's me," said the voicemail message on Penny's phone later that afternoon. "I know it's short notice, but I wondered if I could take you to dinner this evening. I've spent the day reviewing Bethan's case notes."

Rather to her surprise, Penny found herself looking forward to dinner with Gareth. His kindness the night before had been just what she needed, when she needed it, and something seemed different about him. He looked more relaxed, more approachable. Maybe her recent experience with Michael had helped her see him in a different way. He picked her up just after seven and they drove the short distance into town.

"How did the wedding preparations go this morning?" he asked.

"Oh, fine. Just the usual last-minute panic. Bridesmaids in a flap and everybody running up and the down the stairs shouting,

'Has anybody seen my eyeliner? Can somebody do these buttons up?' The cake wasn't right, the mother changed her mind about the flowers. The bride isn't very girly, she's part of the local horsey set, so I think she went along with some of the arrangements just to please her mother."

"Who's her mother?" Davies asked.

"Heather Wynne Hughes. Married to Evan, local farmer. Beautiful home. Lots of money there."

"There usually is, when horses are involved."

The Italian restaurant was crowded but they were shown to a table and handed menus. After a brief discussion, they gave their order to the waiter and Davies poured each of them a glass of cold, crisp white wine.

"I'm not going to discuss the Catrin Bellis case with you here, because it's too public," he said in a soft voice, "but at some point soon I would like to have your thoughts. The higher ups want to see this case wrapped and I don't have a lot of time."

"I don't really have any thoughts," said Penny. "Or what thoughts I do have are all over the place. But I keep coming back to that map. I think her murder is linked to the map but I just don't see how. It would really help if we could decode it. Dorothy suggested it might lead to something hidden or buried."

"Let's think about that whilst we enjoy our dinner."

They kept the conversation light and neutral throughout the meal. When their coffee was served Davies studied the half of the map that Haydn had provided, and the drawings taken from the slate fencing in Bluebell Wood.

"You can't do anything with a silly map like this unless you have the starting point, and it seems to start with this thing here that looks like a bee, except the stripes go the wrong way." He folded the papers but instead of returning them to her asked, "Do you mind if I hang on to these?"

Penny shook her head. "That's fine. I've got copies."

He tucked them in his pocket and signaled for the bill.

"Will there be someone in the police department who can decipher that?" she asked.

"I don't think so. I expect it will take someone with local knowledge to work it out."

"In that case, I've just thought of someone who might be able to help with this," said Penny as Davies withdrew a credit card from his wallet.

"Who?"

"Our friend the rector. Thomas likes puzzles."

"Why don't you ring them and invite them for Sunday lunch tomorrow? They can bring Robbie and we'll find a nice country pub somewhere. The Black Bull, maybe."

After a brief conversation, Penny pressed the button to end the call.

"Bronwyn says Robbie isn't feeling well so they'd prefer to stay home. She wonders if we could have the pub lunch another time and would we like to have Sunday lunch at the rectory tomorrow? Bronwyn was planning to stay home from church, anyway, because of Robbie. I said we would. Twelve thirty. Is that okay with you?"

"It's just fine. Shall I pick you up or meet you there?"

"I'll meet you there. I like a walk in the morning."

After he'd dropped her off at home, she thought about Gareth, and how happy she was that he'd invited her to work on the case with him. It was starting to feel like old times, the same only different. And for some reason, better.

231

Thirty-three

The morning walk through the timeless landscape of fields and grey stone walls edged at this time of year with purple wildflowers and ferns invigorated her and she arrived at the churchyard gate where Gareth was waiting for her flushed with a sense of well being. Together, they walked to the rectory.

"Come in, Penny and Gareth. Lovely to see you both. Glad you could make it. Come through."

With her cairn terrier Robbie at her heels, Bronwyn Evans led them into her tidy sitting room with its lovely leaded windows that overlooked the river and offered them a sherry.

"Thomas should be home from church in a few minutes," Bronwyn said. As Robbie started barking, Penny commented that she was glad to see he was feeling better and Bronwyn gave them a little grin and said, "That'll be him now."

The door to the kitchen opened and closed and a moment later Thomas Evans appeared in the sitting room. He extended his hand to Gareth and smiled a greeting at Penny as his wife reappeared in the doorway. "We're ready if you'd like to come through to the dining room," she said to Penny and Gareth. "Thomas will have a quick wash and be right with us."

The old-fashioned dining room was dark, compared to the adjoining sunny kitchen. The walls had been papered in a deep magenta, somewhere between a burgundy and rich red. An oak sideboard took up one wall and the oak table in the centre of the room with eight chairs had been set for four. At the entrance to the sitting room a longcase clock ticked away the seconds. As the group took their places around the table, the clock struck one.

Bronwyn carried in a large white platter with two chickens on it, surrounded by roast potatoes. She set this in front of her husband, then returned to the kitchen for vegetables, gravy, and bread sauce.

When she was seated the rector said grace and began to carve the chicken.

"I tucked a little rosemary under the skin," Bronwyn remarked. "A little of that goes a long way, but I do think it adds a nice flavour."

"Jessica Hughes had a sprig of rosemary in her wedding bouquet yesterday," said Penny as she passed her plate to the rector.

"It's for remembrance, rosemary is," said Bronwyn. "I wonder who she was remembering. Sometimes a bride will do that if she has lost a parent, say."

"It was an interesting wedding," said Thomas. "The groom is quite a bit older than Jessica. A horse breeder, apparently. I'm not sure the parents completely approved. Her mother in particular didn't seem completely happy."

"No, she wasn't," said Penny. "We were at the farm in the morning helping them get ready."

The meal continued with easy conversation, and while Bronwyn served coffee and a lemon tart, Davies reached into his jacket pocket and produced the maps.

"I wonder if you'd have a look at these," he said to Thomas. Penny explained the history of the two maps—one from Haydn Williams and the other from a slate fence—and Thomas took out his reading glasses. He moved his plate and cutlery to one side, and smoothed the maps in front of him. "Let me see then," he murmured. Bronwyn finished pouring coffee and took the pot to the kitchen, and then returned to peer over her husband's shoulder, her hand resting lightly on it.

The rector traced the little drawings with his finger, studying each one as he went.

"Right," he said, after a few minutes. "They're two halves of a map made by a couple of local boys, you say."

"We're especially confused by the first figure that looks like an insect, or possibly a bee," said Davies.

"I don't think that's an insect," said Thomas. "I think it's a swaddled baby. When I first saw it, it put me in mind of the little marble tombstone of the infant Sydney Wyn, laid to rest in 1639 in the chapel of our very own church, right here in Llanelen." He took off his glasses and looked from Gareth to Penny and then back again.

"So if I'm not mistaken, the trail on your map starts right here in the church. Why don't we finish our coffee and then see where the map takes us?" He took a sip of coffee. "Assuming

I'm right, of course. I may be completely off base. But we'll find out."

He beamed at his wife. "That was a lovely lunch, my dear. You quite outdid yourself."

Thirty-four

Thomas, Penny, and Gareth walked along the short path that led from the rectory to the church. Gravestones on either side indicated fairly recent burials and on their left, the River Conwy sparkled in the warm afternoon sunshine.

A century or two ago, the Wynne chapel was part of the main body of St. Elen's church attached to the chancel but at some point an elaborate wooden rood screen with the amusing motif of pigs eating acorns had been installed to separate the two. The chapel was accessible now only through its own entrance. The carved, arched wooden door creaked on its black iron hinges as the rector pushed it open and they stepped down onto the uneven stone floor straight into the fifteenth century.

Sunlight streaming in through mullioned windows, set high up in the thick stone walls on all four sides of the building, did its best to push the darkness to the dusty corners. The air had a close, almost mossy smell from centuries of old wood, incense, and candle smoke, a distinctive odour often found in old churches sometimes referred to as, "God's breath." The atmosphere was pleasant and peaceful with a sense of solitude and quiet reverence. The birdsong in the churchyard faded into stillness.

As their eyes adjusted to the reduced light, they made their way past the bottom half of a stone sarcophagus, said to be part of the coffin of a medieval Welsh prince. The walls were covered with engraved brasses and pieces of statuary, carvings, and monuments sacred to the memory of men and women from various branches of the Wynne family who had lived and died hundreds of years ago.

The rector pointed to a memorial depicting an infant in swaddling clothes, the vertical yellow veined folds in its marble garments speckled with sunlight.

Penny and Gareth exchanged a quick glance. "You're right, Thomas," said Gareth. "This could be the first drawing on the map."

On each side of the figure was carved a shield and beneath the sculpted child was the inscription: *Here lieth the bodie of Sydney Wyn daughter to Owen Wyn Esq. which was borne the 6th of September and departed this life the eight of October fallowing Anno Dni 1639.*

And on top of the shield on the right lay a sprig of dark green rosemary.

"Oh," exclaimed the rector. "Isn't that interesting! We were just talking about rosemary and look at that." He picked it up and brushed its needle-like leaves across the palm of his hand. "It feels quite fresh," he said. "I suppose Jessica could have left it here yesterday after her wedding as a tribute to her family."

He shrugged. "Right, well about that map, then. What would you like to do?"

"Well, why don't we have Penny pace it out and see what happens?" said Davies. All three pored over the map. "It says one hundred after the first drawing, so I'm guessing that means one hundred steps."

"But starting from where?" asked the rector. "The door of the chapel or the baby memorial?"

"Let's try the memorial," said Penny. "After all, that's what he drew. If he'd meant the door, surely he would have drawn an arch to represent the chapel door?"

The two men murmured agreement, so Penny positioned herself beside the memorial. "And I have to remember to take child-size steps," she said. As she took the first step the rector counted one. By sixteen she had reached the door of the chapel.

"Which way now?" she asked.

"To your left," said Davies. "You're meant to keep the river on your right." He looked around. "It's hard to say, but I think these figures are sheep and it may be that when this map was drawn the area on the other side of the river was common land with grazing rights. Where the cricket field is now."

Penny was now on the black asphalt path that ran through the churchyard with the rectory just ahead of her. The door opened and Bronwyn came out with Robbie. She waved at Penny and the two joined the little group.

"How's it going?" she asked.

"We're on step sixty-seven," said the rector. "There doesn't seem to be any instructions as to what we're meant to do now."

"Let me see the map again," said Bronwyn. She studied it for a moment and then looked toward the rear of the church.

"I think you should go over there," she said, pointing at a rho-dodendron bush.

"And why do you think that, my dear?" asked the rector.

"Because this little drawing," she tapped her finger on a circle with dots on top of a rectangle, "looks like a clock."

"Of course!" exclaimed the rector. "How could I have missed that?"

"What is it?" asked Davies.

"Just keep walking Penny," said Bronwyn. "Here, Robbie and I will guide you. Thomas, let us know when we reach one hundred." Bronwyn rotated Penny's body slightly and she paced a few more steps.

"One hundred!" called out the rector. "Stop!"

Penny had reached the grave of John Owen, the town's famous clockmaker who was laid to rest in the churchyard in 1776. "So somewhere around here is whatever the boys thought worth burying and recording the spot?" asked the rector.

"It looks that way," said Davies.

The rector surveyed the churchyard. "But it could be any-where! How on earth would you find it?"

"Or maybe nothing's buried here at all," mused Davies.

"Well, what are you going to do now?" asked the rector.

"I'm not sure yet," said Davies. "But we won't be doing any-thing officially just now. Thank you, everybody. I think that's good for today."

The five of them, counting Robbie, walked back to the rec-tory. "We need to get ready to go out," the rector apologized. "We've got a hospital visiting appointment at three. One of my parishioners has asked to see me. Something's troubling her and people often find as the end approaches that they need to get something off their chest."

Penny and Gareth thanked them for lunch and departed.

"Well, that was a most interesting experience," said Thomas as he and Bronwyn tidied up the kitchen.

"Never mind that," said his wife. "What's up with those two? Are they back together, do you think? I was dying to ask Penny, but didn't think I should. But I was very surprised when she called and invited us to lunch. I wonder if there's any hope that they might rekindle whatever it was they had."

"I'm not sure," said Thomas, "I don't think they're together in a romantic way, but he's devoted to her. That much is obvious, even to me."

Thirty-five

Shortly before eight the next morning Bronwyn and Robbie set off on the first of their daily walks, leaving Thomas to prepare breakfast, ready for their return. He was looking forward to a quiet Monday, first catching up on parish business and then catching up on his sleep with an afternoon nap.

Just as he spooned a couple of dollops of his wife's favourite marmalade into a small glass bowl, the kitchen door opened and Bronwyn stuck her head in. "Thomas, you'd better come and see what's happened in the churchyard."

He set the bowl at her place on the table. "Why, Bronwyn, what is it? Is it Robbie? Has something happened to Robbie?"

"No, Thomas, Robbie is just fine. But either giant moles invaded overnight or someone's been digging up the churchyard. Come right now, Thomas. You're going to want to see this."

He hurried out into the churchyard and followed his wife to the grave of John Owen. Half a dozen large, deep holes had been dug at the base of the church and around the grave.

"Oh, dear," he said. "We'd better get these holes filled in. A visitor could trip over one or fall into it and sprain an ankle or something."

"No, Thomas. Think about it. This could be a Significant Development." She emphasized the words "significant" and "development" as if each merited a capital letter. "We'd better call Gareth Davies so he can decide if this is important or not. And what's more, he won't want people trampling all over the scene, so we'll have to close the churchyard to visitors until he's seen it. And anyway, as you say, it's a safety hazard. So I suggest we post a sign saying the churchyard is closed until one o'clock. How about that? That will give people who want to visit time to do something else this morning, have a bit of lunch, and then come back this afternoon."

Thomas put his arms around her. "Whatever would I do without you?" he said. "Now I suggest that you and Robbie forgo your morning walk and you come home with me and we have breakfast whilst we wait for Gareth. Fortunately I haven't made the coffee yet, so we'll make a bigger pot in case he and his team, if he brings one, would like some."

"Yes, very glad you called," said Davies. "And quite right not to let anyone into the churchyard until we've had a chance to assess it. See you in a few minutes and the coffee would be most welcome." Davies hung up the phone in his office, slipped on his jacket, and walked down the hall to the canteen where PC Chris Jones had just joined the breakfast queue.

"Sorry, Jones, no breakfast for you. At least not here. I'll explain on the way, and the good Mrs. Evans will have coffee waiting for you."

They arrived a few minutes later at the rectory, where a hand-written sign on the padlocked gate apologized for the inconvenience but the churchyard was closed for the morning. Just as he was getting ready to ring the rectory to let Thomas know he'd arrived, the kitchen door opened and the rector himself scurried toward them. When he'd unlocked the gate Thomas held out his arm in the direction of the clockmaker's grave.

"Yes, I can see the digging from here," Davies said. "Well, Thomas, I would say that at the very least we've got a case of vandalism. I wonder what else we'll find. Come on then, Jones. Let's check it out." Jones murmured something that the rector didn't quite catch. "He's desperate for coffee," Davies said to the rector. "We'll send him over to the house to ask Bronwyn to pour him one and he can join us in a couple of minutes."

Davies and the rector walked to the grave and contemplated the holes that surrounded it. Each one was about one foot across and of the same depth. The dirt that had been removed from the hole was piled up beside it. They walked slowly from one hole to the other, peering into each one.

"It must have taken someone a fair bit of time to do all this," Davies said to the rector. "And they couldn't have done all this in the dark—they would have needed lights. You didn't hear anything in the night? See any strange lights moving about?"

The rector shook his head. "No, sorry. Wish I had. Our bedroom overlooks the river, so we wouldn't have heard or seen anything in the churchyard. I'm a sound sleeper but if Bronwyn had heard anything, she would have woken me up."

A few minutes later, carefully holding one of Bronwyn's

kitchen mugs to avoid spilling any of its precious contents, a smiling Jones glided across the churchyard and joined them.

"We're going to need every one of these holes examined," Davies said, "and the dirt piles as well, obviously, in case someone left something behind. A button, a hair, a fingernail, a glove, a tool. Hell, maybe even a phone. I doubt we'll be that lucky, but stranger things have happened."

Jones set his coffee mug on a nearby slate chest tomb and pulled out his notebook. "And request a photographer, too," said Davies. He sighed. "Of course the real problem is we have no way of knowing if they found what they were looking for. Whatever that might be."

"There's something going on at the church this morning," Eirlys told Penny as she slipped on her pale pink smock.

"What do you mean, 'something going on'? This early on a Monday morning? They can't be having a fete or something like that. That would be held on a Saturday."

"Oh, no, not that kind of something. Something different. I could see some people in the churchyard milling about when I walked by this morning. So I walked down past the alms-houses to get closer and there's a sign on the gate that says the church is closed this morning."

"Oh, well, maybe it's a funeral. Although come to think of it, of course not. Why would they close the church for a funeral?"

Eirlys shrugged and turned her attention to the small bag she had taken with her on Saturday to Jessica Hughes's home manicure. She pulled out a couple of bottles of polish and set them on her worktable.

"If anybody's looking for me, I'll be back soon," Penny said.

She crossed the town square and turned toward the church where a small crowd had gathered outside the gates.

"Nothing to see here," a uniformed officer told them. "Move along now."

"What's happening?" asked Penny, catching a glimpse of Davies near the church. The area around the clockmaker's gravestone had been cordoned off with blue and white police tape.

"Nothing for you to worry about," said the police officer. "Just carrying out a routine investigation."

"Would you please tell DCI Davies I'd like a word with him," she said. "My name's Penny Brannigan."

"Know him, do you?" he asked.

"Yes, I do. I'm sure he'll talk to me."

The officer walked off to the grave where several people, wearing white protective overalls, were working. He spoke to PC Jones, who accompanied him back to the gate where Penny was waiting.

"Morning, Penny," he said, and then explained to her they were investigating the mysterious overnight appearance of several holes in the churchyard. "We don't know what they were looking for, or if they found it," he concluded.

Penny thanked him and returned to the Spa. The morning passed quickly and at noon Victoria, Eirlys, and Penny gathered in her office to discuss creating a mobile wedding unit so they could deliver that service while keeping the Spa open.

"I'd like to work the mobile unit," Eirlys said. "It's fun to get out and see other people's houses and I like being part of the wedding excitement."

"Was Jessica Hughes a particularly difficult bride?" Penny asked Eirlys.

"No, I don't think so. I had to work really hard on her hands, though. They were so rough and I don't think she's used to wearing makeup. She was nice to talk to. If you like horses, that is."

"What was her room like?" asked Penny.

"Really big. About the size of my parents' room and mine put together. Filled with trophies and rosettes. She's won a lot of competitions. She said it runs in the family. Her mother doesn't ride, but her grandfather and great-grandfather did. There was a picture of her great-grandfather, I think she said it was, on a horse during the war."

"I don't think they used horses in the Second World War, so must be the first," Victoria said. "Great-great-grandfather, possibly."

Penny shuffled some papers on her desk and pushed them to one side in a neat pile and set her phone on top of them.

"Oh!" said Eirlys. "You've got one, too!"

"One what?" asked Penny.

"One of those papers with the funny drawings on it."

"What do you mean, 'too'? Who else has one?"

"Jessica. I saw a drawing that looked just like that in her room."

Thirty-six

I wasn't snooping or anything," Eirlys continued. "Jessica left the room at one point so I looked around for a bit."

"The way you do," encouraged Victoria.

"Well, it's not like it was in a drawer and I opened it," said Eirlys. "It was just sitting there on the table. There's a little seating area in a kind of alcove and it was just there. I thought the drawings looked like something from *The Hobbit*."

"Do you know where Jessica is now?" Penny asked.

"Well, on her honeymoon, I guess. She told me they were going to Ireland to look at horses."

Eirlys looked first at Penny, then shifted her gaze to Victoria. A small line appeared between her eyebrows.

"Why are you asking me all these questions? Did I do something wrong?"

"No, you didn't," Penny reassured her. "It's just that the paper you saw might be important, that's all. We might have to tell Detective Chief Inspector Davies about it because it may be connected to a case he's working on. One thing, though. The paper you saw. Was it a photocopy, do you know? Did it have a smooth edge like this?" She pointed to a paper on her desk.

"I don't know about the edge, but it couldn't have been a photocopy. I'm pretty sure it was written in pencil." Her head tilted back slightly and her eyes moved up and to the right. "It was written on lined paper, like you get in a school notebook."

Penny paused for a moment while she considered the significance of what Eirlys had just said.

"I think we'd better leave the discussion about the mobile wedding service for later," she said. "Eirlys has given me a lot to think about."

"In that case, can I go now?" Eirlys asked. "I was hoping to meet a friend for lunch."

"Yes, off you go," said Penny. "And take your full lunch hour."

"Well," said Penny when she had gone. "Now we have to work out what to do next."

Victoria slid her phone over to her.

"It's not that difficult. You phone him and tell him what Eirlys just told you about Jessica."

"I don't think it's that simple. If Jessica's in Ireland, she couldn't have dug up the cemetery last night."

"So how did the map get on a table in her room, then?"

Penny thought for a moment. "Could one of her parents have left it there?"

"Well, I don't know about that. But I do know this for sure. You have to ring Gareth. If this map is somehow connected to the death of Catrin Bellis, as you keep telling me it is, he needs to know. And what's more, there could be fingerprints on it, that could crack this case wide open." She picked up the phone and held it out to Penny. "Go on. You know you want to. And if you don't want to, you have to."

"Oddly enough, for some reason I don't want to. There's something missing."

"Oh, yes? And what's that?"

"The first half of the map that belongs to Haydn Wiliams. The left side. If someone in the Hughes family does have the right side of the map, well, it's useless without the other half. That's the whole point of tearing the map in two. So each person who owns a piece of it is an equal partner in whatever the map is concealing because both halves are necessary to finding it. And if it was a Hughes family member, whether it's Heather or Evan or Jessica, he or she couldn't have known to dig in the churchyard unless he or she had the first part of the map."

"Well, that's easy, then. Haydn Williams and his friend and neighbour Evan Hughes are in it together."

"Oh, I don't think so. Haydn is so naïve, and I certainly can't see him being part of a plot to kill Catrin Bellis for a piece of paper. Besides, I think he fancied her. I think he was looking forward to getting to know her better." Penny shook her head. "But of course you're right about telling Gareth about the map in Jessica's room. I'll do that now and he can sort it."

"That's right," said Victoria. "That's his job, so let's leave him to it. And meanwhile, let's get on with ours."

A few minutes later the man himself rang to tell Penny that police had found nothing of interest in the churchyard holes. "But someone was definitely looking for something," he added.

251

"I found out something," she told him. "Eirlys saw what could be the other half of the original map at the Hughes farmhouse."

"Oh, I know that look, Mrs. Lloyd. You've got something to tell me."

Mrs. Lloyd dipped her hands in the soaking water and beamed at Penny.

"Indeed I do," she said. "You'll never guess. I've only just heard myself. They were trying to keep it quiet, I guess."

"They? Who were keeping what quiet?"

"The Hughes family. Their daughter, Jessica, was married on Saturday. Such a big to do for such a horsey girl, in my opinion. Anyway, apparently the marriage didn't take and she came home that very night to her parents." Mrs. Lloyd laughed. "You don't hear of that happening very often these days!"

"But what about the honeymoon in Ireland?"

"There was no honeymoon. There was no nothing. She's back at home with her parents and I have no idea what happens next. Can they get the marriage annulled, do you suppose?"

"Well, maybe once she's had a bit of time to think it over, she'll give it another go," said Penny.

"Well, I suppose that's possible," said Mrs. Lloyd doubtfully. "But I've been wondering why she agreed to marry that man in the first place. I think her parents, her father in particular, must have pressured her into it. Apparently the fields of the two farms adjoin and he liked the idea of one big spread."

"I'm not sure you're right about the parents pressuring her, though. I don't know about the father, but Heather told me she wasn't keen on her daughter marrying him. Still, what interests me right now is the honeymoon. Are you sure Jessica didn't go to Ireland?" Penny asked.

"Well, I can't be sure," Mrs. Lloyd replied. "I'm just telling you what I heard."

"Of course." Penny worked in silence for a moment, and then, changing the subject, inquired after Florence Semble. "How's Florence getting along? Still getting used to the idea of owning all that wonderful art?"

"Oh, not much has changed with her," said Mrs. Lloyd. "Still the same old Florence. She does spend a bit more time out of the house, though. She's become quite chummy with Jean from the library. You know, the lady who found Catrin Bellis's body."

"Oh, yes. Did she find a place to stay?"

"She did. A nice little room right across the street from us, if you can believe it. That was quite the traumatic experience for her. Something you'd never dream would happen to you. You're just going about your business, finding a place to live, and you happen upon a murder scene."

"No, you wouldn't expect that to happen to you in a million years," agreed Penny.

"I'm sure she thinks about it a lot. She was in such a state when we found her. The police interviewed her soon after, I think, while her memory was fresh. I wonder if she's remembered anything since. Sometimes things come back to you when you least expect it, don't they? Somebody says something, or you see something and it reminds you of the very thing you've been trying to remember."

"Yes," said Penny thoughtfully, "yes, sometimes things do come back to you, with a little prompting."

"I thought when it happened that Florence and I might be

253

able to solve the mystery but of course we don't have the resources that the police do, so we decided to leave it to the professionals," said Mrs. Lloyd with a slightly crafty look at Penny. If she picked up on the little dig, Penny did not show it. "But I have my suspicions, though."

"Oh, yes?"

"Well, that married man I saw Catrin with. Brad Driscoll, it was. As I said to Florence it's the oldest reason in the book. The mistress says, 'I want you to leave your wife and marry me,' and the man says, 'I can't do that because of the children,' and the mistress says, 'Then I'll tell your wife about us,' and he feels he has no option but to kill her." Mrs. Lloyd gave Penny a sorrowful look. "To silence her, you see."

"Well, that's certainly plausible," said Penny, "but of the two, I would have picked Tegwen as the more likely killer. She goes to Catrin's home to confront her because she thinks Catrin is having an affair with her husband, they argue, and in the heat of the moment, it all gets out of hand and poor Catrin ends up dead."

"Oh, no, Penny. As I explained to Florence, if she found out her husband was having an affair, her first thought would be to kill him, not Catrin."

Penny laughed. "I can't help thinking, though. Is Brad Driscoll really the kind of man worth killing for?"

It was Mrs. Lloyd's turn to laugh. "Is any man?"

With the manicure finished and Mrs. Lloyd on her way, Penny rang Davies to tell him that according to Mrs. Lloyd, Jessica had not gone on honeymoon, and could have been at her parents' home on Sunday night when the churchyard was vandalized.

"I know," he said. "I saw her there today. Look, I can't really talk now, I'm in the car, but perhaps we can meet up later."

"Let's," said Penny. "Because something Mrs. Lloyd said has given me an idea."

"Jessica told us she'd come home Saturday night when we went round to ask about the piece of paper found in her bedroom," said Davies. "Oh, and by the way, I'm sorry, but she wasn't long in figuring out who must have seen it there. We dropped poor Eirlys in it, I'm afraid, but I told her that it wasn't Eirlys who told the police about it. We still haven't been able to establish how it got there or more importantly, who put it there. Now tell me your idea."

"Mrs. Lloyd said something like someone can make a chance remark or do something that triggers a memory, and that got me thinking, so I just wanted to put it to you in case you think it might have some merit."

When she had finished explaining what she had in mind, Davies nodded.

"We're just a little bit ahead of you," he said. "We've been thinking the same thing. What is that old proverb? 'If you want to catch a fish, stir the waters'? Now, I can use your help in setting it up, but once events are in motion, you have to promise me you'll stay well out of it and let us do our work. And you'll have to follow instructions exactly. No thinking for yourself. You're very well meaning but you have to leave it to us."

"Of course," said Penny. "Now we just have to—"

Davies interrupted her. "Sorry, 'of course' isn't good enough. I know what you're like. I need your absolute assurance that once this starts to go down you'll stay well out of it. Don't stick your oar in. Don't interfere. If you do, you could jeopardize the whole operation. Now, do I have your word?"

"Yes, you do," said Penny.

"Now how can we make sure our suspects know about this, I wonder. It needs to be done in a casual, conversational kind of way. They mustn't suspect anything. Do they ever go out for dinner, I wonder?" Davies asked. "We could mention it in a way that they would overhear."

"The best way might be through Haydn Williams," Penny said slowly. "I could find a reason to visit him, let him know that Jean's remembered something critically important to solving the case. He'll be sure to pass it on to Hughes. Oh, and then there's Jean, of course."

"We've already spoken to her. She's agreed to help but is understandably rather anxious. But remember, you need to stay well out of it. If you don't, Jean could be in great danger."

Thirty-seven

*T*he next afternoon Penny and her sketching partner, Alwynne Gwilt, with a sheaf of drawings under their arms, once again walked up the unpaved road that led to Haydn Williams's farm. Finding an excuse to call on him had been the easy part. Getting him to commit to a time had been the challenge.

"Hello, Haydn. It's Penny here, Penny Brannigan, yes. Alwynne and I were wondering if you'd be home tomorrow. We just wanted to pop in for a few minutes and show you the sketches we did at your farm. Thought you might like to see what we came up with," Penny had said while DCI Davies listened, his arms folded and eyes closed. At the end of every sentence he nodded encouragement.

Penny listened for a few minutes while Haydn explained all

about the busy day he had planned. He and Evan Hughes were thinking of buying an award-winning ram together and were going out to inspect it. He wasn't exactly sure what time they'd be back, but finally suggested four o'clock. He should be back by then but if not, they should just make themselves at home until he arrived. The kitchen door was always open and they wouldn't have to worry about Kip as he'd be with the men. He never missed the chance of a ride in the Land Rover, did Kip.

There had been some discussion about whether Penny should go alone, but Davies had decided it would look more natural if Alwynne accompanied her. And although he didn't anticipate any trouble, the situation would be safer with the two of them.

Haydn wasn't home when they arrived, so following his instructions they let themselves in. They didn't have long to wait until the sound of the Land Rover rocking its way up the rutted lane was followed by excited barking and then Kip raced into the kitchen, followed by two men.

Haydn greeted them, and headed straight for the cupboard to pour himself a whisky. He offered a drink to his companion, Evan Hughes, who shook his head.

Penny and Alwynne had laid their sketches out on the table and the two men bent over to examine them.

"I like this one," Haydn said, pointing to a sketch by Alwynne, who unable to resist, gave Penny a teasingly triumphant smile.

"What about mine here with the little black sheep?" Penny asked. "Oh, it's nice, too," said Haydn. "Did you enjoy yourselves that day? Do you get out sketching much?"

They talked about the sketches for a few minutes and then Penny skillfully brought the conversation round to the real point of their visit.

"I heard there's been a development in the Catrin Bellis case," she said.

"Really?" said Haydn with a quick glance at his friend. "What's happened?"

"Well, apparently the police are going to do a reenactment of the crime. You know, with actors. They film it and show it on telly in hopes it will jog someone's memory. They're doing it because apparently there's a witness who arrived on the scene soon after it happened and they're hoping she'll remember an important detail. She may have even seen the killer. Who knows?"

"How do you know all this?" asked Hughes. "You seem very well informed."

"Oh, everybody in our Spa's talking about it," said Penny with a smile she hoped didn't betray how nervous she was. "You know what women are like. At the Spa we're always first to hear all the interesting bits of news making the rounds.

"But this time it's going to be a little different," she continued. "Although they use actors, the real person who discovered the body will be on hand in case seeing it all so vividly helps her recall an important detail."

"Do you know who this person is?" asked Haydn.

"Yes, her name's Jean. She works in the library."

"And when are they going to do all this?" asked Evan.

"Tomorrow, just after one o'clock, same time as Catrin's body was discovered. They do it at the same time as the actual crime so everything looks the same and hopefully, people are in the same place as they were on the day it happened. You know, if you were just coming back from lunch for example.

"And apparently the actress playing Jean will even be

259

wearing her clothes. They like everything to be as near as possible to the real thing."

Penny packed up the sketches. "Well, Haydn, thank you again for the lovely day we had sketching here."

"Do you need a ride into town?" asked Hughes. "I'm going in anyway to pick up my wife."

"Oh, no, thank you," said Alwynne. "We've made arrangements, thanks. My husband will be here in a few minutes to pick us up."

"How did it go?" Davies asked. Alwynne's husband had dropped Penny off at the Spa and she'd walked the short distance to the police station where Davies was waiting for her.

"Very well, I think. It was even easier than we thought it would be because Evan Hughes was there, too. I explained everything and they both seemed interested but I couldn't really get a reading on either of them."

Davies rested his chin in his hand and said nothing.

"Do you think the killer will turn up?" Penny asked.

"Oh, yes," said Davies. "I'm very confident he'll be there. It'll be just too good to miss. You've heard how arsonists like to attend their own fires? It'll be like that. And besides, I think we're dealing with someone here who has a pretty good opinion of himself. Most murderers aren't really all that clever." He grinned at her. "We just let them think they are. And we let them think we're a little thicker than we really are."

"There's something I've been wondering about," said Penny. "If the killer escaped through the back door, as seems likely, why are you filming at the front of the house?"

"We'll be filming the front door as the killer goes in, and the secondary location at Mrs. Lloyd's," said Davies. "The killer likely went in the front door, and out the back, so we hope someone saw him or her in one or other of those places.

"Right," he added. "Let's do this and see who comes out of the woodwork."

Thirty-eight

T hyme Close had been blocked off to vehicles, but people on foot were being allowed in and told to stand behind the metal barricades that had been erected on the pavement opposite the front door of Catrin Bellis's house. A small film crew milled about, setting up a camera on a tripod, laying cable, and checking details on a clipboard.

Penny and Victoria stood behind the barricade, with Jean Bryson between them, both hands clutching the top of the barricade. Penny stole a glance behind them and nodded to several acquaintances, including Haydn Williams and the Hughes family.

As spectators continued to arrive, DCI Davies positioned himself at the back of the crowd, now two and three deep in places. In his casual clothes, he blended in with everyone around him; only his eyes, constantly scanning the crowd would have suggested he was anything other than a curious onlooker.

Jean Bryson's eyes were busy, too. She peered anxiously toward the end of the street, then turned her gaze to Catrin Bellis's front door, then back to the end of the street.

And then, after a crew member called for quiet and the crowd fell silent, a woman turned into the street and all eyes turned toward her. Wearing Jean's coat over her purple plaid skirt and lavender-coloured blouse, she walked slowly down the street, occasionally glancing at a small piece of paper in her hand. The woman in Jean's clothing checked the paper one last time and then walked up the path that led to Catrin Bellis's front door. She pushed gently on the door and then entered the house.

A moment later, two other women entered the street and Penny stifled a little gasp. It was Mrs. Lloyd and Florence themselves. She raised an amused eyebrow to Victoria, who made a little gesture with her hand.

When Mrs. Lloyd and Florence had almost reached the end of the street, the woman playing the part of Jean Bryson ran screaming out of Catrin's house, Mrs. Lloyd and Florence turned around, and the woman ran up to them. The three stayed as they were, frozen in place, until the director called "cut." The crew examined their monitors, exchanged a few words with one another, and then, apparently satisfied that they'd captured all the action, began to pack up their equipment. Many people in the crowd who'd been been filming the filming lowered their mobile phones. DCI Davies walked around the edge of the crowd to join Penny, Victoria, and Jean.

"Is that it?" asked Penny.

"Yes, for now," he replied, not looking at her. He touched

her arm and spoke in a low voice. "Get ready. Here we go. Don't say anything now." And then, in a louder, normal voice, he said, "We're moving now to Rosemary Lane to capture the second part of the event."

Jean, standing beside him, clutched at his arm and turned slightly so her profile was visible to the people behind them. "Before we go, Inspector, I've just remembered something. Seeing this has brought it all back, just like you hoped it would. I did see someone. He was in the kitchen."

"Oh, well done," said Davies, smiling encouragingly at her. "I'm sorry I've got to speak to the director about the next segment, but we'll send a police officer over to you right away." He turned to Penny. "Look after Jean until the police officer gets here, will you?"

He moved off and Jean turned to Penny. "I'm not feeling well, and I want to go home and lie down. It's just across the street from Mrs. Lloyd's so I'll be fine. No, please, don't come with me. I'd rather go on my own. I'm fine." She hurried off and disappeared.

The growing crowd followed the film crew into Rosemary Lane and watched as a running man came into view, carrying a white quilt, which he dumped over the stone wall in front of Mrs. Lloyd's house. Mrs. Lloyd herself and Florence stood across the street as the action unfolded.

"Oh, if only I'd been looking out the window at that moment," said Mrs. Lloyd. "Imagine! I might have seen the killer himself dumping the quilt. The nerve!" The man playing the killer then disappeared down the street while an actress dressed up to look like Dilys arrived less than a minute later, picked up the quilt, and walked off with it. The filming ended and once again the crew replayed the action on their monitor. When they were satisfied they'd captured everything satisfactorily, they began to wrap things up and the crowd drifted away.

DCI Davies walked over to Penny with a smile tinged with relief. "What now?" she asked.

"We wait."

"We wait until it's broadcast?"

"Oh, it'll never be broadcast. Those weren't even real actors. Police officers with an interest in amateur dramatics." He checked his phone. "Shouldn't be long now."

"What's going to happen?"

"My phone's going to ring and when it does, we'll have caught our killer."

Thirty-nine

Jean Bryson left the street door slightly ajar and climbed the stairs of a small house across the street from Mrs. Lloyd's. She entered a bedroom just off the landing and sat in a comfortable chair beside the narrow bed. Flowered curtains fluttered in the afternoon breeze as she took a sip of water from the glass on a bedside table.

The weight of a foot carefully placed on a creaky stair was the first indication that someone was coming. Jean held her breath and waited. A moment later the door to her room opened slowly and a man entered.

"So you've come for me," Jean said. "I thought you might. It was you I saw in the kitchen, wasn't it?" The man said nothing but took a step closer. "It must have been," said Jean, "or why else are you here? You must have followed me." She sighed.

"Well, what have you got to say for yourself? You killed that poor Catrin Bellis, didn't you?"

"No," said Haydn Williams. "I didn't. I came to warn you that you're in danger because he's on his way here. You have to get out of here and go to the police. I'll go with you."

"Who's on his way here?" said Jean, standing up.

The door opened and Evan Hughes filled the frame. His face was a mask of confused anger. He looked from Jean to Haydn.

"What are you doing here, Haydn?" he demanded.

"Just having a word with this lady. About you."

At that moment Det. Insp. Bethan Morgan emerged from the adjoining bathroom.

"Can you explain what you're doing here, Mr. Hughes?" she said.

"I saw Haydn come here and I followed him. I wondered what he was up to."

"That's not quite true, now, is it?" She beckoned him over to the window and pointed to the street below. "Look down there. Do you see the film crew? The director? The camera operator? They're actually police officers and they've been keeping a very close eye on you today. They watched you in the crowd. They watched your family. And they really watched Jean here." She gave a little wave out the window and made a gesture with her finger pointing downward.

She turned to Jean. "We can't thank you enough for helping us today. If you go down the stairs, a police officer is waiting to take you across the street. Mrs. Lloyd and Florence have a nice cup of tea waiting for you, or something stronger, if you prefer." She touched Jean lightly on the back and opened the door for her.

"And Haydn, we're going to need to speak to you but you

should leave now, too." As she finished speaking DCI Davies entered the room.

Haydn paused in the doorway and turned back to look at his friend, still standing in front of the window. Their eyes met and Haydn raised his hand in a resigned gesture of regret.

He made his way down the stairs and slowly emerged into the street. The crowd had started to disperse but one person, a woman with red hair and a sympathetic smile beckoned to him.

"How'd it go?" Penny asked.

"Awful," said Haydn, shaking his head. "I still can't believe it."

"Come on," said Penny. "Let's go and get you a nice cup of tea."

"I'd rather have a whisky," he replied.

"I'm sure that can be arranged," said Penny, indicating Mrs. Lloyd's charcoal grey house. "You're very welcome to join us here."

Florence opened the door and ushered the two into the sitting room. Jean and Mrs. Lloyd were seated together on the sofa. Penny joined the rest of the women in a cup of tea and Mrs. Lloyd poured a generous glass of whisky.

"I hope it's all right," she said holding out the glass to Haydn. "Left over from Christmas. Now then, we're all dying to know all the details. How did you know to go to Jean's place?"

"I'd had my doubts about Evan for a little while," Haydn said, after taking a deep draught of whisky. " I knew he'd seen my half of the map and he kept banging on about the other half. And then when Catrin was killed and the quilt went missing, I started to suspect him."

"Why didn't you go to the police?" Penny asked.

"Because I couldn't bring myself to believe that he could

269

actually do that. I've known him all my life. He's a good dad, he tries to be a good husband, and he's one of the best sheep farmers in the area. Your mind just won't go there about someone you know so well. Someone you know and like. Someone you respect, look up to, even. And maybe you are in denial about it. I'm not explaining this very well, but until today it just didn't seem real."

"And what happened today?" asked Penny.

"After the re-creation, Jean turned to the policeman and said she'd just remembered something, and Evan said something under his breath. It took me a moment to work out what he said, but he said, 'She knows' and then I could tell by the way he looked at her, that it was all true. And he gave her such a hard, cold look. I've never seen anyone look like that before. And then Jean left, and I was afraid for her, so I followed her and saw her go into the house. I knew then that she'd be all right because Evan couldn't hurt her if I was there. I didn't know there'd be other people there, too."

He held up his empty glass and Mrs. Lloyd refilled it.

"I don't know why he did it," Haydn said. "I was very sad when Catrin died. I'd known her a long time from back when we were at school and I always thought she was special. I was just starting to think about asking her out. It's all just such a stupid shame. Two lives ruined. More if you count Evan's family." He paused for a moment and then repeated, "Such a shame."

Everyone remained silent. Finally Mrs. Lloyd said, "You know, Florence, I think I might have a glass of sherry now and some of those little biscuits I like, if we've got any in." She looked around the room. "Anyone care to join me?"

Jean held up her hand.

"Evan Hughes, I'm arresting you on suspicion of the murder of Catrin Bellis," intoned Det. Insp. Bethan Morgan. "You do not have to say anything. But it may harm your defence if you do not mention when questioned something you later rely on in court. Anything you do say may be given in evidence."

"Now listen to me, Hughes," said Davies. "We kept you up here until the crowd dispersed but your wife and daughter are down there waiting for you. We can do this one of two ways: with or without handcuffs. What's it to be?"

"Without."

"Right. We'll be taking you down to the station for questioning but first, I want you to tell me one thing. What you were looking for in the churchyard. Did you find it? Yes or no?"

"I think you know the answer to that."

"I want to hear it from you."

Forty

So," said DCI Davies, "you found what you were looking for. Tell me about it and why it meant so much to you."

In front of them was a square package, wrapped in ancient leather. An earthy, damp smell rose from the table and filled the small interview room at the Llanelen police station.

Evan Hughes, on one side of the table, stretched out both arms to the package, touched it lightly, then sat back in his chair, and his mouth slightly open, gazed at the ceiling. After a long moment listening to Hughes's shallow breathing, Davies made eye contact with the police officer beside him, and then tipped his head at Hughes.

"Answer the question, please, Mr. Hughes," said Det. Insp. Bethan Morgan. "Tell us about this package and how it came to be in your possession."

Hughes crossed his arms and remained silent.

Bethan stood up and pulled on a pair of latex gloves. "For the recording," she said, "I've just put on a pair of latex gloves and I'm unwrapping the leather from the parcel." She peeled back the leather, revealing a rough green casket. Its base was about the size of a hardback book and it stood about eight inches tall. She opened it and removed a small leather drawstring purse. It was softer, less pungent, and a paler colour than the exposed leather that had protected the casket. She untied the drawstring and tipped the contents of the pouch onto a piece of leather beside the casket. Twelve large pearls rolled out. "For the record," she continued, "I've opened the casket and removed the contents. One leather pouch containing what appear to be twelve pearls of good size."

"Mr. Hughes, how did these come to be in your possession?" Davies said.

Finally, he spoke. "We dug them up."

"And 'we' would be?"

"My daughter, Jessica, and me." And then he added, "She just knew that some treasure had been buried. That's all. She knew about the map but she didn't know where it came from."

Seizing on what mattered most to Hughes, Davies continued. "Mr. Hughes, this is all going to be easier on your daughter and wife if you tell us exactly what happened."

Hughes let out a long exhalation that sounded like a sigh filled with resignation and relief. "I'm glad it's over. How much do they know?"

Davies ignored the question and pointed to the object on the table.

"I ask the questions here, Mr. Hughes. Not you. Our forensics revealed traces of ancient leather in one of the holes in the churchyard. We haven't sent this for a proper appraisal

274

yet, but unless I'm very much mistaken, that's ancient leather. And also, unless I'm very much mistaken, it's a valuable artifact. So you need to tell us everything you know about it."

He stood up. "I'm going to give you a few minutes to think things over whilst I arrange a cup of tea for you. And when I come back, you'd better start talking. And if you want your solicitor present, we'll arrange that. But we're going to get this done, Mr. Hughes, and we're going to do it now."

With his solicitor beside him and a cup of tea in front of him, Hughes began to unravel the story of how the casket of pearls came into his possession.

"Since I've known Heather, there's been this story about how her great-grandfather, as a boy, was cheated out of something. They never quite knew what, but it was said to be valuable. Precious. Something to do with two other boys who kept something from him. They all went off to war together, but two were killed and only Heather's great-grandfather came home, so he never found out what it was. There was talk of a map, so when Haydn came into the pub that night flashing half a map that the Antiques fellow had found in his clock, and I saw the date on it, I knew that it had to be part of the map. I took the map to the loo with me and photographed it. Then all I needed was the other half."

He took a sip of the now tepid tea and glanced at Davies who nodded to him to continue. Det. Insp. Bethan Morgan did not look up from her notebook.

"At the Antiques evaluation I overheard the appraiser telling Catrin there was something in the quilt she'd brought. I didn't know if it was the other half of the map, of course, but her great-grandfather was one of the three boys, and the quilt dated from about that time, so it was possible. I went round to ask her about it, but she got very stroppy with me. All I wanted her to do was look in the quilt and see if the map was in it, but she refused. I tried to grab it from her, but she fell and hit her head on the hearth. She tried to get up and that's when things got out of hand."

His hands, wrapped around the empty tea mug, trembled and his voice shook. "I grabbed the poker and hit her with it," he said. "I meant to hit her hands to make her let go but she ducked and lunged at me and I ended up hitting her head. I didn't mean to kill her." He winced. "If I could take it back, I would, believe me."

"We all do things we aren't proud of," said Davies. "It's just that some things are worse than others."

Bethan looked up. "And then you grabbed the quilt, left by the back door, and dumped it in Mrs. Lloyd's front garden?"

Hughes nodded miserably.

"When did you pull the map out of it?" she asked.

"As I was leaving. I went through the kitchen, picked up a knife, and slit the seam open."

She looked at Davies. "Any more questions?"

He shook his head. "That'll do for now. Mr. Hughes, do you have anything you'd like to add to what you've just told us?"

"I still don't know how I could have done it. But I did. What's going to happen to me?" asked Hughes.

"You'll be charged with the murder of Catrin Bellis," said Bethan. "If you'd like to see your wife, I can notify her. We can even drive her here, if she wishes."

Hughes made a scoffing noise. "I doubt she'd come. She won't want anything to do with me now."

After Hughes had been escorted back to his cell, Davies and Bethan Morgan remained seated in the interview room.

"Why would someone who has everything—a beautiful home, family, nice life—what would motivate him to do something like that?" Bethan said.

"Because people who seem to have everything sometimes want a little more."

As the green of the valley turned grey in late-evening shadow and the parade of restless clouds bringing the occasional bursts of rain had been blown away, Davies tidied up his desk, said good night to his colleagues, and left the station.

"So it's over," said Penny, holding the door of the Spa open for him. "You got your man."

"We did. Evan Hughes has confessed to killing Catrin Bellis."

"Well, that's good. You can wrap up this stage of your career by cracking one last case."

Davies smiled. "Well, officially, it won't be me who solved it. I suggested to Bethan that she return to duty for a few days so she could wrap up the case and get the credit for it."

"Did you really?! That was wonderful of you."

Davies looked serious. "Not really. It was her case and she did all the work early on. I wonder if it was the right thing to do, though. I hope I didn't just prop her up for now and next time, when she's on her own, she'll be in over her head. Because she was definitely floundering this time."

"There's a few minutes of daylight left," said Penny. "Let's go for a little walk beside the river."

She locked the Spa door behind them and they pushed open the squeaking gate, then crossed the town square.

"And what did you mean, exactly, when you said 'this stage' of my career?" Davies asked as they entered the churchyard.

"Oh, I think you'll be looking for something else to do before too long," said Penny. "I don't think you'll stay really retired. I can't see you spending your days puttering about in your garden. You'll find some new projects to throw yourself into."

"Well, you may be right. And for my first project, I thought I'd fix that awful squeaking gate at the Spa. It's been driving me crazy for months."

Penny laughed as they seated themselves on a wooden bench and watched the river flow by for a few minutes. Then she turned toward him, facing upstream, with the churchyard on her left. She rested her arm on the back of the bench and gazed toward the chapel, surrounded by graves.

At the roar of approaching aircraft they lifted their faces to the sky. Two fast-flying, streamlined black jets flew directly ovehead, banked, and then disappeared into cloud cover.

"RAF jets from Anglesey on maneuvers," said Davies. "There was an RAF station here during the war."

"Do you ever stop and think about all the people who were here before us?" she asked. "The RAF crews who attended church here, in their blue uniforms, during the Second World War, for example. Who might have walked that very path when they said good-bye to their wives?"

Davies nodded. "Or the townsfolk turning out for the 1776 funeral of the local clockmaker," he said.

"Or small boys who for some reason, buried their treasure near his grave over a century ago."

Forty-one

July 1900

The long summer vacation stretches out endlessly when you're young. Day after languid day, filled with swimming and riding your bicycle down shady country lanes, the bright green leaves overhead casting dappled shadows across your friends' faces. Picnics of bread and cheese and an apple that taste so good, so special, simply because you're eating out of doors beside a fast-flowing stream bordered with wild flowers and it's summer and you are ten years old and enjoying every moment of this heady, delicious freedom.

This was the first summer Wilfred Williams had been allowed out on his own, to explore the fields and forests that bordered his family farm. With his black and white Border collie, Fran, by his side, he walked the pathways that led to the adjoining farm where his best friend Herbert Bellis lived. On some days they were joined by the third member of their little gang, Sydney Wynne, but more often than not Sydney's mother would come to the door with excuses why he couldn't go with them. His grandmother was coming to tea and he had to stay clean and tidy for the whole day in his Sunday best until she arrived. On another occasion, she explained that he had been very naughty, had disobeyed his father yesterday so for punishment he would have to remain inside all day today, working on sums and reading passages from the Bible.

In truth, his overprotective mother was extremely fearful of the dangers to which those other two boys might expose her precious child; she imagined all kinds of terrifying possibilities, each more awful than the last: her innocent, naïve boy would brush against a stinging nettle and spend the rest of the summer with a burning, itchy rash, or he would lose his grip and tumble out of a tree and suffer a terrible head injury that would leave him an invalid for life, or worst of all, fall into the River Conwy and get swept away, only to wash ashore downriver, drowned, his lifeless body sprawled on a reedy bank.

So on a sunny day at the end of June, when Herbert and Wilfred knocked on the kitchen door of the Wynne farmhouse, his mother, dressed so much better than their own mothers, told them that Sydney couldn't come out with them that day. "He's poorly," she said. They thanked her and walked away, pausing for a moment to look back at the house. Sydney waved to them from an upstairs window.

"Doesn't look poorly to me," said Herbert.

"Well, never mind him," said Wilfred. "More strawberries for us!"

They hopped on their bikes and raced off down the country road, passing the Jones's farm, and turning into a small lane that ran alongside it. About half a mile up the lane they stopped, leaned their bikes against a tree, and cut off across a hay meadow. The tall, multi-coloured grasses gave off a warm, dry, slightly musty smell as they danced softly in the summer breeze. After a couple of minutes they reached Mrs. Jones's expansive strawberry patch.

"Do you think we should?" asked Herbert.

" 'Course we should. Look at all she's got. She'll never miss a few."

They bent down and picked a few plump red strawberries, warm from the sun, and popped them in their mouths where they burst, releasing a delicious trickle of juice. Eagerly and greedily, moving down the row, they picked more. Suddenly, Herbert stopped.

"Here," he said. "Come and see this." A triangular piece of something brown stuck out of the ground under a plant.

"What do you suppose it is?" he asked as his friend bent over it, his hands resting on his bare knees.

"Let's find out!" He knelt, bare knees in the dirt between the rows of strawberries, and began digging around the object with his hands. Herbert joined him and soon they had cleared away enough dirt to free most of the object. Together, they pulled it out of the earth, and brushed away the dirt. The strawberries were now forgotten.

It appeared to be a bulky parcel of dark brown leather, wrapped around something shaped like a box. The leather gave off a pungent, dank, earthy smell that spoke of a long time buried.

The boy slowly unfolded the smooth but cracked and brittle leather, revealing a small, casket-shaped box. It was black but when Wilfred rubbed the side of it with his shirt cuff, a dull green patina was revealed.

"Gosh!" said Herbert. "What do you make of that?"

"I don't know," Wilfred replied. Across the meadow the small figure of Mrs. Jones appeared, her white apron fluttering in the gentle breeze and a large basket tucked under her arm.

"She's coming to pick her strawberries," whispered Herbert. "We'd better hightail it out of here. What should we do with the box?"

"Give it here," said Wilfred. "We'll bring it with us and work out what to do with it later." He tucked it under his shirt and the two boys were soon flying down the road toward home on their bicycles.

When they reached Herbert's house they ran upstairs, eager to examine the box. They placed it on his bed and knelt on the floor, examining it from every angle and admiring it. Its small hasp was in place, unlocked.

"Open it! Go on!" said Herbert.

Wilfred slowly lifted the lid and peered inside.

"There's a bag or something," he said.

"Well, go on, then. Give it here!"

He pulled out a leather purse with a drawstring around the top. He was just about to pull the drawstring when his mother's voice reached them from the bottom of the stairs.

"Herbert!" his mother called. "Are you up there?"

"Yes, Mum!"

"Is Wilfred with you?"

"Yes, Mum!"

"Well, it's time he was heading home. It'll be teatime soon and his mother will be wondering where he's got to."

When the diminishing sound of her footsteps indicated she had retreated to the kitchen, Wilfred pulled the drawstring open and tipped out the contents.

"They look like those things ladies wear around their necks or on their ears," said Wilfred. "Pearls, I think they're called. My *nain* has some. She wears them to chapel on Sundays and when it's a do, like me da's birthday."

He picked one up, rolled it around in his fingers, and held it close to his face to examine it. The afternoon sun picked up its iridescent, creamy hue and bathed it in a rich, warm glow.

The two boys exchanged concerned looks.

"What do you think we should do with them?" asked Herbert. "Should we show them to a grown up?"

"Nah, we can't do that," replied Wilfred. "They'll want to know where we got them and we'll have to tell them we were in Mrs. Jones's strawberry patch. And then I'll be in for it with me da."

"Maybe we could put them back in her patch," suggested Herbert. "You know, just put them back where we found them and no one's any the wiser."

"But if we get caught, then they'll think we was trying to steal them. We've got to hide them somewhere while we work out what to do. I can't have them in my room because me mam goes in there all the time."

"Same with me," said Herbert.

"Let's have a think," said Wilfred. He studied a picture of Jesus hanging on Herbert's wall and then, a flash of relieved inspiration crossed his face.

"I know!" he said. "Where is it that they're always digging holes?"

Herbert raised his shoulders in a vague shrug.

"The churchyard, you great lump!"

"Herbert! Let's be having you! Come downstairs this minute and get washed for tea! And as for you, young Master

Wilfred, I'll not be telling you again! It's time you were off home! If you're not here by the time I count to ten, I'm coming up." There was no mistaking the tone of Herbert's mother's voice and the two boys stood up.

"Hide this somewhere safe for tonight and meet me tomorrow morning, soon as you can get away, in the churchyard," said Wilfred.

"Look!" said Herbert. "Over there, by the church. Someone's already dug a hole!" They made their way over to it, and peered in. On the other side of the churchyard, with his back to them, an elderly man in heavy woolen trousers and a white shirt was knee-deep in a grave. He carefully placed shovels of dirt to one side. Occasionally he leaned his shovel against the side of the grave, removed his cloth cap and wiped his brow with a white handkerchief that he then replaced in his pocket. After resting for a moment or two, he continued with his task.

"This here's the grave of the man who made all them clocks," said Wilfred, pointing down at it. "Me *nain* showed it to me and said I should be really proud to come from Llanelen because of him. We got one of his old clocks in our parlour."

"What's this hole for then?" asked Herbert.

"Don't know. Maybe he's going to plant a bush or something in it when he's finished over there." He pulled the parcel from under his coat, and after pulling the leather wrapper tightly around it, set it in the hole. The boys then covered it loosely with handfuls of dirt that had been placed beside the hole, leaving space above it to accommodate whatever the hole had been dug for.

"Right," said Wilfred. "Now we have to mark the spot so we'll know where to find it again."

"Let's start from inside the chapel," said Herbert. "At the stone baby."

They counted off their steps to the hole where they'd placed the box and then wheeled their bikes out of the churchyard and headed for home. The gravedigger, now standing deeper in the grave, leaned on his shovel, watching them leave, and then wiped his brow with his handkerchief. A moment later another shovel full of dirt topped up the pile on the edge of the grave.

Hot and out of breath by the time they arrived at the Williams's farm, they leaned their bikes against the lambing shed and while Herbert drank a glass of water in the kitchen with Wilfred's mother, Wilfred ran upstairs to fetch a school notebook and a pencil from his bedroom.

"What have you boys been up to this morning?" she asked.

"Oh, nothing much. Just rode our bikes for a bit," Herbert replied. He smiled his relief when Wilfred reappeared and after thanking Mrs. Williams for the water, the two boys ran outside.

"Don't slam the—" she called after them, but too late.

"Let's walk up to the little hill that overlooks the stream," Wilfred suggested. Perched on the side of the hill, Wilfred handed the notebook and pencil to his friend.

"You're better at drawing than I am," he said. "You do it."

So Herbert drew a map according to Wilfred's instructions showing where the box was buried. "And draw a clock to show the clockmaker fellow's grave," he said. When the map was finished, they studied it to make sure it was as good as they could make it and then Wilfred solemnly tore it in half. "You keep half," he said, "and I'll keep half and one day we'll go back together and get it."

Herbert wrote his name on the bottom of his half. "Do you think we should tell Sydney?" he asked.

"Nah," said Wilfred. "But let's just tell him we buried some treasure and he'll never guess where, but there's a map shows where it is. And all he has to do is find the map!"

Laughing, Herbert tucked his half of the map in his pocket just as Wilfred's mother came to the kitchen door. "Wilfred, time to come in for lunch," she called. "You'd better go," said Wilfred to his friend. "I'll see you tomorrow. I've got to help da with some chores this afternoon."

Herbert jumped on his bike and disappeared down the road. Wilfred entered the kitchen and was about to sit down for lunch when his mother pointed at his knees.

"That's two days in a row you've come home with filthy knees," she said. "What have you been doing?"

"Nothing," said Wilfred.

"Well, get upstairs now and get washed for lunch. And I'll want to see those knees clean when you come back down."

Wilfred marched out of the kitchen, fingering the map in his pocket. As he passed the parlour the clock struck one. He rolled up the map and approached the clock. His mother had left it slightly out from the wall when she'd dusted behind it so he reached round and stuck the map in a hiding place he'd used before, the space created by the moulding round the bottom of the clock. He knew the clock offered better hiding opportunities up where the dial was, but he couldn't reach that high. He continued up to his bedroom, had a wash, and then rejoined his mother in the kitchen. His father had arrived home from his morning's work in the fields and ruffled his son's hair.

"Coming out to work the sheep with me this afternoon, lad?" he said, buttering a piece of bread and setting it on Wilfred's plate.

"I am, da."

His mother ladled a small serving of mutton stew on their plates and the little family bowed their heads in prayer as Mr. Williams said grace.

Forty-two

A couple of weeks later, with the official start of summer, Penny and Gareth were enjoying a picnic on the somewhat remote tidal island of Llanddwyn, connected to southwestern Anglesey by a stretch of sand that disappears beneath the waves at high tide.

Named after Dwynwen, a fifth-century Welsh princess and the country's patron saint of lovers, the legend-rich island features a rugged coast with sandy coves hidden under large rock outcrops. They'd walked for about a mile at low tide along a pristine beach, stopping every now and then to examine an interesting shell, until they reached the spit of land that connects to the island at low tide.

Once on the island, they walked past friendly, shaggy ponies that roamed freely in the tall grass, and continuing the gentle climb, came to the stone ruins of the sixteenth-century chapel erected in Dwynwen's honour. They continued on until they reached the top of the island, with spectacular views across to the majestic mountains of Snowdonia.

Now, they were sprawled on a green plaid rug beside a white lighthouse overlooking the sparkling blue Irish Sea, happily munching the lunch Penny had prepared and Gareth had carried: sandwiches, cheese and biscuits, grapes, and strawberries.

"They're local, those strawberries," said Penny. "Caron Jones brought them into the Spa yesterday. The Jones farm is just down the road from Haydn Williams and the Hughes's place."

Gareth took a bite of one, setting the little green leaves on the edge of his plate. "Delicious," he said. "Did you know that it was her son that Jessica Hughes married?"

"Oh, the one-day marriage that didn't take, as Mrs. Lloyd put it? No, I didn't realize that's who it was. I guess it's not going to work out."

"No, it doesn't look as if it will."

"I guess Jessica's got a lot on her plate right now, with the legal fallout from her father's arrest," said Penny.

"She does. Catrin's house has an offer on it, but the legality is questionable. She didn't have a will, so her estate would go to her closest living relative."

"Which would be Evan Hughes."

"Right. But because of what's called 'the slayer rule' he can't benefit from his crime, so everything goes to Jessica, even though he hasn't yet been convicted of the murder. But she has said she couldn't possibly keep it, and will donate everything to benefit charities that care for horses and donkeys."

"That's very good of her." Penny poured tea from a flask and held the cup out to him. "And would I be right in thinking it's Bethan who's made an offer on the house? I could tell she quite liked it, even with everything that needs doing to it."

"She has. It'll be a good home for her as well as investment. And of course she'll get it at a good price, what with someone having been killed there. That kind of thing tends to put off a normal buyer but it doesn't really bother her because she helped bring the killer to justice," Davies said.

"Well I'm sure Jessica will be glad she needn't have anything more to do with the house, although she's still got to organize the auction of the contents. And of course she couldn't keep the bronze casket with the pearls."

"That was the most amazing thing. The expert that the local museum brought in to do the appraisal was floored when he saw it was Roman."

"Someone told me a long time ago that the Romans loved pearls from North Wales and some were even sent back to Julius Caesar, but who would have dreamed they'd turn up the way they did."

They were silent for a moment, listening to the sound of powerful waves crashing into the rugged rocks below them.

"There is something I wanted to tell you," Gareth said, breaking the silence. "Bethan tells me that they've found the cyclist who hit that artist professor, Michael Quinn, on the path by Lake Sarnau." He watched her reaction. She showed no emotion. "If the case goes to court, you'd likely be called to testify."

"I'd be fine with that," she said smoothly, giving him a steady, reassuring smile.

"So have you got anything special planned for the summer?" he asked.

"Not really. You?"

"As it happens, I do. Turns out you were right about my not lasting too long without a job, so I've agreed to do a bit of contract work. You're looking at the new head of security for the Llanelen Royal Autumn Agricultural Show."

Penny laughed. "That's terrific! You'll be very good at it. They're lucky to have you."

"Actually, they've never had much in the way of security before, but with the increase in rural crime, including theft of valuable animals, the organizers thought they'd better do something about that. So I'll be attending meetings and learning as much as I can about the show over the summer. I'm quite looking forward to it, actually. I've always admired farmers. Not just for the work they do, but for the type of people they are."

Penny checked the time on her phone. "I've been thinking," she said. "About Catrin's things that will be going up for auction. I was thinking I'd like to buy her little carriage clock."

"Why would you want to do that?" asked Gareth.

"I've never taken much notice of clocks, but over the past couple of months I've really come to appreciate them. Especially the longcase kind." She held up her phone. "You show me a piece of today's technology that will still be keeping perfect time two hundred and fifty years from now and looks as beautiful as one of those John Owen clocks."

"They can be noisy, you know, those longcase clocks. Winding up to strike the hour, ticking and chiming all day long in your front hall or sitting room or wherever you keep it."

She laughed. "I don't have a front hall and there's no room for a longcase clock, but I could give a pretty carriage clock a good home."

A long afternoon stretched out in front of them. They still had lots of walking and exploring to do, so Penny began gathering up the lunch things. A few strawberries remained in the plastic box that she now held out to Gareth.

"Let's eat these up before we go." As he bit into the ripe fruit, she looked up at the blue sky and then across the sparkling water and remarked, "Nothing says summer like ripe strawberries."

"Except, maybe, days like this."

"I wonder how the map got in the quilt," Penny remarked as they placed their lunch things in the backpack and Gareth hoisted it over his shoulders.

"We'll probably never know for sure," he said, as they set off on the steep, uneven path in the direction of the Celtic cross. "But when I was a boy, my grandmother lived with us and my father set up a quilting frame for her in the front room. All day she'd sit there, in front of the window, sewing these tiny little stitches. Beautiful quilts she made. So I expect someone in the Bellis household was making a quilt, the boy thought it would be a good hiding place, tucked the map inside it, and the woman making the quilt sewed it in. She might not even have known it was there."

They walked on in silence, surrounded by breathtaking natural beauty, and as they paused for a moment to look back the way they had come, toward the sea and the lighthouse, she slipped her hand into his.